A Dose of Murder

The Big Pharma Series

By Lotus James

LIFE GARDEN
PUBLISHING INC

Lotus James

A Dose of Murder – Big Pharma Series
Copyright © 2022 Lotus James

ISBN: 978-1-7359745-5-2

This is a work of fiction. Names, characters, places, incidents, and events are either the product of the author's imagination or are used fictitiously. Any resemblance to actual persons, living or dead, is coincidental.

Produced by:
Life Garden Publishing Inc.
P.O. Box 333
Borden, IN 47106 USA

Table of Contents

Chapter 1 ~ Going Home

Saturday, November 30, 2019

Haley pushed the handle and exited directly into the parking garage. No matter how many times she walked out the employee door, fear set in. It was a temporary sensation, sometimes with the hair on her neck tingling along with tension in her stomach. Her blue eyes met with the guard on duty. She smiled at him, grateful for his presence. Fortunately, she now had a reserved parking spot close to the security office.

She took a deep breath of the outside air and her stress level began to drop, just as someone's blood pressure would go down if administered nitroglycerin. Clicking the FOB on her key ring, she slid swiftly into her vehicle, locking the door. Shifting into reverse, Haley eased her blue Honda out of the reserved spot in the hospital garage. The security guard was kind enough to wait, making sure she exited safely. Smiling at him again, she pushed the driver's side window button, lowering it. She was glad to finish another long shift and grateful the guards were attentive.

"Thank you so much. Enjoy the rest of your day."

The guard smiled back with a nod. "No problem. You enjoy your time too."

She began her descent into the darkness of the parking garage toward the exit.

"Hey Siri."

"Uh huh?" the app responded.

"Send Jack a message."

Siri asked, "What do you want it to say?"

"I just left work."

Siri responded, "Your message says I just left work. Ready to send?"

"Yes, send," she commanded.

Touching the steering wheel's audio controls, her favorite play list was there waiting. The music cranked, a welcome distraction as she made her way out of the garage and into the day's traffic, which was a tad lighter than usual since it was late Saturday afternoon in downtown Atlanta.

This was the first time she had worked through the Thanksgiving holiday — three days of patient care with over 38 hours in. The extra holiday pay was welcome, but taking care of the needs of the newly born arriving each day made shifts feel shorter. Rewarding as it was to assist these beautiful newborns, she would never delude herself about the heartbreak that occurs when one doesn't make it. Unfortunately, Haley knew on a personal level how it felt with the miscarriage she had suffered. Carrying a child, giving birth and then losing it … that was a huge grief she prayed she would never experience.

Staffing changes at the old Mercy Hospital since the Lowen corporate buy-out had many of her friends moving to University hospital where the pay was commensurate and employees did not have to relearn everything they already knew. With Lowen taking over, the upper management had added what some felt was nothing but corporate nonsense. While they had tried to not change the branding of the hospital too much, the takeover included a name change to Lowen Mercy Hospital. Jokingly, Haley called it "lovin mercy". Some days, it was anything but that. She hoped she would not lose track of friends that had moved on to University. It would take some scheduling and effort for that not to happen.

With the loss of staff, someone had to step up and be there during the Thanksgiving holiday. Working Thursday through Saturday, only coming home for short periods to sleep, she missed the Thanksgiving Day festivities with Jack and her in-laws. At least she had a video call with her Aunt Molly and Uncle Mike in Valdosta. It was short and sweet, but she said hello to them just before they were ready to dive into desserts.

Haley thought about how she would not take the Christmas shift, even though she loved putting the little Santa hats on the babies born that time of year. Family was important, and that holiday was not one she would negotiate on.

Picking up speed, she merged onto the freeway and began the trip home. The weather was typical autumn, sunny but chilly. She purposefully left the heat off in the car. If she turned it on, she'd likely become more tired than she was now. What she needed was a good hot shower and something to eat.

Jack seemed to truly miss her presence with his family for the holiday, saying it felt odd. Thank goodness he had brought home sumptuous leftovers — enough for both to dine on for two days. Haley missed Sharon and Joe. They had become like surrogate parents to her from the very start. She also would have loved to have caught up with her brother-in-law and his wife, Sarah, and their clan.

She did not miss being questioned at dinner on whether she and Jack had experienced any luck in having a little addition to the family. Everyone meant well and was eager about another pregnancy. They were trying to make that happen. She and Jack wanted to get pregnant again. The miscarriage of a little over a year ago left her devastated for a while. She moved out of pediatrics at Mercy for five months, before finally wanting her position in the department back. Touching and caring for those babies only reminded of her child that didn't make it.

If the tester doesn't turn blue sometime over the next year, she and Jack agreed they would consider in vitro.

Haley had some hesitation over the idea, not wanting to have triplets. One baby at a time would be ideal for this couple.

Jack and Haley had purchased a home that was too large for the two of them after the miscarriage and the "incident" that happened while she was pregnant. Jack was determined to project her into the future where they would have a family together. While her drive to Mercy was longer, she worked three days a week. This put Jack closer to Chadwell Pharmaceutical's complex on the outskirts of Atlanta.

The first thing he wanted to renovate was the master suite. It was nice, but he wanted that space to reflect them as a couple. The master bedroom and adjoining bath were made to feel more sensual in every way possible. They were magnetically attracted to one another. For Haley, Jack pushed all the right buttons with her visually and tactilely. The renovation was a way of Jack making his mark on the area, Haley thought. Plus, it was so luxurious. It made each feel like jumping each other's bones. Certainly, that would create more chances for a pregnancy. Who can argue with that, Haley thought?

Jack's new favorite spot to corner her was in front of the long mirror in the bath. Both found something very intoxicating about watching themselves joined in ecstasy. Jack had thought of so many things to make it special, including music speakers, ambient lighting, and a steam shower with multiple heads. He took the design over the top though with the waterfall faucet. Combined with the faux stone tile and carefully placed live plants, it sort of felt like being in the jungle.

"Now, I can jump into that jungle shower," Haley said out loud to herself. "I have the next four days off."

But Jack would leave for South America on Tuesday morning. She knew that would give them all day Sunday to be with each other and part of Monday when she imagined he would be busy on the phone. It had been a while since Jack made an expedition and never one where he took three team members from his department. Haley thought about helping him pack and plans for a delightful meal that last evening together.

Jack's position at Chadwell Pharmaceuticals kept him constantly engaged either in the laboratory performing research, writing scientific papers, and sometimes traveling into the field. He was now working on something quite substantial, but secretive. Because of proprietary rules about information, everything was always secret until perhaps right before a formal announcement. Still, Jack would hint from time to time about the nature of his work. This time, however, he had been silent lipped. This project had risen to a more important level, even though it commenced a while ago. Jack was diligent about not taking a chance of speaking on the phone or over the Internet with anyone about it. This gem of a discovery had to be kept in the tight circle of his team and two executives at the company.

With both working long hours, Haley determined she might have to take a leave from nursing if their little bambino — no, not if — when their baby finally arrived. Jack was not easily replaced at his job. As Chadwell's chief research scientist, he earned three times Haley's salary. They could afford to allow her to stay at home with their child. And that would make for a more relaxed mama who was available to work on producing a sibling.

Proceeding from the interstate onto her exit, it was a short drive now to the country retreat of a home Jack and Haley found. Making a turn onto the cul-de-sac, Haley noticed her neighbor, Alex, trimming weeds around the mailbox area. She waved, and he waved back. Rolling down the window, she idled the vehicle beside him. "Did you guys have a nice Thanksgiving?"

Alex showed his wide smile. "If it was any better, I couldn't stand it. Delicious food and fine company. How about you?"

"I worked from the holiday through today. Jack had dinner with his parents and family. It was a bit strange, but I was so busy at the hospital, it didn't feel like Thanksgiving anyway. Do you know how many new babies we had after their mothers ate more than usual for Thanksgiving? Just take a guess."

Alex put his finger to his mouth and looked up as if the answer would come from the blue sky above. "I'll guess ten."

Haley shook her head. "Close! We had ten mothers, but eleven babies. Twins!"

"Haley, how can you take care of eleven babies at once? Jeez!" Alex said, with a puzzled look.

"Well, sometimes they cry and have to wait their turn. There are three of us in the unit right now, plus a trainee. Most of the mothers have their babes staying in the room with them. That helps. I am tired, though."

Alex nodded. "I bet you are. Anything you want me to tell my other half?"

"Tell Jessie I will have to catch up with her after Jack leaves for South America. He flies out Tuesday morning."

"Will do. Feel free to drop by before then if you guys want some company." Alex said.

Haley readied the vehicle to move again. "Thanks, but I think we have plans to do some shopping and veg out at home. Talk to you later!"

Making her way toward the house, it pleased her each time she arrived home as soon as the structure came into view. Selling the condo was the best decision. The only thing she sometimes regretted was the steep backyard. Haley felt it could be difficult terrain for children to play. Jack said they would have powerful leg muscles. She thought of having some of the yard leveled out, but not without losing some of the beautiful live oaks and tall pines. There was a grassy area out front and to one side that was fairly level for play.

Pulling into the garage, she turned off the vehicle, grabbing her bag. As soon as she entered the kitchen, comforting food aromas hit right in her hungry belly. She gazed at Jack, who was standing with a glass of wine in one hand and a potholder in the other.

"There you are. Haley, I am so glad you are home. I've been laboring all day on this huge turkey meal for you," he joked.

Matching the mood, she kissed him and patted his shoulder. "Oh, you poor thing. I just had dinner prior to leaving work."

Jack's smile faded. One could say his mouth looked like it was drooping on one side.

"Not really, honey. Just teasing you in return. Labored all day, huh?"

He hugged her tight and whispered in Haley's ear, "I may have had a little help from my mom."

Melting into his embrace, Haley giggled softly.

"Let me get my jungle on and then we shall talk turkey and eat it too, okay?"

Jack knew that was her little slang term for showering in the rain forest inspired bath.

With a playful pat on her behind, Jack said half sternly, "Get to it, beautiful lady. Dinner will be served in thirty minutes."

Chapter 2 ~ Dinner & Dessert

Grabbing the turban hair wrap and bath towel, Haley stepped out of the glass and stone shower onto the bath mat. After quickly wrapping her hair in the turban, she dried and applied moisturizer at the same time. Long hours at the hospital had a way of depleting all of a person. At the sink, she worked on removing what mascara had pooled under her eyes and cleaned her face with a special cleanser. She then worked eye and night cream onto her face and neck, respectively. No makeup tonight.

Haley brushed her teeth and gave her wet hair a comb out. Trading the wet towel in, she slid into some silky pajamas which would absorb the chill in the fall air and still feel nice to the touch — Jack's touch.

"Did I make it in time or am I fashionably late?" she called, entering the dining area.

"You are right on time, my dear. Please, have a seat. I only have one more item to fetch from the kitchen."

"Jack, this is beautiful. You're using our wedding china and the candles you gave me last Valentine's Day. I feel so special."

"Only because you are. I'll be right back."

Jack returned with a silver bucket chilling her favorite white wine. "Allow me," he said as he poured her a glass.

With a huge smile, Haley lifted her glass, inhaling the bouquet.

"Do you think I should indulge in this, Jack?"

"A glass or two will not hurt you. Since you are not pregnant now, it will be fine."

She knew this and didn't know why she felt like she needed his permission. Perhaps it was in hope of reassurance. If anything went wrong with a future pregnancy, she wanted to make sure it was not her fault and all decisions were made jointly. That sounded crazy to even think like that. Regardless, she would have just a few sips to celebrate this surprise dinner he had pulled together, and then no more.

The wine was fabulous. It had been many months since Haley drank anything alcoholic. The selection he had made was a perfect match for the meal laid out before her.

Jack joined her at the table and they filled their plates with the tasty leftovers her mother-in-law, Sharon, had packed for him to bring home. The turkey was moist, and she had obviously roasted it with the right amount of herbs and spices which carried over into the stuffing. The sweet potatoes were soft and yummy -- like a dessert unto themselves. Haley had some of her spinach salad and famous green beans.

Jack noticed Haley gazing off into space. "Penny for your thoughts?"

His question broke her stare. "Oh, honey, I don't know what I'm thinking. It's been a long three days with only six hours' sleep between shifts."

"I'm glad you're here and have time to relax. I won't be disturbed with anything tomorrow from the company. Sunday is our day," he said firmly.

"Jack, twins were born this morning at the hospital," she said excitedly.

"Fraternal or identical?"

"Fraternal girl and boy," she answered. "What if we did have twins, Jack?"

"Nothing wrong with that — little Jack and Haley juniors. I know we are going to get pregnant soon. Ready for pie?" Jack asked, smiling.

"Honey, I'm feeling like a stuffed turkey at this point. I better wait on that. Please, go ahead if you want some."

Jack sliced the pumpkin pie he had picked up at the grocery. "Uno momento senorita," he said as he walked toward the kitchen. He grabbed the can of whipped cream from the refrigerator and shook it. Without warning, he came over and playfully squirted a bit on Haley's open cleavage area above the v-neck top. She laughed softly as he playfully licked the whipped cream from her body, tickling her with his tongue right in the center. Her neck and head tilted back toward the dining room chair as she felt his mouth caressing her up the neck and toward her lips. He slid his tongue inside her mouth and slowly kissed her deeply.

"I've missed you, baby."

"I've missed you too," and Haley kissed him back with as much intensity.

Suddenly, she became self-conscious about the dining room curtains being open. Breaking the lock he had on her mouth, she pulled her head to the side. "Close the curtains, Jack."

Dutifully, he hurried over to the window and drew the drapes together. Turning back to her, he smiled precociously and his eyes held desire as they met hers. Taking her by both hands, Jack motioned for her to rise from the chair. They stood, tightly embraced, as his hand slid down her back toward her waist and pushed away the elastic top of her silky pajamas. Haley could feel how hard he was, and knew now was probably the best time. If they only teased each other for an hour or more, she might be too tired later.

It felt right to go with the desire between them now. She raised his shirt, feeling the muscles in his powerful arms and tapered chest. Kissing his hard abdomen, Haley moved her lips up his body along with her caresses. He sighed and his breath became heavy, sounding almost labored.

Jack's movement was smooth as he methodically glided her pajama pants down and lifted the silky shirt over her head. Clearing an area on the dining room table, his muscular arms lifted her to a sitting position. Pressing his body in between her legs, she teasingly asked, "Did you forget about your pie?"

"Not at all," he chuckled, grabbing the can of whipped cream. "Lie back Haley. It's time for dessert."

Chapter 3 ~ Sunday Shopping

Sunday, December 1, 2019

Haley awakened slowly, noticing the sunlight drifting in ever so slightly. Turning over, she stretched her hand toward the opposite side of the bed, feeling for Jack. He was already up. Tempted to roll over and catch just a little more dream time, she suddenly sat up, remembering he would leave in two days. Today was their day, and she wanted to make the most of it. As she was rising, the door opened.

"There you are, sunshine," Jack strolled in. "Stay right there, babe. I have a surprise for you."

"Can I go to the bathroom?"

"Yes, get that over with and then get right back in bed."

She did as he requested, curious about his motives. More bodies entangled together like last night? Haley was not sure if she felt ready for that just yet. She decided to quickly brush her teeth, just in case.

After freshening herself, she opened the curtains just enough to let in a little more of the day's radiant sunshine. Scurrying back to bed, she slipped naked into the sheets. Hearing Jack's footsteps on the hardwood as he came toward the room, she glanced toward the door as it pushed open wide. Jack was beaming, carrying a tray and placing it in front of her with coffee, two boiled eggs, toast with strawberry jam, and freshly sliced tender peaches.

"Oh my, what a delicious surprise."

Jack was beaming like a schoolboy delivering breakfast to his mom on Mother's Day.

"I bet you didn't think I had it in me, did you? Your private chef and waiter last night and room service this morning."

She laughed, adding, "It is out of character as you are always in a hurry, making calls, sending emails and on the go in the morning."

"Today is our day, Haley. I want you to relax and feel pampered. Of course, I'll be around tomorrow before the trip. But you know, the day before I leave town seems to have a different vibe."

"Yes, those days do indeed feel a little busier," she agreed with a half smile.

"What about you?" she inquired. "Are you going to join me in bed for this fine feast? You said our day and I want to pamper you as well."

Slyly, he smiled. "You can pamper me all you want."

She had just bit into a juicy slice of peach when he bent over and kissed her on the cheek and then again on top of her head.

"Sounds like you have planned our day." She held out her hand to him. He squeezed it tightly and kissed the top.

Finishing breakfast, Haley went to the master bath once more. Jack watched her intently, and she knew his eyes were fixated on her backside as she left. After relieving herself, Haley hoped perhaps she was pregnant already. But she also knew that coffee made one urinate frequently. Placing her hands on her lower abdomen, she glanced down the wall of mirrors and prayed, "God, give us a child again — one that is strong and makes it."

"Haley, I am going to fall asleep if you don't get your cute little ass in here now," she heard Jack call. Bored easily and not content with moments alone doing nothing, she rushed back into the bedroom to find him lying completely nude on his stomach.

"Look at you," she said, half giggling. "Ready for a massage, or will that put you back asleep?"

"Please don't tease me, Haley. I know promising massages is your way of leading me on."

She reached into the armoire and selected lightly scented almond oil. Pouring a bit in one palm, she rubbed her hands together to distribute it as evenly as possible and warm it as well. Beginning with his shoulders, she lingered long on the specific areas where he felt more than a little rigid and balled up. Haley closed her eyes as she imagined her thumb and fingers erasing his tension like butter melting under her touch.

"Oh babe, that is so good. I did not know how tense I was until you touched me."

"You are a bundle of nerves, honey. All being carried on your shoulders. I'm glad this is helping."

She continued making her way down each side of his back and then coming back up the spinal column area. Jack moaned as his face continued to completely relax with eyes closed, mouth gaping open a bit. With the stress he carried around, Haley loved seeing him enjoy this moment in time. Honestly, there were not enough of these occasions in their life.

Slowly working her way down, she now fixated her healing touch on his strong buttocks. Haley found Jack so handsome, not a beefy muscular type, but more of a lean man with muscles filled out nicely in all the right spots. She compared his hard body to her soft one, realizing she could not pinch an inch of fat on him anywhere. She supposed that was due to all his nervous energy.

She became aroused, as she made tight circular motions on Jack's behind. But she would wait. She continued to caress and massage Jack's legs and then feet until he was like a rag doll under her touch. As she was close to being finished with his feet, Jack pulled from her suddenly and turned over. His manhood was bulging and she could not resist making her way toward it. She massaged his full, stiff flesh, smiling playfully. He twitched with delight. Inching her body upward while staying skin to skin with him, she made her way to his face and kissed him deep, thrusting her tongue into him.

Breaking the kiss, Haley looked deep into his hazel eyes. She felt so much emotion well up inside of her. "I love you so much, Jack."

He returned the gaze. "Baby, you cannot know how much I love you."

Haley felt a sweet intoxication as they fell into one another once again. When Jack and she made love, it felt like an incredible union where they melded into one.

Jack fell asleep within minutes afterward, as Haley lightly stroked his chest and rested her head on his shoulder. Watching him snooze, her eyes watered softly. *Damn, I am lucky to have Jack. He is so giving and loving. One day, this gorgeous man and I will have a family.*

Quietly rising and slipping from the bed, she decided this was the best time to shower and get her face on for the day. It never took Jack long to get ready for anything, except perhaps his overseas trips.

No more emotional watery eyes, she thought, stroking mascara on her lashes. *Jack will be back from South America soon enough and you just need to have fun with him today.*

She chose skinny jeans and a red cowl neck sweater. Haley then slipped into the kitchen and called her mother-in-law, Sharon, thanking her for the Thanksgiving dinner she sent her way. Jack awoke, showered, and was ready to leave the house in no time.

They headed toward the Alpharetta business district. Both had missed supporting local businesses the day before on Saturday, but thought they might try to find something they needed today. Traveling south on Main Street, their first stop was Alpharetta Outfitters, where many fishing enthusiasts often sought gear and equipment.

Jack put the car in park and looked at her. "Gotta get some gear for wet conditions this time. We will harvest right along the banks of the Tapajos River. He jumped out and came to the passenger side of the vehicle, opening the door for her. The store was laid out and merchandised nicely. Even if you were not an outdoor enthusiast or fisherman, it made you want to buy something. Jack chose an item new to him, special boots designed for operating in the river featuring technologies he had not used before. He also snagged two pairs of neoprene wet wading socks.

Haley turned toward the front of the store and noticed a man outside one of the display windows staring at her instead of the items for sale. He glanced away when their eyes met and pushed his hands into his pants pockets. She tried not to think anything about it, knowing she tended to imagine things happening since her incident. Haley turned back toward Jack and the salesperson, who was demonstrating all the features of the special boots. When she turned around again, the man was gone.

Jack put the large purchase on his American Express. As they strolled out of the store, she pinched his arm and said in her best exaggerated southern accent, "Did I ever tell you that you're high upkeep, buddy?"

He laughed as they got back into the Jeep to head to their next location a few streets away. They parked in a public parking lot and then walked, hand in hand. The sun provided some heat today, even though temperatures were beginning to take a dip.

They strolled through several boutiques looking for things each might want to give others for Christmas. Haley noticed a store with what appeared to be handcrafted jewelry. Jack could tell that Haley wanted to check it out. "Let's look inside," he suggested.

The hippie vibe was definitely going on as numerous chimes announced their entrance. Patchouli, sandalwood, and another scent Haley could not place gave the shop a distinct aroma. It wasn't subtle, but she liked it. There were glass cases of beautiful handmade pieces sorted by the materials involved in creating them.

She was drawn to a particular case that was tagged *Luck - Protection - Fertility.*

Haley perused the selections as an older lady moved in place behind the counter. "Let me know if you would like to see anything in the case," she said.

"Yes, I will. I'm curious to know what you have for fertility."

The woman's eyes met Haley's. She then looked at Jack. It was almost uncomfortable except that she had a very kind look on her face. "It is said that the second chakra rules creation and fertility," she said, pointing to a chart on the wall showing each chakra area. "While many stones can help with this, I recommend those that match the color vibration of this chakra. Gemstones in the orange color palette would be fertility helpers, like carnelian." Her hand reached for a beautiful pendant of polished stone wrapped in copper.

"Hold this piece and see how you like it."

Haley took the stone from the lady and examined it. "Would this be something to wear on a chain around my neck?"

"You could do that, yes. But the closer it is placed to the second chakra area, the better it will activate and balance the energy there. I could make it into a piece worn at the waist or a bit below that."

"How often would I need to wear it?"

"When you feel like you need a little boost to your creative side or sexuality."

Haley glanced at Jack, who was more than a little skeptical. "What do you think, honey?"

"Oh, you know me. If I can hang out with a shaman in the rain forest and believe their powers and rituals with plants and feathers, who am I to say it doesn't work? Couldn't hurt."

"What about for the man? Should he wear a stone as well?"

"He can use carnelian, but if he would like something different, we can go that way too. Let me see what I have that would be good for him."

She pulled out a small wand like stone. It was fairly crystal clear in the middle, with cloudiness at one end and gold orange hues at the pointed end.

"This is citrine. Not only will this help the second chakra area, but it will also give him added strength and virility."

"Okay, I'm sold," Jack said, slightly smirking. She wrapped the crystals in tissue paper for each and included instructions for caretaking of the stones.

"Oh, one more thing. What do you have for protection, especially when traveling?" Haley inquired.

"Well, there are many stones for traveling. For instance, those going by plane often use malachite. Amethyst is good to have in your pocket as an all around protection piece. Let me show you both."

She pulled out a vivid green heart with swirls and an amethyst cluster. "Take a look at these."

Haley and Jack both felt the stones in their hands. They looked at each other and Jack said, "We'll take both."

Their next stop had to be the always anticipated Kilwins on Market Street. From the moment Haley entered, the aroma of chocolate and caramel overtook her senses. She chose the sea salt caramel and a dark chocolate truffle, grabbing some coffee as well. They both sat smiling, but silent, slowly savoring the sweets and balancing it with their beverages.

Jack broke the silence. "Don't you think it's odd that we have not seen any tree ornaments for sale?"

She paused with gooey goodness in her mouth. "Well, we have not been to all the stores. Could be a few that have ornaments."

"True, but rather than walk through every street and store, do you want to go by the mall and see if our old standby vendor is set up there for the holidays?"

"Sounds like a good plan."

It was tempting to purchase more chocolate delights to take home, but they dutifully resisted. As the couple made their way to the Alpharetta Mall, Jack got lucky and snagged a parking spot fairly close to the main entrance. The business they had purchased an ornament from the last two years would be set up as a kiosk in the middle of the mall if they were selling their wares again this year. Haley hoped they would be. This was turning into an annual event for them to purchase a new ornament each year. Haley knew that not all men were sentimental, and this was something she really loved about Jack.

Luckily, the vendor was set up at the mall again. They slowly made their way around all four sides of the large kiosk, trying to find the perfect ornament to add to their collection.

"Oh Jack, I love this one and it almost looks like our house, if by some miracle it snowed. Look, it lights up as well."

"It does resemble our place. Let's see if they can engrave it with our last name."

"Great idea!"

Jack stepped toward the cashier. "Hi, we want to purchase this ornament, but wondering if it could be engraved here on the front of the house with our last name?"

The clerk took the ornament from Jack's hand and felt its composition. "I'm a little worried about engraving this one, as it is not metal. It could crack."

"Oh, that would not do," Haley interjected.

"One solution is that we can reproduce your name on clear backing. It is like a sticker but with more staying power. Here, I can show you some examples," the clerk said, reaching behind him.

Jack and Haley looked over the ornaments he offered.

"I think that would work. Haley, what do you think?" Jack asked.

"Let's do it. Our last name is Foster."

Once the ornament was completed, they shopped the first floor of the mall. Haley hesitated for a moment at Emani Maternity store gazing at their displays. Jack gently nudged her. "Do you want to go in?"

"Not today. We'll wait."

He could hear the combination of desire and hesitation in her response.

"I want to buy you something, Haley. What do you want or need?"

"Ahh, that's sweet." She thought for a moment. "I would love a new pair of boots. Something stylish, but comfortable."

"Okay, let's do it. Lead the way."

She found the perfect pair of boots with a low heel in a light shade of brown. Haley determined they would match her light colored fall jacket. Jack purchased another pair of hiking boots identical to those he had, but the design was a little different. The manufacturer had stopped making the style he liked the most.

Making their way toward the entrance they originally entered, Haley noticed the same man who was outside the window at the Outfitter store sitting on a bench, looking at his phone. He glanced up at her as they passed by. Suddenly, she felt something. Dread crept into her stomach and the surrounding air became suffocating. They continued walking toward the exit. Haley grabbed

Jack's arm. "I don't feel good. My heart is racing and I feel like I can't breathe."

"What's wrong?"

Gasping for air, she said, "Just get me to the car."

Chapter 4 ~ Perplexed

$\mathbf{G}$rabbing Haley firmer now by the hand, Jack walked swiftly with her to the car. He was grateful they were not parked far away. Opening the passenger door for her, he helped her inside and made his way to the driver's side. He had not seen Haley like this for a while. The ravages of post- traumatic stress seemed like they would not go away. Jack had done everything in his power to make Haley feel safer, including secretly putting three different guards on a personal bonus at the parking garage of Mercy hospital. Haley could leave that place. She didn't have to work, but he was also always behind her decisions, even if they created a challenge.

They had moved from the urban condo to a beautiful home that was relatively secluded but still had a few neighbors. He had installed a state-of-the-art security system. While Jack had obtained his concealed carry permit, he was not prone to carrying a gun all the time. He was not carrying now. He could not determine what or who may have triggered her this time, but he was on guard and felt a bit of adrenaline rush through him, as well as curiosity in the situation.

Inside the car, Haley melted down. He gently stroked the inside of her left hand as he held it. *Helpless. I am so damn out of sorts when she is out of sorts. I don't know what to do.*

Her mascara was creating black tendrils down her cheeks. Searching the car, he handed her some tissue and tried to inquire what was wrong. She couldn't tell him yet. *This is frustrating, but I must be patient now. I'll wait for her to speak.*

Finally, and with emotions overflowing, she poured out the dread she was feeling, including the description of a man who had initiated it knowingly or unknowingly. It was probably the latter and only mere coincidence this guy had been in two separate places they had also visited.

Jack wanted to believe there was a dangerous man following her or them, just to prove her right. Yet, logically, why would anyone do this? He was worried about Haley and felt she needed additional therapy. *It's going to be difficult for me to tell her that, but in a gentle way, I must. The day has been so perfect. I have to find a way to get her back to her real self, not the one ridden with anxiety and fear.*

Chapter 5 ~ A Live Tree

The cool November breeze brushed Haley's face as they made their way to the car. Fight, flight, freeze. Instinctively, her body knew the drill. Not being a fighter, she had been known to freeze. This time, she just wanted to flee.

Once in the vehicle, her emotions exploded, releasing the tension, but leaving knees that felt like gelatin. A waterfall of tears rolled down her cheeks, and Haley hoped she was wrong, overreacting to the situation. Between sobs, she kept telling Jack she was sorry.

"What is it, honey? Talk to me." Jack handed her tissue and reached for her left hand. "Are you having an attack?"

She nodded affirmatively, feeling as if she couldn't make words right now. Everything was too frightening, and the man was still close enough in proximity that it made her feel possibly watched or in danger.

Stuttering, she finally raised her voice. "Just get me the hell out of this parking lot."

Dutifully, Jack started the vehicle, backed up, and revved the engine as they made their way toward the main highway. The further he drove, the safer she felt.

"Jack, just listen, and try not to judge. I'm sorry if I am being crazy."

"Okay, yes, of course. Talk as you feel ready."

Wiping her face and grabbing another tissue, she gently blew her nose.

"When we were at the first store in downtown Alpharetta where you purchased the wet gear, I turned toward the front of the store and there was a man standing outside one of the display windows. Instead of looking at the items in the window, he was definitely staring at me. He quickly looked away. I thought it was probably nothing, but took note of it. Now, as we were leaving the mall, he was sitting on one of the benches, looking at his cell phone. It was the same man, and he looked at me again. I feel like he is stalking me, or possibly the two of us."

There was silence in the car for a few moments.

"Go on," Jack coached.

"I don't know if I am overreacting, but I don't think so. This heavy feeling of doom came over me. Jack, I can't tell whether I am just being triggered by this or if he is really a bad guy."

There was another small stretch of silence in the car. Finally, Jack spoke. "Honey, I don't know whether to find the guy and grab him by the collar or what? It could be something, but most likely it is a coincidence. Lots of people are out shopping on this holiday weekend. He could have been in two public areas that we were. Perhaps he recognized you from the first store and that is why he looked at you the second time. As for staring at you, well, I would do that if I didn't know you. You're an attractive woman."

A wedge of irritation mixed with tears filled her throat. "You think I'm crazy."

Somewhat defensively, he quickly replied. "No, no, I don't. I think you have been hurt and victimized, and your feelers are out because you don't want anything to happen like that again. Nor do I -- listen, you are safe. You are with me and while I'm gone, you will be safe. I'll have Alex and Jessie watching out for you. If you feel the need, go over and stay with them for a while or even to my parent's house. Whatever it takes for you to feel and be safe."

Silence engulfed the vehicle again as Haley processed his stance. Staring out the window, she felt like a child being consoled by an adult that she was not seeing a monster in her room in the middle of the night. It was a trick of light, her imagination getting out of hand. Inside, she knew Jack was being rational. *A man looked at me twice in two different locations today. That is all that happened. Right?*

Jack squeezed her hand tightly. "Make an appointment to talk to your counselor this week. Okay, babe? I think it might help. I cannot tell you how disturbing it is for me to have to leave on this trip with you in turmoil."

She squeezed his hand back. "Yes, I will call tomorrow. I'll be fine, Jack. I'll be fine."

Jack switched on some light jazz on the satellite radio, and it helped to calm the mood. They were far away from the man now. Haley thought about her reaction, realizing she did need to get a grip and calm down.

Jack glanced at her momentarily, still trying to keep an eye on the road. "Do you still want to go to our favorite restaurant?"

"Honestly, if we could just pick up something tonight and take it home, that would be great."

Jack nodded, understanding how she felt. "Let's do it, I'm starving. What sounds good?"

Haley thought for a moment. "For some reason, I always crave pizza after a couple of days of turkey and Thanksgiving fixings. Does that sound good to you?"

"Perfect! How about take and bake from our favorite pizza maker?"

Reaching for her phone, Haley said, "I'm calling them now to put in an order. Thin crust or stuffed pizza?"

"Let's go with the stuffed. I feel like I could eat the side of a building."

"Done!" she replied, feeling as if the thought of pizza itself had been enough to clear much of the mood.

Jack pulled into the shopping plaza where the pizza restaurant was located. In the parking lot, there was a large portion sectioned off with a business selling live Christmas trees.

"Let's get a live tree, Haley."

"Do you think it will last until Christmas?"

"Sure it will, as long as we keep it watered. You can help with that while I'm gone, huh? I can get a head start on trimming the trunk and getting the tree in place while we are baking the pizza. After we eat, I'll start on the lights. It will work out fine. We can do it."

Jack and Haley walked through the aisles of trees, finally choosing a beautiful blue spruce about seven feet tall with a fairly straight trunk. He motioned to one of the men selling the trees that this was the one they had chosen. Jack paid him and pulled a blanket from the back of the jeep to lie on the roof under the tree. Two men from the tree business help him tie it down and secure it.

Haley felt there was something magical about this time of year. Taking home pizza and a tree to decorate were welcome distractions. It was a lovely gesture, and she understood her husband was working on her psychologically. She supposed it was good that someone was helping. She felt doubt about her ability to do normal things, like shopping, without having some sort of imaginary crime scenario seeping into her conscious awareness. Jack had a way of making her so happy and he knew how to take her mood further away from where it had been some minutes before.

Once home, Haley preheated the oven and removed the plastic wrap from the pizza. With preheating time, it would be ready in about forty-five minutes. Jack had already single handedly carried the tree from the top of the car, setting it just outside the garage where he would work on trimming the bottom in preparation for the tree stand. Haley decided she would go to the basement and fetch the stand and lights to save him some time. She also brought the packages in from the car.

To further the mood, she cast a Christmas music play list to the living room speakers. In her mind, things were beautiful right now. She felt so grateful. What more could she want, snow possibly? She turned the television on and found a Christmas screen saver that alternated snow scenes. It was a perfect complement to their festive change in mood and what she needed for this last full day together with Jack.

The doorbell rang and she ran to the door. Jack stood rustling with the large spruce and she opened the door wide. Haley had set the tree stand in a nice, prominent area where the tree could be admired from almost every view. Jack tilted the tree to the side and had Haley place the base of the tree stand on it. He then lifted the tree, still gripping it, and asked her to step back and view it from different points in the house to see if it was straight.

"A little to the left, honey ... just a tad," she said. Jack adjusted it and she went to three different areas to inspect again. "That's it, and this is going to be the best tree we have ever had."

Jack smiled, "I think so too. Can you get down there at the base and start turning the screws on the trunk? I will hold the tree in place."

Haley did as requested until it became really difficult to turn the screws with her bare fingers as they begin making their way deep into the trunk. Jack bent down and helped her along. Once he felt the fit was tight enough, he looked at her on her knees next to him and leaned forward with a quick kiss.

The timer on the oven went off just then, and they both giggled like children, stealing a secret under the tree only to be caught by the bell.

Chapter 6 ~ Time Together

Haley really enjoyed the toppings on the pizza more than the crust. She would never eat the edges. "Where will you stay in Brazil?" she asked.

Jack finished chewing, "The first night, we will stay in a very nice hotel. The next morning, we fly into the forest by charter plane. We will stay at a low key place, not outfitted as nice as the place you and I stayed during our honeymoon. Ethan and Lance will be visiting the rain forest for the first time."

"Exciting, I treasure our trip there for our honeymoon." Haley knew that she and Jack were different from some couples when it came to travel destinations. Perhaps it wasn't romantic like Italy or Paris, but it was memorable and real as you can get.

"I'd have to agree, babe. I actually carry a lot of memories of us there each time I go."

"Really? Why didn't you tell me that before?"

"I don't know. I suppose by the time I get back to you, I've left my thoughts raining upon the jungle floor," he said, smiling.

"Or swinging from tree to tree, my monkey man?" Haley made primate sounds and mimicked the small monkeys with her arms.

Jack snorted. "See, this is why I love you. You're never afraid to let your hair down."

"Oh, you want to see me with my hair down, huh?"

"I want to see you putting our special ornaments on our new tree. I'm going to work on getting the lights on first," he said.

Haley wrapped the remaining pizza and placed it in the refrigerator. Jack emerged with a large tote marked "tree lights" and began unpacking and checking each strand. "Amazing, all strands are working. This is the first year that's ever happened in my entire life. Normally, there are at least a couple of strands having issues."

Haley smiled, quickly loaded the dishwasher, and wiped down the counter and table. She then joined Jack in the living room and helped place all the lights on the tree. The lights were all clear, but that is what they liked, as it made everything feel brighter.

"Oh Jack, I almost forgot. There is a tote where I put the new garland I purchased after Christmas last year. The tote is red and it should be labeled."

Jack nodded. "Come with me and you can help bring up a tote too."

They both descended the steps to the basement, into the storage area where all the totes were neatly lined up on shelves. "There it is," Haley said, pointing.

Jack grabbed the red tote, and Haley searched for the large one with the ornaments. Naturally, it was located on a top shelf.

"Damn, I don't know why we don't keep a step stool down here. I need to remember to pick one up when I shop again."

Jack was able to get the tote down and it was much heavier than the red one with garland inside.

"Here, you take the garland. I've got this."

The tree began coming together quickly. As each step progressed, they would pause and admire how it was becoming their joint creation. Haley felt like she and jack were generating nostalgia for the future — something they would always have fond memories of. This was very important to her as she had grown up without a father figure to help with things like live Christmas trees. Toward the end, there was no one to decorate a tree with her. Her mother had taken over father roles as best she could, given her circumstances financially, physically and emotionally.

"Hey, why are you looking so forlorn?" Jack asked, jogging her out of a faraway look.

Haley made herself snap out of it. Living in the past … that was a bad idea. *Stay in the now,* Haley thought.

What has been is over and what we are creating now is what counts.

"I'm fine. Just realizing how special this is to do together. I love it!"

As Bing Crosby crooned *White Christmas*, Haley found a can of spray-on snow. She shook it and dotted the window panes around the back of the tree with a little of the white stuff.

"Jack, how tired are you tonight? We've been going all day."

"Oh, I could be persuaded to catch a second wind. What do you have in mind?"

Haley glided over to him, wrapping her arms around his neck. "Let's go to the rain forest jungle together. I want to feel the humid air and watch the steam rise." She kissed him deeply and he groaned.

"Did you set the alarm?" he asked.

"No"

"I'll do that now," he said.

Making their way toward the master suite, both were eager to shed their clothing and feel the pulsating water on their bodies. Haley stood, feeling Jack standing behind her. He brought his mouth toward the back of her neck and moved her wet hair out of the way. His breath was loud and strong, almost animal. She could hear him inhale intensely, as if he wanted to breathe her into him, and she would let him. As his soapy hands explored her breasts, stomach, and between her legs, she closed her eyes and imagined they were in a lush jungle together.

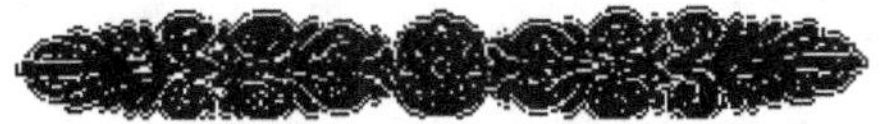

Jack stroked Haley's back and thought about what a fierce, but quiet, beauty this woman he loved held. Her issues she dealt with were understandable and it was good for her to have a third party like her therapist to talk with.

Haley turned on her side facing him, and held onto his shoulders. She looked him in the eyes. "Honey, I have to admit, I am more than slightly curious about your work this time."

"Haley, I feel it's better if the secret stays in the closed work group I have around it. You understand that, don't you?"

"Of course, but who in the world would I even mention your secret to? Even though I am in the medical field, I don't go around talking about possible new pharmaceuticals."

"I will tell you only so much. In that way, you can know how big this possibly is. But, don't ask me specifics, Haley. I won't share that. Agreed?"

"Agreed, Dr. Foster," she smiled and wrapped her bare legs around him, pushing her hips toward his.

"Now, you know this is very unfair to take advantage of me while you are seducing me all over again, don't you?"

"Mmmm, I might admit that it could be a little coercive."

Jack grabbed her buttocks and squeezed them, and then let out a gigantic sigh.

"Haley, I isolated something. Initially, it was a plant we gathered by accident while harvesting. I didn't even know what it was, just a stray plant hanging onto our harvest. It's tricky to cultivate in our climate or the greenhouses. Sercy had success, but we need more of the plant. That's why I have to go back to the rain forest. I can't tell you anything else about the project."

"I understand. Jack, I am so proud of you."

"Baby, you are what pushes me to want better for you, our children we will have, and everyone in this world. This could possibly be such a game changer medically, that this information is on a "need to know" basis only at Chadwell. Nothing is to be known about it outside of the company. Do you understand how secret it must remain? Competitor companies would kill for this information."

"Yes, I will speak of it to no one, Jack."

"Good. I have taken considerable efforts to make sure any information and notes I have on this are hidden within secure files and not emailed or spoken of even on the phone. Everything is backed up in a secret hiding area here in this house. That's how important this is."

"In our house, where?"

"Someplace very safe from anyone who might try to get to it. Don't worry yourself with it."

Chapter 7 ~ Jack Worries

Monday, December 2, 2019

Despite the end of a beautiful night together, Jack's dreams had been wrought with turmoil. He woke, trying to recall a string of dreams that all seemed to be woven together somehow. In his mind, it was like trying to peer through thick mist with only glimpses of people in action. Emotionally, the dreams felt like a tremendous tug of war. He was on one end of the rope, unable to see what was on the other end. But he feared it was something drawing him into an invisible swamp.

He snapped out of the daze of confusing dreams. It was Monday morning now and Brazil was calling him away. As much as he hated leaving Haley, he had to make good use of his time today to prepare for tomorrow morning's flight. This day would not be spent at Chadwell, but tying up loose ends and handling items by email or phone with Evan Mitchell. Even though he had issues with the guy, he was designated to step in for Jack during his absence.

Evan was a couple of years younger than Jack and extremely dedicated to Chadwell. His ambition was apparent and at least once he had worried the guy had attempted to set up a triangulation situation between Jack and the higher ups. Luckily, he had been able to quickly diffuse the tryst and retain superiority over that particular project and his role in general. Still, the fact that he realized this about Evan made him hesitant, leaving things in his hands. But he also knew the guy was the type that would elbow his way in, regardless. It was better to just let him have some authority and put some limits in place, thereby controlling how much damage Evan might do to a project or employee relations.

Evan was good at his chosen work — very good, but he seemed to have philosophical differences from Jack, especially related to profit over safety and efficacy of a final product. While Jack wanted to help people with the drugs the company created, risks needed to be minimized. Studies must be thorough. Jack would stay with results when a potential drug left his lab. He would analyze the data from the studies to see how the animals were affected. Likewise, if it moved onto human trials, he would monitor the data from the volunteers carefully. Evan didn't seem to want to take a patient approach with trials, but to rush them through skipping steps. Jack knew this could create profits for drug companies initially, but also could cost them much more down the road because the drugs were not properly dosed or vetted.

He also needed to speak today with Alex or Jessie, the neighbors next door. He still had quite a bit of concern about Haley's ability to stay steady with her emotions. Jack was not positive, but fairly certain the incident she was imagining with the guy at the mall was pure coincidence. Yet, he could see how the pattern of the man looking at her through the first store window, and then glancing at her again as they were leaving the mall could trigger Haley.

If the guy was up to something nefarious, what was it exactly? Most men would not stalk a woman who was with a man, or at least that's what he thought. He had never really researched this. Jack wondered why the guy seemed to hang around the storefront or at the mall, instead of actively engaged in shopping. Perhaps he disliked shopping and was waiting for his wife, who was in the store. It was these questions that would then ferment scenarios in his mind — just like in Haley's. He had to remain objective, yet diligent about her safety.

He understood, but realized how much the attack was still deeply affecting her. If they did not need more of this plant, he would not be making this trip at all. He thought about seeing if Haley could join him last minute — just to keep her with him. But this trek would be a bit more treacherous in the rain forest than what she experienced on their honeymoon. Time was short to pull it all together. She would have to give notice at work and obtain the right gear for the trip.

If she could stay focused on planning the holidays, allowing that to take center stage in her mind while he was gone, that would be ideal. He would mention this to Alex and Jessie. It wouldn't be a bad idea to get his parents and brother- and sister-in-law involved too. Without telling them about Haley's latest episode, he would just ask them to plan something with her while he was gone, since she could not make it to Thanksgiving.

Overall, he wanted to get the plants out of Brazil, packaged properly and overnighted back to Atlanta. Once he and the team returned to the states, he could lose this tense feeling — a tension that was crawling from his lower spine up to his shoulders and neck.

Jack showered, shaved, and brushed his teeth. He was pulling on casual sweats when his olfactory meter went off the chart. Something was beckoning him to the kitchen.

Chapter 8 ~ Haley Cooks

Awake first, Haley grabbed some coffee and prepared one of Jack's favorite foods. While waiting on the bacon to fry, she sliced the tomato, along with thin onion slices. She popped some bread in the toaster and rinsed lettuce for the BLT sandwiches. Haley flipped the bacon and put some finishing touches in place by wrapping a gift she had for Jack to take on the trip. She had assembled a first aid kit with extra items because, well, you never know. Just for the sake of good luck, she also wanted to make sure Jack wore the green heart-shaped malachite stone they purchased together.

The bacon finished frying and she assembled the sandwiches. She then searched through various craft supplies. She found some leather string and used that to attach the wire wrapped malachite stone, making sure the length was a good fit for Jack to wear around his neck. Taking a small piece of leather cord, she attached it to the wire wrapped amethyst. He could keep it on his key chain for good travels.

Jack walked into the kitchen. "I have not left, but you've got me feeling homesick."

"Could it be you're smelling bacon?" she giggled.

"I didn't know how much I was craving it until the aroma drifted into the bedroom."

"Well, sit down and let me serve up a bacon, lettuce, and tomato sandwich for you."

Jack sat at the breakfast area in the kitchen. Haley brought him a huge sandwich with mayo and thin onion slices on the side. "I didn't know if you wanted onion on it or not. You know I love it."

"This is scrumptious, thank you."

Jack nearly inhaled his sandwich along with a cup of coffee and was about to head for the sink and dishwasher. Haley was still munching along on her sandwich and she called out, "Wait, honey. I'll do that today. Besides, I have something I want to give you. Please come and sit down with me for just a moment."

Jack placed his plate on the counter, but grabbed another cup of java.

Haley lifted a gift bag she had tucked beside her ankle, setting it on the table. Smiling, she pushed it toward him. "It's no big deal, Jack — little things." She knew Jack would feel bad if he had nothing for her that he was presenting in this manner. Had he forgotten that he just bought her new boots, their yearly Christmas ornament, a fertility stone and a real Christmas tree?

Jack opened the first tissue wrapped item — the green malachite stone which had been fashioned into something he could actually wear. "This is awesome, babe. I will definitely keep it around my neck the entire trip." He opened the second smaller tissue wrapped item finding the amethyst stone.

"All I could find was the craft leather string to use for now. We can do something more permanent later. I thought you might want to keep the purple stone on your key chain. That way, you almost always have it on you."

"Great idea. This is so thoughtful. Well, I hope they work," Jack chuckled.

"There is one more thing inside that bag."

Jack placed his big hand deeper inside the gift bag and pulled out the larger gift. Opening the surrounding paper, he found Haley had assembled a comprehensive, but lightweight, first aid kit. "Yeah, that's what I'm talking about. Honey, you should sell these. This is put together with so many useful items. And I like the way you refashioned a cd holder into a portable kit. This could really come in handy anytime, but especially in the rain forest." He hugged her and gripped her tightly. "I love having my own personal nurse."

Haley picked up the breakfast mess in the kitchen, putting the dishes away and pouring the grease from the bacon into an old coffee can. She loaded the dishwasher and pressed start. In the meantime, Jack was in his adjacent office. She could hear him on the phone with

Evan Mitchell. He was going over final things with him for keeping up the regular work at Chadwell.

Evan was a strange bird — never married, but definitely seemed to be into women. More than once, he had been flirtatious with Haley, but she brushed it off or ignored him. It was not so much what he said, although he was always complementary. It was more how she would notice him staring a bit too long, which she would initially sense from her peripheral vision, only to turn and see he was looking directly at her. That, combined with the comments from him, felt a little too personal. Surely, he knew she was completely in love and dedicated to her husband.

While Jack was busy on his laptop and phone, she returned to the master bedroom to help him pack. She knew the phone call with Evan would take a while as they went over last-minute things the department had going on. Being second in charge, Evan would handle anything that came up while Jack and three team members were away.

After about forty-five minutes of packing, then reorganizing things, Haley felt she had finished helping as far as she could. For travel, she had a tendency to over pack on any trip and he had a tendency to under pack. The smallest item could have huge importance to you in a remote location. She went over the list she kept on her cell phone and made sure everything was there. Some items would seem strange to a customs or TSA agent going through the bag, but there was nothing illegal. Jack had a separate duffel bag containing large burlap bags. Twenty-five bags took up quite a bit of room, but it was necessary for gathering any plant life he wanted to ship back to Chadwell with proper government clearance. He had stashed some other things in the duffel bag as well.

Looking at the clock, time seemed to fly. Haley began feeling some anxiety and trepidation about Jack leaving and being alone. She would not relay that to him. Obviously, the chemicals he was trying to isolate and do something with from that stray plant stalk were important. She needed to relax today and enjoy this time until Jack would return, which could never be soon enough.

After sending what he hoped was the last email, Jack shut down his laptop. "Okay, babe. I am finished with everything except two phone calls."

"Great, I'll be in the kitchen. I'm making one of your favorite dinners tonight."

"Yummy, well, I will let you surprise me, although the smells from the kitchen may give it away."

"Only if it covers the bacon smell from this morning."

"What are you talking about? I love that bacon smell, woman."

Jack partially closed the door to his office for privacy.

He picked up the landline phone and rang his brother first. "Jason, need to ask you a favor, brother."

"Shoot," said Jason.

"As I mentioned at Thanksgiving, I'm leaving in the morning for my trip. Haley had a minor episode last night while we were out shopping. Nothing too bad, but I know she is still grappling with things. Can you or Sarah plan to spend time with her while I'm gone? I know she would love to see the kids since she missed everyone at Thanksgiving. Maybe you could get mom and dad involved too."

"Sure thing, Jack."

"I hate to ask as I know you guys are as busy as the next person, but I thought if you have any holiday events planned or even shopping, that might be a good thing to invite her to as well."

"Let me get with Sarah. We'll look at December's schedule and put some plans together. This is not an issue at all, Jack. I'm glad you called me. We'd love to see Haley."

"That's great. I know she could benefit from being around people she knows and loves."

"Don't worry about it, brother. I will have Sarah contact her once you are on the way."

"Thank you. It's good to have family and friends I can count on in my absence. I will get with you when I return."

"Sounds like a plan. Have a good trip."

Jack needed to call their closet neighbors. Since the move here, Alex and Jessie had become a big part of any social life he and Haley embarked upon. He rang their number.

"Alex, how you doing, dude?"

"Hanging in there like a hair in a biscuit. How about you stranger?"

"Couldn't be better. We purchased a live tree last night on a whim and put it up after chowing down on some pizza. The reason I'm calling … perhaps Haley told you, I'm making another trip down to the rain forest. The plan is I will be gone about ten days total. I was wondering if you could both just keep an eye on Haley and the property while I'm gone."

"Of course, Jack, we would do that even while you are here."

Jack lightly chuckled, "I appreciate that, my man. Truly, I do," He lowered his voice to almost a whisper, "It's just, you know, Haley is periodically still experiencing some issues … PTSD from the incident."

"Yep, I know, and we will stand like guard dogs around here. Luckily, we are on a quiet cul-de-sac almost in the middle of nowhere. It would be hard for anyone to pull anything off, but I know she is still processing through that."

"Alex, I really appreciate it. I'll try to bring something unique back for you and Jessie. Take care, my friend."

"You take care as well. We'll have dinner together when you return."

"Sounds great. I look forward to it."

Haley only caught the tail end of the conversation and knew Jack had spoken with Alex. She lowered her chin and looked wide eyed at Jack as soon as he ended the call. She knew Jack was asking them to look out for her. Haley bent over Jack's desk toward him, sporting a genuine smile. "Thanks honey. I am so glad we moved out here and have them as neighbors."

"Me too, babe. Me too."

The smell of beef pot roast floated from the kitchen into Jack's office. It had Jack salivating. "You're killing me, Haley. Bacon this morning and beef tonight — damn!"

She smiled and continued working on the meal preparation. "Should be ready in about twenty minutes, Mr. Carnivore. Your main suitcase and back pack are laid out on the bed. I think the packing is good, but you should check it, especially if there is anything in the suitcase that you would rather have in your backpack. I put the first aid kit in the backpack so you can reach it easily."

"Will do. Thanks for all your help, beautiful," he said as he made his way around the kitchen island to hug her. He held on extra long and breathed in her scent. She smelled like vanilla and honey, a refreshing combination even for such a carnivorous guy. "I love you, Haley. You are more than I deserve."

Haley lit the candles on the dining room table and pulled the drapes, giving them total privacy in the room. She plugged in the Christmas tree lights and stood admiring it for a few seconds, appreciating that the tree was visible from their dinner spot. A crisp, clean pine scent was evident now as the tree was taking over as the star of the room. The woodsy aromas were light, but still strong enough to overcome the aromas of the kitchen.

If she could slow down time, she would make dinner last an eternity. Haley didn't want tomorrow morning to come, but she knew he had to go. She would not be selfish and allow Jack to know how much she didn't want him to leave. Life was comprised of trade-offs, and this was one of them.

Still, just having his touch each night was something she was missing already. Tonight, whether or not they made love, she wanted to be as close to him as she could get. If she could just hold this moment in time. But like many joyous times she had shared with Jack, deep down she knew to just savor it while it was happening and then commit it to memory. There would be many more special moments with one another. Regardless, she wanted to meld as tight with him tonight as she could.

Chapter 9 ~ Savor

Haley was showing Jack in every way, with her culinary activities and gestures, that she appreciated him. While it made it even more difficult to leave, he was also driven to find the elusive plant that contained promise for so many. He would take healthy samples of it, noting the conditions it grew within and any other important information. He would need to speak with the elders of the indigenous people and find out who knew the most about it — or anything at all. Who was the keeper of knowledge about this plant?

Within the rain forest, there were millions of plants and many had never been categorized by western science, much less tested for chemical composition and attributes. However, the locals often had much wisdom to impart about the use of such things living so close within nature. He would need an interpreter as well. It was customary and gracious to offer gifts to the tribe, bestowing it to the ancient knowledge elder first and allowing them to make distribution and use of it as they deemed appropriate.

Jack had packed these items separate in his duffel with the burlap bags for collection. It included loose teas and tobacco, along with several yards of brightly printed broad cloth. For the children present, he had gathered small trinket toys. He zipped up the last bag. Hopefully, he had all he would need.

Leaving the master bedroom, Jack went to join his wife for the last evening they would share until his return. Haley had thought of everything. Light ambient music played, the tree and candles were lit, along with a tempting array of food set in the middle of the dining room table. They had not dined in this room very often, saving it for very special occasions. Using it two nights in four days was a record for them.

Haley did not like feeling you outdid her in being the giver in the relationship. If so, she was quick to step forward. Her nature was to give, and he loved that she operated in such an unselfish way. She deserved everything that was good in life and then some. Delicately, he would need to ask her if she had made an appointment with her therapist. He might wait until they were on the way to the airport tomorrow to do that. There is nothing he wanted to say or do to interfere with the great vibes they were experiencing together on this last evening for a while together.

Haley was nowhere in sight, so he busied himself with placing the piece of amethyst on his key chain. He was already wearing the malachite stone on leather around his neck. The song changed to something slow and sultry. He lifted his gaze as Haley floated into the living room in a light blue full-length gown that was completely sheer. Her breasts were clearly visible but the love patch between her legs was covered in a g-string which revealed her beautiful buttocks as she slowly and seductively twirled, making the gown fan out. Her long, wavy dark blond hair was cascading in tendrils, occasionally shielding the sight of her breasts like a teasing curtain that swayed back and forth. As she came closer, Jack could feel the surge in his blood flow and heat rising into his chest. She smiled, twirling once more, and he noticed the carnelian stone attached to the top of the g-string.

Coming close and standing in front of him as if for inspection, he was almost breathless at her beauty. "Your fertility stone," he said, not knowing what words to say.

"Yes, I wanted it to stay on me for good luck."

"Well then, I suppose I will have to work around it," Jack smiled wryly.

"First, we must take care of your appetite."

"Which one?" Jack laughed.

"The one connected to your stomach, honey."

Haley floated again, this time toward the dining room and its long candlelit table holding a beautiful layout of tossed salad and beef stew. Jack followed her in a partial trance. She looked like a goddess in that gown with her hair flowing freely instead of tied back. He had to touch her. This woman, his wife, was a vision — a fantasy come to life.

"Wait, let me hold you," he said, reaching for her

Jack wrapped his arms around her waist. "You make me feel like the luckiest man in the world. Hell, I am the luckiest man in the world."

Haley giggled. "I suppose I share that in common with you, except I'm the luckiest woman."

He pulled out her chair and looked on with desire at her beautiful back side as she sat down. Jack bent forward and turned his head toward her face. Softly, he put his lips to hers and gently licked with his tongue. Haley placed her right hand on the back of his neck and pressed his head toward her, making the kiss deeper. Jack plunged his tongue inside, enjoying the wet taste of her. Sensing this could get out of hand quickly and he might forfeit the dinner she had worked so hard on, he pulled away and gazed into her eyes.

"Honey, you make it hard to focus on this fine dinner you've prepared, but I will try."

Jack was smitten after the first bite of stew. Slow cooked with aromatic herbs and a hint of citrus, the meat was tender and fell apart easily when touched with his fork. She had included tender new potatoes and baby carrots. The salad was a perfect blend of spinach, romaine and baby kale leaves with finely diced cucumber and red pepper. Haley had made his favorite salad dressing blend and added some sunflower seeds, cherry tomatoes, and feta cheese. Devouring the food, Jack began feeling a little more grounded. It hushed him in an earthy, satisfying way as they ate silently with only the music moving in the background. Still, Haley was opposite him and she was the end prize, the dessert for this king's meal. Her gaze would meet his periodically and her eyes seemed to touch him as surely as if she were putting her lips to his.

When Haley was present, no other woman existed. She was a paradox to him and constantly intriguing. Her long blond hair perfectly framed her girl next door face with wide blue eyes. Haley's body had skin so smooth covering all the right curves for him.

Inside, Jack felt a wild emotional pull now between wanting to linger and stay like this with Haley forever and knowing that he had to change his mental attitude, taking a more serious approach to the trip and business he had ahead of him. *This time we have now is just another moment, one that again passes too quickly. I want to savor it and burn it into my memory.*

Chapter 10 ~ Leaving

Tuesday, December 3, 2019

Waking with the alarm, the two lovebirds flew out of bed and showered together, more for expedience than intimacy. There had been plenty of the latter around last evening. Haley thought about how Jack had repeatedly made love to her during the entire night. She worried whether he had slept long enough. It didn't matter now. They were into this day — the time when he would leave for a while and be so far away from her. *Don't think about that now. It's time to be supportive and not clingy. Jack needs to focus on what's ahead of him.*

Breakfast was quick with store-bought banana nut muffins and coffee outside on the deck overlooking the backyard. The weather had experienced a warm up from the usual cooler temperatures this time of year. She checked the forecast on her tablet. "High here today is going to be about 77 degrees," she told Jack.

"Wow, that's a quick switch," he replied.

"Well, you know this area. Weather changes fast."

Indeed, the weather could be unpredictable. They peered into the backyard where a funnel cloud had touched down a month earlier, a spin off reaction from a hurricane down south that had degenerated into a powerful tropical storm by the time it made its way north from the Gulf of Mexico into Georgia. The wind was savage, taking four of the over one hundred foot tall pine trees down. Their trunks were twisted at the thick base, uprooted, and splintered into large limb fragments and pieces. Many of the homeowners in the area had damage. Luckily, it had not affected the house.

"It would be nice if the insurance company would be a little swifter about taking care of the trees," Haley said.

"The insurance company is probably going to try and wiggle out of this, Haley. I'm not going to worry about it right now. It will be fine if they drag their feet as winter is coming on. Come closer to spring, either I will deal with the cleanup or someone the insurance company approves."

With traffic, Haley had allowed about an hour and twenty minutes to get to the airport. The couple left in her Honda, traveling down Highway 19 toward I-85 south. About an hour away, she would merge onto I-75 and the Hartsfield-Jackson International airport was shortly thereafter.

The ride was quiet, with low music playing inside the car. Jack broke the silence. "I want to make sure you don't forget to make an appointment with Laura, your therapist."

"I happen to be going there at 1:00. I messaged her over the weekend and she was able to get me in today."

"That's great. I should have known you were a step ahead of me."

"I am going by the hospital first. They're having a free continuing education class. I might as well take advantage of gathering my points for that. It will help me kill some time before the appointment."

"Sounds like a good plan. Knowing how things go at the airport and with my departure time, I probably won't be in the air until your class is about over."

"Jack, I don't want you to think I don't care because I am not coming into the airport for your departure."

"No, honey, I don't think that at all. The Atlanta airport is too big, crowded, and crazy for you to even worry about it. We'll have to say goodbye at the curb where you drop me off, babe. I can handle it, but no matter where we said our goodbye's it would feel intense."

Haley maneuvered the vehicle to the curb for Jack's airline departure area and put the car in park. She turned to look at him and they both had a long moment of gazing into the eyes of one another. No words were necessary now. Haley pushed the button to pop the hatchback, and Jack grabbed her hand. "Give me a goodbye kiss, beautiful," he whispered. Each shifted their torsos, meeting in the middle over the console. Jack's lips covered hers. He held the back of her neck with his right hand and moved her with a little more pressure toward him, making the kiss deeper. As it broke, he saw her eyes welling up with tears. "It's going to be okay, babe. I will be back."

"Call or text me when you arrive in Brazil."

"You know I will, honey. I've got my satellite phone with me in case I have service problems with my cell phone. I'm going now. Keep busy and keep smiling. I love you!"

Haley watched as he climbed out of her car and walked around to grab his bags out of the back. He shut the hatchback and waved goodbye.

Go! Just get out of here before he sees you breaking down. Don't make him feel so bad for leaving on a business trip.

Haley waved, blowing a kiss back to Jack - put the car into drive and drove away from the airport.

Haley left the continuing education class at the hospital and used the sky walk over to the building with doctor's offices rather than leave her coveted reserved spot in the garage. From there, she could take the elevator down and walk a block to her therapy. Once out on the sidewalk, the sun was bearing down with some welcome heat on her face and arms. She thought about how everything felt fine right now. She was safe. But she still needed to talk to Laura.

Once inside her therapist's office, she sat in the chair she preferred, the comfy one that actually rocked a bit. She found that rocking slightly made her feel more at ease. It had actually been a helpful tool from the very beginning. It was at her first therapy session that Jack had accompanied her. She would always be grateful to him for that and while unusual, it helped her to be able to begin to relate to Laura the story of the incident. It also assisted Jack in understanding the depth of post traumatic stress and how she might be affected going forward. Laura had been there through the loss and feelings she needed to process about the pregnancy and miscarriage. All of it had been helpful to keep Haley moving forward.

As she was able to cope better, appointment intervals had moved from weekly to once per month. However, with what occurred over the weekend, both she and Jack felt like an appointment now might be wise.

"Haley, you look wonderful. What do you think about this sunny warm-up we're having today?" Laura asked.

"It feels really nice outside. Jack and I had a quick breakfast outside this morning and then I took him to the airport. He's going to be gone about ten days on a rain forest trip for work."

"Oh wow! Someday, I might go on one of those guided tours of the rain forest. Sounds exotic and intriguing to me."

"You would probably love it. And, yes, I would do the guided thing there."

"So, your text sounded a tad urgent. What's going on that you felt like coming in today?"

"I had an episode Sunday."

Haley retraced the experience for Laura, telling her the impressions she received from the man who had appeared at two different locations and her physical reactions. Laura listened, scribbling a few notes on a notepad she held, occasionally adjusting her glasses on her nose.

"Haley, I will not say anything to invalidate the feelings you picked up. I will say that right now, we do not know if there is anything to it or not. Since your attack in the parking garage, you will naturally be looking for unusual patterns that people may have around you. You will listen closer, looking around you more often. Overall, you will have those intuitive feelers out more than most people. This is a good thing because you are in a position where you do not want to become anyone's victim. Sometimes it is also a hindrance because we put coincidences together that may have no relation. It could have been a total coincidence. We just do not know for sure. In the past, we spoke of things you can put in place around you to make you feel more confident and safer.

What do you have right now that helps in that way? I know you have mentioned some before, but let's go over it again."

"Well, when Jack is with me, he can carry a firearm. I have not felt confident about that yet, but maybe I need to consider embracing owning a weapon that would suit me and learning to use it correctly. I'm just not crazy about it, but I will consider it again. We have an excellent security system in the house with cameras, glass breakage detectors and more. I do feel somewhat safe at home, even when Jack is away."

"Okay, you say somewhat safe. Why not totally safe?"

"Well, if someone wanted to attack me and they broke in to do so, I may have a warning, but perhaps it could be a while before the police arrived. I think about that."

"So, you are wondering how to ward off someone or defend yourself until authorities could arrive?"

"Yes, when I run scenarios through my mind, I think of where I could hide in the house. I have great neighbors I could call. Nevertheless, I have some significant fear. I see the security system as a great deterrent, however, for anyone to try."

Dr. Miller paused, making a note. "What about away from home, such as work or going to the grocery?"

"Occasionally I stop by a grocery and I really have not had any adverse reactions or feelings from that. Most of the time, I have the bulk of the groceries delivered on one of my days off. The cost is offset by the gasoline and time I would use to do the shopping myself."

Dr. Miller pressed her for more information. "What about your work?"

"At work, I often have initial anxiety when I enter the parking garage, whether I am going into work or leaving. Many times, I walk with other medical personnel out or in. But sometimes that doesn't work out. I just try to breathe through it when I'm by myself. Fortunately, I was assigned a reserved spot close to an entrance and the guard's office. That has been a really good thing for me. Plus, I notice when I leave, the guard on duty will actually come out of the office they sit in and see that I am leaving the garage. It's one of the reasons I stay at that job. Sometimes I feel funny about everyone knowing what happened, but I just try to tell myself not to worry about that. It could happen to anyone."

Making more notes, Laura states that it sounds like Haley has filled a lot of gaps that could give rise to her post traumatic stress. "The thing is, you will come into situations where something — usually just a strange anomaly, triggers those feelings again. This is where you could choose to double down on your internal calming practices. This will be especially important if you are alone when PTSD strikes. Of course, you can always call someone who understands to try and walk you through it."

"Yes, I know what you are saying. If Jack had not been with me on that shopping trip, I probably would have been either cowering in the car the second time I saw that man or driving like a maniac to get away. Could have been a little of both. The problem is I don't want to call our family or friends each time this happens. Granted, it has not occurred frequently, but I feel silly when it is nothing but my overactive imagination."

"I understand. We have a group of women that deal with varying levels of post traumatic stress. They meet once a week. It could be a good place to meet others, perhaps make a buddy or two that you could call. This would be someone who would totally understand. What do you think of that?"

"When do they meet?"

"They meet in a few hours from now. I alternate with another therapist in guiding the group each session. It would be from 5:30 to 7:00 on Tuesdays. Would that work for you?"

"Yes, I'll give it a try."

"Okay, I will put you down as an attendee. Do you want to come today?"

"Sure. I need to eat something and I'll kill some time until then. Thanks, Laura. And, thanks for squeezing me in today."

"Oh, you are welcome. Do reach out to me if you need anything. The group meets on this same floor in Room 214. "

Haley rose from the extra comfy seat, grabbing her bag as she made her way toward the door. It had been worth it to see Dr. Miller today. Coming here made her feel more confident.

Chapter 11 ~ Heading South

Jack focused on moving swiftly from the curb, away from Haley. *Just keep walking. You'll speak to her again in a few hours.* The airport was packed with travelers for business and pleasure. It was easy to spot the travel intentions of most. He focused on figuring out why people were traveling as he waited in line to check his bags. His eyes spotted a well dressed older couple and decided they were grandparents on their way to spend time with grandchildren. Suited business men were interspersed throughout the crowd with shiny shoes and clothing that said they were meeting ready as soon as they departed their flights.

As he made his way to the airline counter, he checked three bags that were thankfully not over the weight limit. He had early check in, but stood in the security line longer than usual even so. Obviously, it was just another busy day at the Atlanta airport. These places always seemed to have a loud, but low hum of voices, wheeled luggage rolling along, and the occasional cry of a baby or toddler. There were repeating announcements over the intercom system. As he walked to the departing gate, he noticed Ethan, Sercy and Lance huddled together talking.

Waving him down, Sercy was the first to spot Jack approaching. "Oh, the boss is here, you guys. We have to change the subject now," he said loud enough for Jack to hear.

"Hmmm, I thought my ears were burning. Well, I hope it was good for you three," Jack smiled.

"Seriously though, Jack, did you find out where we are staying the first night?"

"Yes. Our hotel is the Hilton Sao Paulo in the financial district. They were able to arrange transport to the small airfield we will fly out of tomorrow as we make our way into the rain forest."

"Good deal," Lance said.

Their plane was already at the gate, and they began lining up for first-class passengers.

"This is the first time I've flown in first-class," Ethan said, with a bit of anticipation.

"My virgin experience as well," chuckled Lance.

First in line, Ethan smiled and turned to them, "Well, we are on Chadwell's dime, so why not?"

"I will be interested to know what you think of the first class experience. Enjoy, it's going to be all downhill after that," Jack smiled facetiously and then added, "Seriously, it's going to be about fifteen hours in flight on this plane. First Class may seem uncomfortable after a while. But hey, here we are."

The line began moving, and they walked down the passenger boarding bridge, entering the first-class cabin. Each of the team members held a type of anticipation in their eyes that almost looked as if they were excited boys leaving home for summer camp. Jack sought to bring them back to earth before they even hit the sky. "I hope you guys brought plenty of wet gear. We will probably have a lot of rainy, wet days. Not as bad as March or April, but still the rain picks up in frequency this time of year."

Lance and Sercy had chosen seats together across the aisle from Ethan and Jack.

"I hope what I brought can withstand the tropics," Lance said. "I have to say first-class travel is poised to spoil me. These seats totally recline, don't they — like into a bed?"

Jack chimed in. "They do, and that table folds out into a fairly large desk area if you need it." The first-class area was richly appointed, with beige leather seats that were very soft to the touch. Everything looked as if someone had spent a great deal of time engineering the ergonomics of each area. It was beauty and functionality blended with total comfort.

Sercy chuckled. "Better see if the Hilton has those free little shower caps when we check in tonight. We may need to up our game, Lance."

Lance laughed heartily. "Oh, just the vision of us all in clear shower caps in the rain forest. You crack me up, Sercy."

Jack and Ethan glanced over at Sercy, and they all had a huge laugh. Those passing through first class to their seats were taking notice of the guys, wondering what could be so humorous when a woman approached them, frowning. "Are you laughing at me?" she asked, staring a hole through Lance.

"No ma'am. Not at all. Just making conversation between us about our trip."

She twisted her mouth as if she did not believe Lance and proceeded down the aisle toward her seat with her carry-on bag.

"Okay guys. We're already having too much fun and some people think it's at their expense. Let's talk about something more serious until we're off the ground at least.

Sercy gave Jack a mischievous smile. "Sure, let's talk about how Evan Mitchell is probably going to fuck up the entire department before we get back." Everyone sighed.

"No doubt!" said Lance.

Jack brushed his fingers through his hair. "I hope not."

They all knew it was within Evan's nature to be the kid who wanted brownie points from the teacher or higher ups all the time. He would do anything to shine, including throwing everyone else in the department under the bus to make that happen. There was something about the guy that just sucked the humor out of the room — or even a plane.

"I guess the good news is we don't have him on the trip with us, Jack," said Lance.

Jack smirked. "See, there's always a bright side to things."

The guys settled in and made themselves comfortable with things they had brought along, either to read for work or pleasure. Lance told everyone he had downloaded an audio book and was going to try to listen to the entire thing on the way to Brazil.

Sercy tapped his fingers and said, "How long until lunch?"

Jack smiled, shaking his head. Sercy just looked at him like a kid in the back seat wondering "when will we get there".

After fifteen plus hours in flight, the four scientists would land at São Paulo-Guarulhos International Airport.

Chapter 12 ~ Therapy

Haley grabbed the soup and salad special for dinner. She refilled her lemonade and made her way out of the restaurant back toward the medical building where she had spent time earlier with her therapist, Laura Miller.

She took the stairs up to the second floor and found room 214. Opening the door, she saw a room that was spacious, with low ambient lighting and chairs in a circle. Heads turned as she entered and her therapist, Laura, stood and greeted her.

"Haley, you decided to join us. Welcome! Have a seat wherever you like in the circle. Everyone is almost here." A few more women arrived over the next few minutes. While Haley felt slightly anxious, it was reassuring that Laura was there leading the group.

"Okay, everyone, we will get started. We have two new participants joining the group today. Haley and Jasmine." Haley noticed the other ladies seemed sweet, quite welcoming, in fact.

"Let's go around the circle and give a first name and how long you have been dealing with PTSD. You are free to add anything else you want, as well." Laura looked to the lady on her left and said, "Will you start?"

"Hi, my name is Clarice. I have been dealing with PTSD for about 18 years when I was raped and held captive for over a week."

Wow, Haley thought. Clarice added nothing else to her story. The next in the circle shared. "My name is Morgan. I was the victim of a burglary at the store I worked at. We were tied up and held at gunpoint. No one was hurt, but the fear of it all is something that keeps messing with me. This happened a little over a year ago."

One by one the ladies all had stories, many Haley considered more horrific than her own. She felt so bad for some of these women. She also felt safe enough to share what had happened to her.

"Hi everyone. My name is Haley. I was leaving work at the hospital, walking through the parking garage, when a man with a full face hood ran up behind me. I was sixteen weeks pregnant. He knocked me to the ground and hurt me. He said things to me I didn't understand then and still do not know. It felt very personal, like he was specifically after me, but he could have just been mentally imbalanced. I'm not sure if it was random, or I was targeted by him. A group of nurses came by and stopped him from possibly raping me. He took off running and was never caught. I was brought inside the hospital and admitted. I lost the baby a few days later." Tears flowed as Haley briefly retold and shared her experience. "I have been doing pretty good handling the PTSD, but sometimes I have strange fears come over me which don't seem rational to others."

A table sat in the middle of the circle with notepads, ink pens, and three boxes of tissue. The lady next to her rose and brought tissue to Haley.

"Thank you" she said softly, still sobbing.

Everyone was quiet while they waited to see if Haley would share anything further. Finally, the group leader spoke.

"Haley, thank you for sharing your harrowing experience with us. I know I can speak for all of us when I say how sorry we are that you endured such an awful attack. By letting us know what happened, it gives glimpses for the other members into what you are dealing with. We are all here to speak and help one another with support."

Haley wiped her cheeks and nodded. Her eyes, now red and blurry, glanced at the other women. All had their eyes on her and most, if not all, gave expressions of support.

"Thank you everyone. I realize there are many who had more traumatic experiences than I. What happened to me was so out of the blue that it shocked me to my core, and now I feel ever watchful. My goal is to get to a place where I feel more assertive about my surroundings and even offensive if I feel I am being followed or stalked. The problem is, I have had things happen where I feel like someone is following me — actually see them — but I cannot know for sure or accuse people that may be doing nothing."

Haley went on to tell the group about the shopping experience with her husband over the weekend. "As you can imagine, my husband wanted me to come back to therapy for support on this. In my gut, I felt like seeing that man the second time at the mall was a little too coincidental. More than that, I just got this strange vibe. I cannot get on the offense with that bit of information when it really might be coincidence."

One of the group members asked, "Can you remember exactly what you felt the second time you saw him?"

Haley nodded. "Yes, physically, my stomach felt like something invisible pierced it and I was almost nauseous. In my mind, I felt terror and just wanted to flee the building as quickly as possible."

The therapist interjected that she sees this as a natural reaction from either a real stress situation or imaginary. The mind does not know the difference. "You mentioned you would like to be more proactive about your safety, on the offense, I suppose, versus the defense. Is that correct?" Dr. Miller asked.

"Yes," Haley nodded.

The therapist continued. "Most of us are wired to have the reactions we do based upon our personalities and conditioning. Right now, you have experienced wanting to flee brought on by your autonomic nervous system, is that right?"

"Yes, but I have also felt frozen to do anything at times," Haley added.

"Okay, here is something to consider and if anyone here in the group has done this, I'd like you to please share any outcomes or results. Many people after being attacked begin training in martial arts, which not only gives them confidence to react in situations, but skills to know how to proceed against an attacker. Can someone who has experience with this share what they know?" Dr. Miller requested.

A very petite lady raised her hand. "Yes, I have been training since I was raped three years ago. At first, I had no confidence that I could defend myself. One of the first things I learned, however, was how to keep myself calm under extreme stress so I could think clearly and rapidly about my next decision or move. Right now, if an opponent comes at me, I feel I could take on most. If they have a gun, I don't know. If they have a knife, maybe. But, I was like you. I froze or ran and many times running and getting away from the situation is the right thing — the best move to make. I will tell you something else. I trust my gut — what you felt in the mall — more now than ever."

A lady with brown hair and eyes spoke up. "Can I share an idea? If you had been shopping alone and had that experience and feeling, the most proactive thing you could do would be not to leave the mall right away. Instead, you could go into a store or two, perhaps back track to another section of the mall and see if this person is still turning up around you. I wouldn't hesitate to go to the mall security office and ask for an escort to my vehicle, either. Please understand. I am not criticizing, just thinking how you could be safer if alone. Luckily, you had your husband there, and that is usually a big deterrent for a predator."

Another woman spoke up. "Yes, if you can flee safely, there is nothing wrong with that. But I understand you are worried if you are being paranoid or not. So what if you are? Better safe than sorry."

The room erupted in sounds of agreement.

Haley glanced at the petite lady who had spoken first. "Where do you go for training?" she asked.

"There is a well-known studio in the Buckhead area. I'll give you the name of it. If this is something any of you are interested in and want to come watch a class, I can get that arranged."

She continued, "I think a lot of people believe you have to be a black belt or have tremendous experience to defend yourself. In reality, being able to stay calm and think quickly, plus know a few simple moves to disarm an assailant can really save you. Let me tell you a brief story that happened a few weeks ago to another lady who attends the school. She was standing outside the supermarket at an ATM when she was approached by a girl. The girl stepped right up behind her and poked her finger into this lady's back and demanded money. The lady, who has not trained that long, was able to breathe, stay calm and think about what to do. Suddenly, she went into full mode."

The petite girl continued with the story as everyone listened. "Turning slowly, she asked the girl calmly. How much money do you need? This took the girl off guard a bit at her supposed compliance. The girl looked dumbfounded but said $400, probably knowing that is a withdrawal limit of cash at many ATMs. Okay, said my friend and she stomped the hell out of the girl's foot one time, which threw her back a moment. Then she threw her elbow into her face. She then side kicked her in the knee, forcing it into the back of her leg and as she lurched forward, she grabbed her by the head and drove her knee into her face. Fortunately, someone sitting in their car had seen the altercation and called 911. This time, police arrived quickly, although often they do not. The girl was carrying a knife in her pocket and had been holding up elderly people in the area as well."

All the participants cheered and Dr. Miller nodded but spoke up. "Listen everyone. I want to remind you we have spoken of many methods in this group for handling PTSD and actual situations that could occur. Let's be mindful that not everyone can or will take self-defense classes. They are only one tool in a vast array of things to curb the effects of PTSD and keep us safe."

Dr. Miller went on to speak of ways to calm and center one's self during an episode of PTSD and some ladies shared their success in doing this as well. Haley listened intently. She had tried some of the methods with some success. Sadly, she did not stay dedicated to any particular method or put in real practice with anything. Perhaps what she really needed was someone to make her more accountable, like a coach or mentor. Instead, she had been going about life simply hoping nothing ever happened to trigger an episode. Obviously, that was not a solid plan. She definitely wanted to check out the self-defense classes.

Chapter 13 ~ Evan Mitchell

Evan removed his jacket and tossed it over the large brown leather chair in his living room. It was his favorite place to sit, where he could think about things and make plans. The wheels were now in motion that would change his career and life. Directly and indirectly, it would affect many others as well. Jack's idealism about saving the world with his new concoction would be nipped in the bud, he chuckled to himself.

In a way, it was Jack's own doing. Evan was only assisting Tellinger and the Board of Directors at Chadwell with damage control. He had not devised the specific plan to cause Jack's demise. He was only following orders on the plans made by others. Hopefully, he would soon be a member of the board, as promised.

Walking toward the windows overlooking the condominium clubhouse and pool area, he stopped at his wet bar and poured a glass of scotch. Kicking off his shoes, he made his way back to the brown leather thinking spot. Evan reached forward and lifted the black knight from the onyx chess set in the middle of the wood and glass coffee table. He moved the piece in an "L" shape, three up, one over and took the white knight. A smile spread across his face as he leaned back against the soft leather and propped his feet up beside the chess set on the table.

He had to give props to Jack, though. He had isolated something that could be an absolute miracle drug. The trouble is it would also dilute the profits of Chadwell Pharmaceuticals and every other company like it. It would diminish the need for biological research and funded grants in many labs worldwide. Damn, even the medical machine would be affected by Jack's miracle drug. Doctors, nurses, hospitals would suffer lost profits with such a quick patient cure. Cure was a dirty word not generally allowed in the medical model. It was, in some cases, an illegal word. Jack's "cure" could continue to create lost revenue all the way to the undertaker and graveyard. Funeral home customers would be on the decline. Jack had so many good intentions that were ultimately bad for business.

Profits were something Jack had never been focused on. While he was a genius and talented at the art of isolating and bringing drugs to market, he either cared very little or did not understand what drove that same market to produce his paycheck and benefits. This is why the intervention had been devised. It had to be and everyone who was for the new drug Jack was developing had to be cut from the program. The mere knowledge of it had to be erased.

Jack did have excellent taste in women. Evan hoped Jack had revealed nothing about the drug to Haley, most especially the specifics. *She's beautiful. I would hate to have her be on the list of those to suffer.*

He drained his glass, rose, and poured another as he glared in the mirror at himself. Setting his glass on the bar, he untied his tie and tossed it beside his jacket. He looked at his reflection intently now, wondering if Haley could find him attractive. He was different from Jack in many ways. Jack's tall stature and dark hair was something many women went for. He was a man who also loved the outdoors.

Evan had adopted a more introverted lifestyle growing up with a sports mania father and brother who outshined him in every way. Athletic achievement counted to his father. Unfortunately for his brother, those hard football injuries had taken their toll on his body.

Evan stayed in shape with regular workouts indoors, primarily. He had learned to develop a taste for dressing well and adopted a certain style he felt reflected "class". Would Haley be attracted to the type of man he projected himself to be? Time would tell.

Yes, Haley would be devastated, and it would take time before Evan would approach her romantically. But who knows what their marriage was like? Could be another one headed for the divorce court in the near future. She might be very unhappy. One can never tell. *Damn, I hope she doesn't know anything about that project. I could be the best thing for her to hold on to, for me to hold on to as well.*

Evan picked up the black knight and ran his fingers over the smooth finish, catching his thumb on the crest of it. *I need to be on my toes and ahead of the game with all of this. No surprises!*

Chapter 14 ~ Back Home

With the day's activities, Haley had slipped out of the loneliness she knew would come over her like a swath of frigid air, cutting her off from the arms and heat of Jack. Arriving home, she turned off the security system and reentered it to be in stay at home mode. Time for her to focus on the next few days. She whipped up a large salad and roasted a couple of chicken breasts in the oven to take for lunches at work over the next four days.

Jack was still in the air and she envisioned him with the malachite stone around his neck, probably snoozing in his seat with his Australian outback hat resting on his chest. She glanced at the Christmas tree and decided to check its water level. It was nearly empty. After retrieving a large plastic pitcher from the kitchen, she filled it with cold water. Haley took a hand towel along with her to catch any excess that would invariably happen when she refilled the reservoir. For some reason, she had not yet ever been able to do this without dripping a little water, sometimes a lot.

The tree lent the right touch to put her in a more festive holiday spirit. Thanks to Jack for his quick thinking because it turned around the mood after the mall incident. One thing was sure, she needed to gain more confidence and know how to react in these situations. Haley looked forward to viewing one of the self-defense classes.

Her phone beeped, and Haley saw a message from her sister-in-law.

Hey there. I'm taking Allison and Eli to see Santa on Sunday. Would you like to come along?

Haley responded. *Yes, they are my only excuse for visiting Santa right now. Ha Ha!*

LOL, can you meet us at our house around 2pm?

Sounds perfect. See you then. I'm off that day.

After all the activities, she found herself lying in bed with her phone that night, waiting to hear from Jack. She knew it might be a while before he and the crew were off the plane and settled into their hotel. She was just dozing off, watching television as it rang. Unknown caller showed up on the receiver. She answered it anyway.

"Hello," she waited for a response. No one said anything or she could not hear them.

"Hello, anyone there?" she repeated.

Click. The connection disconnected.

Haley felt sure the call must have been from Jack. No one else would call this late. Perhaps he was having a hard time getting a good connection. She sat up and resumed watching television. Within a few minutes, the phone rang again with Jack's satellite phone number on caller identification.

"Jack!" she said.

"Babe, I'm here."

Haley sighed. "I'm glad you made it, honey. Did you just call a moment ago?"

"I did. I tried from my regular cell phone but couldn't get through or even hear the phone ring. I grabbed the sat phone and made my way outside to call you."

"Okay, good to know. So, where are you right now?"

"Standing outside the entrance of the Hilton Sao Paulo Morumbi. So glad to be on the ground again. Of course, the flight was long, but then it took nearly two hours to get here from the main airport, but it puts us within fifteen minutes of the smaller one we will fly out of tomorrow into the rain forest.

"What is the hotel like?"

"It's pretty sleek and modern, a huge towering skyscraper in the heart of the financial district. Five stars, for sure. The views of the city here, even at night, are incredible. The decor is very minimalistic, but they have Christmas trees in the public areas."

"Sounds incredible! How is your room?"

"I haven't had time to check it out thoroughly. But it's very modern with warm woods. The bed looks comfy and as soon as I finish with you, I am headed in that direction. Plus, I know you need your rest. It's late. Are you working the same shifts as last week?"

"I am. Sarah messaged and invited me to go with her and the kids for their visit with Santa Claus. I'm looking forward to that on Sunday."

"Sounds like great fun. Take some photos."

"I will. Well, I don't know if you will be able to call me again after tomorrow."

"I think the sat phone will work where I'm going. As long as I am not in too dense of tree canopy, the signal should go through. I love you, Haley."

"I love you too, honey. Go take care of yourself. Eat well and get some rest. And, good luck with your mission, whatever it is."

"Thanks, babe. I'll be thinking of you — a lot. Bye-bye."

"Bye."

Chapter 15 ~ Jack in Brazil

Jack turned, walking back toward the Hyatt's glass door entrance as the sole of his shoes hit the marble floor of the massive lobby. While the space was spectacular, it felt somewhat empty. He could only imagine how sparse everything was once the Christmas decor was removed. Jack realized the vacant feeling was also something he was carrying within himself. He was tired. Something to eat, a shower and bed were in fast order. He made his way to the connoisseur's desk and asked if they had a room service menu. The gentleman spoke English well and offered the menu to Jack. After looking it over for a couple of minutes, he asked if a turkey club sandwich with potato chips and milk could be sent to his room.

"Certainly, I will put in the order now."

Jack entered the elevator and made his way up to his floor. He exited, finding his room number for the second time now, and entered his pass key. Inside, the room was dimly lit and the lights from Sao Paulo rose up the wall of glass windows beyond. Peering inside the bathroom, he noticed it was very well appointed with complementary shampoo and other toiletries, including the proverbial shower cap. He smiled, thinking of Sercy's humor. With these items, he would not have to unpack much, perhaps just his toothbrush and toothpaste. Jack would not be bothering with shaving for awhile now — not until he was back home. Haley would be surprised when she finally laid eyes on him, unless he shaved prior to boarding the flight back.

Jack laid out his clothing he would wear in the morning. The flight was early, and he hoped all the guys set alarms or had wake up calls arranged with the hotel. Regardless, he would rise a bit early, if needed, to wake up their asses. There was a soft knock on the door and he made his way to open it, finding a hotel employee standing there with a service cart. Jack dug into his pants pocket for a tip for the young man and he traded with him for the food, thanking him in Portuguese. Finally, some food. He devoured the sandwich, milk, and chips in record time. He then headed for the bathroom, showering and brushing his teeth.

Sleep was coming slowly for Jack despite the long day of travel. He thought about where he was just twenty-four hours ago with Haley, his arms wrapped around her, spooning her silky skin. He thought about Evan Mitchell and knew the guy had a hard on for taking his position at Chadwell. While he tended to be chummier with the corporate brass than Jack, he still lacked the finesse to come up with actual products that would work. And this potential drug therapy would be such a benefit to everyone.

Jack touched the malachite stone around his neck. He wasn't used to sleeping with anything like this. Nonetheless, he would leave it on throughout the trip, just as he had told Haley he would.

Finally, Jack fell into a deep sleep that would last until he heard the alarm clock on his phone going off. But during the night, he dreamed. Jack could not see what he was fighting, but he felt high emotion, as if fighting for his very life. He could hear the rumble of something dark and low permeating throughout the dream. He saw fire and felt himself running, but he could not see where he was or in which direction he was headed. Everything seemed to have a misty blur around it. Nothing was clear. Still, when the alarm sounded and he woke, the dream feeling hung on even if he could not remember the details.

Chapter 16 ~ Into the Rainforest

Wednesday, December 4, 2019

The hotel van was on time and ready to take all four of the Chadwell employees to the Congonhas airport. Jack was glad everyone was running on time, especially himself. After last night's tossing and turning and little sleep the night before, he could have easily kept hitting the snooze button.

The drive to the small airfield was short compared to the trip from the international airport. Jack tipped the driver and thanked him for getting them there. They found a couple of porters to help them unload the gear and also show them where they needed to go next. The distance to the plane and loading area was not too long. Once there, they watched as the porters loaded the back of the plane with their belongings. A man was approaching and he looked American. This was the kind of trip where you actually met and shook hands with the pilot, a man of mid=fifties.

"Beautiful plane," Jack commented to the pilot as he approached them. "Hi, I'm Jack Foster."

"Nice to meet you, Jack," the pilot replied as they shook hands. "I'm Stan Crossman, your pilot."

Stan touched the plane's exterior as he spoke. "This is a King Air 250. She is gorgeous and fairly luxurious for this size aircraft. Let me give you guys a short tour," he said, walking around to the entrance door.

The plane is pressurized so we can fly higher than many small planes, plus you will feel more comfortable. She has her own digital navigation system, along with monitoring for weather and more. It's a perfect choice for someone who wants to fly quickly and it is very safe. If desired or needed, this plane can land on short runways or even on grass or dirt. You will find the leather seats very comfortable and each one has a window."

The pilot bent inside the plane and flipped out a console beside one of the seats. "Cup holders and a small desk or tray are beside each seat," he added. Once the equipment was loaded, they found their seats. The pilot asked if anyone would like to ride shotgun with him. Jack volunteered and ducked down, making his way into the cockpit area. He was amazed, gazing at all the buttons and touch screens in front of the pilot. The colors emanating from the screens lit up with as much intensity as any video game. It took his mind off the dream, which had been staggering in the background of his mind all during the ride to the airfield. Instinctively, his hand reached up and rubbed the malachite. The pilot noticed. "Lucky stone?"

"Yeah, malachite," Jack chuckled. "My wife gave it to me."

"I'm sorry, horrible at remembering names. You're Jack, right?" Stan inquired.

"Yep, that's me."

"What kind of trip you guys on?"

"We're here for Chadwell Pharmaceuticals gathering some prospective plants for drugs in the rain forest."

"Yes, I saw Chadwell was the client on the intake info."

"Well, you will likely run into some rain this time of year."

"No doubt. Hopefully, we have enough of the right gear. We'll be spending a lot of hours in the field."

"Speaking of hours, I ordered some coffee a bit ago. That's all I'm waiting on before take-off."

Moments later, a young man in his twenties with an airport crew member uniform could be seen walking toward the plane. He was carrying the coffee and walked up the staircase to deliver it.

"Coffee is here. Mr. Crossman, I have enough here for everyone."

"Thanks. That's really thoughtful of you," Stan said.

He handed a tray with five cups of coffee and Jack reached out to take it. He made sure the pilot got his first and then offered it to his coworkers, each of which took one.

"Well, there will be two for you, Stan. I've had my limit this morning. Sitting up front here in the cockpit, I don't need to feel jittery."

"It's up to you. That leaves more for me," Stan said. He smiled and picked up his sunglasses.

"Have at it. I'm good. I brought a water here in my backpack if I get thirsty," replied Jack.

"Everyone, keep your drinks in the cup holders until we are up smooth in the air. Okay, I would say we are ready for takeoff — next stop is into the rain forest," Stan said, as he locked down everything. Jack looked back and everything seemed in order. The door to the plane was closed and locked. Everyone was buckled up and had their coffee in the snug cup holders.

As the engines on the prop plane fired, Jack watched inquisitively as the pilot pushed one button after another and kept changing visuals on the touch screen. Finally, the plane backed up a little, and then the pilot moved her forward toward the runway. It was surprising how much power the small plane had compared to others he had ridden upon. Perhaps it was just where he was situated inside the plane that made it seem that way.

Within minutes they were over a vast carpet of green — the canopy. The view looked unreal, like something out of a movie. It felt so free to be up high, peering into the Brazilian world below. While lost in the thrill, he heard the pilot ask him, "How do you like the scenery?"

"It's out of this world beautiful. Leaves me speechless, really," Jack replied.

He peered back at his mates. Lance was asleep, missing the incredible view. Poor guy must have not slept well last night. Hopefully, he can catch enough shut eye until they reach their destination.

Another five or ten minutes passed by with Jack's face almost glued to the window to his right, occasionally peering out the cockpit window as well. He felt safer looking out the side window. It wasn't that he was deathly afraid. It was just the front-on realization — the visual knowing he was in a small plane gliding through the air. It was exhilarating and unnerving, but the pilot seemed very competent and experienced.

Jack swiveled his head to the left to see how the rest of the crew were doing, only to find all were asleep and missing this incredible view. *Damn*, he thought, *must have forgotten to down their coffees.* He felt the plane dip suddenly and looked over at Stan only to see he was fighting to stay awake.

"Stan!" he shouted. The man's head suddenly dipped and he appeared to be out cold.

Panic set in. They all had coffee, but Jack didn't. Could something have been in it?

"Fuck!" Jack yelled.

He looked at the unusual u-shaped steering wheel and the other instruments. He had no idea what to do. Jack grabbed the microphone headset, which was hanging on the interior for a copilot, and placed it on his head quickly. He pushed the microphone button on the pilot's wheel to try to get in touch with ground control. He had watched the pilot push the button, so he at least knew how to operate that.

"Mayday, mayday! I've got an emergency."

"Air six six three delta whiskey I hear you loud and clear. Do you hear me?"

"Yes, I hear you. The pilot and crew have been drugged or poisoned. I need help up here. I can't wake them up".

"Air six six three delta whiskey uh … roger …uh. Are you a pilot?"

"No, I'm not a pilot. I need to get this plane down safely."

"Air six six three delta whiskey roger that. You're in a King Air, correct?"

"Yes, this is a King Air. Who can help me?"

Jack spoke little Portuguese and the person he was communicating with spoke English but the accent was thick, making it even more difficult to understand over the airwaves.

The response time from ground control was taking too long. Did they have no one there who could help him? Jack decided to move the pilot over into the co-pilot seat so he could have better access to the controls. *Dammit, if they could only get someone who can tell me what to do.*

Finally, a new voice came through speaking clear English.

"Are you a pilot?"

"No, the pilot is unconscious but breathing."

"Are you in his seat?"

"I moved him over to the co-pilot seat. Yes, I am sitting in his seat now."

"It appears you're at 11,000 one one thousand, but still climbing now. We need to find out if the autopilot is on and if so, get it leveled off. Give me a moment to clear your area."

Jack could hear the ground control rapidly issuing instructions to several other aircraft in his area, telling them to move away from that sector.

"Air six six three delta whiskey, are you able to maintain one two thousand?"

"What do I push or turn off? It looks like it's set at ten thousand. I don't know why it keeps climbing."

"Air six six three delta whiskey, can you tell if the autopilot is on or not?"

"It looks like it is and set at ten thousand. Now I'm at thirteen thousand. How do I shut this off?"

"Air six six three delta whiskey understand that we're trying to find some help with that King Air. Stand by"

"Still climbing fourteen thousand"

"Okay, six six three delta whiskey. When you look at the center console there, do you see anything that would disengage the autopilot?"

"I don't know. I see where the autopilot switch is. I can disengage it if you think I should."

"Six six three delta whiskey, roger that. Disengage the autopilot. We're going to try and help you hand fly the plane."

"Okay, I've disengaged the autopilot. Now what?"

"Six six three delta whiskey, I need you to hold the yoke or steering wheel steady for a moment. Can you do that? Hold the yoke level and steady."

Jack grabbed the pilot's steering wheel and it felt like he had grabbed hold of a bear. Trying to keep it steady even for a few moments was a fight. The plane was diving now, heading straight for the canopy.

"Shit!" Jack cursed.

Chapter 17 ~ Devastation

Haley sat at the large semi circle desk area in the hospital unit finishing up chart notes. Her first day back made the time go quickly and while she definitely had momentary thoughts of Jack, she stayed occupied with her tiny, adorable patients. She entered the last few notes into the hospital's system and then logged out. The replacement shift had arrived, and she chatted with the new relief nurse about any patient events and other miscellaneous important things for her to be aware of. Once completed, she turned on her cell phone and made her way toward the parking garage.

While walking down the corridor that made up the long stretch to the building exit, her phone vibrated continually in her hand. She paused, looking down at the texts and phone calls on the screen. The numbers were unfamiliar but local. It looked as if they may have come from Jack's work. She opened the text app.

Please call Chadwell immediately and ask for Evan Mitchell. Urgent!

The next text read: ***Haley, this is Evan Mitchell. I left you a couple of voice mails. Please call my cell phone at this number as soon as you can***

Why would Evan be contacting her? Perhaps he could not get in touch with Jack and thought she might speak to him earlier than he would. Must be something going on at Chadwell that he needs to talk to Jack about. Still, the urgency of it all made her hollow, hungry stomach ache. *Let me get home and I'll give him a call.*

Arriving at the exit door at the end of the long passage, she scanned her badge to be let out of the hospital door. She waved at the guard and he waved back, exiting his area to see Haley to her vehicle. "Thank you again," she said. He watched as she started the vehicle, backed out, and left the garage.

All during the drive home, she thought of Evan's insistence and the messages. She arrived home, entering the garage with her vehicle, shutting the car off and closing the garage door. As soon as her feet hit the kitchen tile, she kicked off her shoes. Washing her hands, she grabbed a yogurt from the refrigerator and sat down at the table to dial Evan's number. He answered immediately.

"Evan, this is Haley. I'm sorry to be so long in responding. I have my cell phone off when I am at work."

"No problem Haley. Are you still at work?"

"I just arrived home. What's up? Are you trying to get in touch with Jack?"

There was a slight pause in the conversation.

"I'm afraid something has happened, Haley. We don't know all the specifics yet, but the plane carrying the crew into Alta Floresta has reportedly crashed."

There was another pause — this time with Haley not responding. Evan's words seemed sincere and he would not do anything like this as a sick joke.

"A crash? Oh my God!" were the only words she could get out.

"We are hoping they have survived it. There are people on the ground now -- a search and rescue team. Chadwell is putting together their own team to conduct a separate search. I am sure it will be mentioned in the media soon, but I wanted to call and tell you myself before you found out about the crash in that manner. I just got off the phone with Jack's parents. Understandably, they have many questions and are in some turmoil, just as I am sure you are."

"Are you sure Jack was on that plane? It doesn't seem real. I, uh, I don't know ...." she began to cry.

"It's definitely the plane the Chadwell employees were on. Haley, we're hoping and praying for survivors. The area the plane went down in is pretty remote. Right now, let's assume that Jack is fine, maybe a bit worse off than when he boarded. I know this must be shocking, but we must keep hope, right?"

"Yes," she sobbed, "I'll be praying."

"Me too. I will contact you again the moment I know something definitive," he said. "Call me if you need anything, have more questions, or just need to talk. Okay?"

Haley clicked the phone off without even saying goodbye. Everything seemed to move in slow motion. The yogurt was no longer appealing. She glanced at Jack's office off the kitchen, viewing his empty chair. What if he did not make it and would never sit there again? Rising, she made her way into Jack's office. She pulled her feet up in the leather executive style chair and hugged her legs. Burying her head into her knees, tears flowed and she prayed earnestly.

God, please let them be alright. Please don't take Jack from me now. And if he is hurt, God, please, please ease his pain.

Haley's head swirled with dizziness and she felt like she needed to lie down. She slowly shifted and moved toward the living room and sat down on the oversized couch. Placing her head between her legs to keep the blood flow there, she cried out, "No, no. I cannot lose Jack. I cannot believe this. This isn't real."

Shifting her position again, she fell onto the couch and sobbed uncontrollably. Invisible pieces of the sky fell onto her as she lie on her right side. "God, no. Please! Tell me this is not real. Please God, this can't be real."

The phone rang a couple of moments later. It was Sarah. "Haley, I just heard. I can't believe it."

"I can't either."

"Are you there alone?"

"Yes."

"Do you want me to come over and sit with you? I know this must be weighing so heavily upon you."

"I … I don't know. Thank you, but let's hold out hope. I feel immobilized. I'm going to turn on the television."

"Look, Jason is on his way home from work and he can stay here with the children. As soon as he gets here, I'm coming out to your house."

"Okay."

There was a part of her that wanted to be alone with this with no one around. Haley wished she could just lie down, sleep, and wake up finding this was nothing more than a bad dream. She had to believe this was nothing but a nightmare.

Chapter 18 ~ The Messenger

Evan looked at the time on his phone. Damn, still no definitive word on the crash. Chadwell's spacious lab felt large and hauntingly empty. Ignoring the feeling, he resumed examination of a small flower with the stereomicroscope, dictating his observations as he made them. Evan tried to keep his mind on his work, ignoring his previous conversations with Tellinger and the other board member. The plane had gone down. Now, they were just waiting to hopefully hear there were no survivors - especially of the Jack Foster variety.

A few moments later, Jack's assistant, Kendra, came into the lab. "There you are. I thought you might be here. Mr. Tellinger wants to speak with you, he's on line three."

"Thanks, Kendra."

He pushed line three on the desk phone next to the computer. "Hello, this is Evan Mitchell."

"Evan, Tellinger here. Word has come from the aviation authorities that the plane has been found. Indeed, it is down on the forest floor of Brazil with no survivors. The bodies seemed to have been hard to recognize from the impact of the fall, plus several huge branches have fallen upon the plane."

J.D. Tellinger relayed this to Evan in a voice that sounded like he was reciting something that he never knew would happen, yet he was the one who had scripted it. The CEO was convincing, sounding surprised about the entire event. Evan wanted to know more. "Did the plane catch on fire?" he asked Tellinger.

"I'm not sure how much fire damage there was, but at least a small amount. With the crushing impact, it would not have made a difference in anyone being able to survive." There was a pause for a few seconds in the conversation. Finally, Evan asked, "What happens next? I will need to contact all the families about their deaths, if that is what you want me to do."

"Since you are now the head of the department, it would be appropriate for you to do so. Be gentle. This is a fragile situation and heartbreaking for them."

"Of course, I will tread as softly as I can with the news. However, we have to stay ahead of the cable news cycle on this."

"Yes, that is important, and I am glad you understand that. I have Shelly Larson, our media relations director, handling all communications on this. If you can be the liaison with the families of your department, this will help tremendously."

"I'll get right on it, sir." Evan sensed that J.D. had not finished the conversation and paused again for the man to speak. "You asked me about what happens next down there on the ground in Brazil. Once any remains are collected, we will pay to have them shipped back to the United States. Any and all personal effects that are recovered may come in a separate shipment later."

"Thanks for letting me know that. I guess that brings up a grim question about funeral arrangements. What should I tell the families regarding this?"

"Well, it sounds as if they could be looking at a closed casket situation. Honestly, I just don't know what we are dealing with as far as the remains. So, this is another delicate area to tread lightly upon with the families. Perhaps you could suggest they contact a mortuary service they would want their loved one's remains shipped to and then have them just stand by. If you can collect the who, what, where for me, I will see that the remains are delivered to the appropriate service."

Evan sighed heavily. "Wow, this is pretty intense subject matter to discuss with their families, but believe me, I'll do my best."

"Good, that's what we need, Evan. It's a freak, horrific tragedy, isn't it?"

Evan's mind was blown with how well J.D. played the part. "Yes, it is."

"Also, there will be questions about what caused the crash. Tell the family members the officials do not know that yet. Once they recover the plane's flight recorder and perhaps any internal recording of the occupants, that will tell a lot more. All of that is out of our hands and with the aviation authorities."

"Okay. Good to know and thank you for calling."

"You bet. I'll be back in touch if I have more information."

Evan twirled his ink pen over the notepad where he had written the specifics from the conversation. He picked up the desk telephone again and buzzed Jack's personal assistant, Kendra.

"Yes," she responded.

"Would you mind meeting me in my office in about five minutes? I need to speak with you about the plane accident."

"Sure, I'll be there."

Evan spoke in a low tone, but audible for her to hear him. "Kendra, please have a seat. As you know, I just got off the phone with Mr. Tellinger." She sat in the chair across from him and looked expectantly for his next words.

"There are no survivors in the wreckage."

Evan paused as he saw she was very shaken to hear this. This was a tightly knit work group, and she had been

Jack's assistant for seven years. Her eyes were watering and her hands appeared shaky.

"I am tasked with meeting with the families of those lost since they were all in this department. Could you please gather full contact information for all families, including anyone they may have put down as emergency contacts? I know you did this already, but this is such a delicate matter. I just want to make sure I don't leave anyone out. So, if you could go over each file that human resources sent up and let me know, that would be great."

"Sure, I will double check each employee."

"Great, and I don't want to stress you further, but I need this soon to stay ahead of what may be reported in the news."

"You got it."

As she turned to leave, Evan stood and said, "I'm sorry. I know this hits you hard as well."

"Yes, yes, it does. I'm in a bit of shock with it all."

"It seems to have that effect. Oh, and please, no speaking of this to anyone at this time to give me time to meet with the families."

Kendra responded with, "Sure. I can't believe it anyway!"

She closed the door and Evan could not help but feel like a traitor. He had to keep his thoughts on what was best for the good of all. Tellinger had pointed out to him every problem with Jack's new drug he had in early development. Jack would not be deterred and if Chadwell would not go along with it, he would have sold the information and technology elsewhere. Tellinger explained that Jack's drug could be detrimental to plans later down the road that were top secret and known only on a "need to know" basis. While Evan did not know what that information was, he trusted that the top brass at Chadwell were telling him the truth.

It was important to meet with all the families quickly. Haley's image danced in his mind's eye. He wanted to keep her in his good graces and would make a personal visit to her home.

He walked past Kendra's desk and could see she was still checking the files. "Just send me a pdf on my phone when you have it all together. I am going right now to meet with Haley Foster."

She gave him a nod that accompanied a look of sadness and great concern.

"I don't envy you," she said.

Evan logged out of the building after passing the security check and fingerprint scan. He made his way through the parking lot of the large complex to his black Porsche, a gift to himself when he received a large bonus a couple of years ago. While that only covered a nice down payment on it, he did not regret purchasing the fine car. He liked things sleek, clean, and well made. Ultimately, that meant expensive.

Evan felt he should call ahead while on his way to the Foster residence to give Haley some notice of his arrival. He dialed the number and she picked up quickly this time. "Hello."

"Haley, it's Evan Mitchell again. I wanted to let you know I am on the way to your and Jack's house. I want to meet with you in person. I should arrive in about twenty to twenty-five minutes. Be there soon."

He clicked off before she could ask any questions, not to be rude, but to be there in person to catch her when he relayed the tragic news.

Chapter 19 ~ The News

Haley thought about what a crazy turn the day had taken. Despite feeling she should know better, she made several calls to Jack on his cell and satellite phones. All went directly to voice mail. Now, Sarah was coming to see her and Evan too. She glanced at the mirror over the table in the foyer. *I don't care how I look right now,* she thought. Regardless, she decided to get out of her scrubs and put some sweats on.

Haley stopped abruptly as she walked into the bedroom. She stood, glaring at the bed, realizing this could be it. Was this a cutoff point in time when Jack would never be with her again to hold and love her? She felt frozen in her steps. *Don't think like that. It's going to be alright. It has to be.*

She could hear a low roar approaching the drive and house. *This must be one of them.* She opened the front door and stepped onto the walkway. A black Porsche sat gleaming in the drive. The door opened and Evan emerged. He walked swiftly toward her and looked more serious than she had ever seen him before. The pit of her stomach pinged with searing pain.

"Haley, thanks for letting me come by. Do you want to go inside to talk?"

"What do you know, Evan? Tell me what you know. I've been watching the news and have heard nothing for sure."

"I do have information, Haley. That's why I'm here. Let's go inside."

"Alright, this way," she said

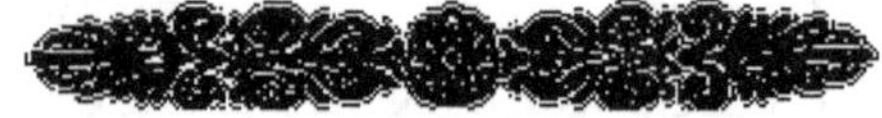

Evan followed Haley into the house and she directed him to sit in the living room across from her on a twin companion couch.

"Tell me what you know."

"It's worse than we wanted to hear or expected, Haley." He watched as her expression went from serious worry to a look of defeat. "The plane crashed in the rain forest in Brazil. I'm told there are no living survivors."

Haley shot up off the couch and screamed, "No, no, no — this can't be!"

Evan suddenly felt like maybe he should have brought along another person to help. He had no idea Haley was capable of shouting like this and having that much anger. God knows he felt guilty as hell. He had helped craft this and bring it upon her world. Evan rose and walked toward her.

"Haley, I am so sorry. I have been tasked by Chadwell to be the bearer of this tragedy to the families. I wanted you to be the first. I'm quickly realizing I may not have been qualified to break this news to you or anyone else."

Haley's arms were folded over her chest and midriff. She looked completely enraged. He could see a vein in her temple emerging through the skin.

Evan continued trying to talk to her. "What can I do right now to help you?" he asked softly and looked into her eyes.

Haley's pretenses and denial began to fade. There was a part of her that felt as if she did not accept this news to be true, it wouldn't be. As if she could control the reality of the crash by just not believing it. She felt herself sink inside as she realized this was real. Haley sat down again on the couch and quickly lay down on her side. The tears and sobbing began. Evan rushed over to her and knelt on the floor at her side. He grabbed one of her hands. "I'm here for you Haley. I don't know what to say, but I am here for you with whatever you need."

The doorbell rang and Evan asked, "Do you want me to get the door?"

"Yes, it's probably my sister-in-law, Sarah."

Evan walked toward the front door and opened it.

"Hi, who are you?" she inquired.

"You must be Sarah. I'm Evan Mitchell from Chadwell. I spoke to your husband on the phone earlier today. I worked with Jack."

Sarah made her way into the foyer and saw Haley lying on the couch, crying.

"What do you mean you worked with Jack? Did you leave Chadwell?" she asked, fearing the answer.

"Please, come in and let's talk, Sarah."

Sarah rushed over to Haley who rose up and hugged her sister-in-law.

"They are saying they didn't make it. No survivors," she sobbed.

Sarah looked at Evan as if to ask if this was true, and he nodded his head affirmatively.

"Oh, honey. I am so sorry. This is devastating. I can't believe it!"

Sarah's eyes became watery, but she tried to be strong for Haley.

"Sit here. I'm going to get you some tissue and I need some water. I'll fetch you some too."

Sarah walked toward the kitchen and opened the refrigerator where she knew Haley stored bottled water. She caught Evan's eye and motioned for him to follow her as well. "Evan, you need something to drink?"

"Yes, I'll take some water."

At the kitchen island, Sarah asked softly, "What do they know so far?"

Evan opened the cap off the bottle, took a swig, then sat it on the island. "The crash was severe and there are no survivors. That is what I have been told. We still don't know why the plane went down."

Sarah was quiet and her eyes watered more. "How has Haley taken the news so far?"

"I think she's having a bit of denial right now. Of course, anyone would."

Sarah nodded her head. "I'll be here with her for awhile if you need to leave."

Evan read her comment two ways. He could tell that Sarah was a strong woman, and she seemed comfortable confronting anyone or making demands. She was giving him both a reason to leave and an invitation to do so.

"Thank you for staying with her until I arrived," Sarah added.

"Yes, of course," Evan said in a low voice. He glanced at Haley still lying down. "I will just say goodbye to her for now and be on my way. I have to meet with the other families, including Jack's parents."

Sarah watched him walk toward Haley on the couch again.

"Haley, again, I am very sorry. Here is my card with my number. If you have more questions or need anything … anything at all, I want you to call me."

Haley reached out and took his card.

"Thanks, I will."

"I am going to meet with your in-laws now."

He looked at Sarah. "Any advice on the easiest way to break the news to them?"

Sarah shook her head back and forth negatively and just looked down.

"Evan, please tell them I am here with Haley or I would be there with them."

Evan walked toward the front door, and Sarah followed him, saying goodbye and locking it behind him. She took Haley water and sat down beside her. She sat up from the couch and took a couple of sips. Sarah looked her in the eyes. "I wish this would go away too, Haley. We need this to not be true. Take my hand and let's pray."

The cable news station played on, and Sarah decided to turn its volume down a bit. Haley looked at her, a bit panic stricken. She seemed to be waiting for some positive word to come upon the television, but none did. Sarah handed her the remote. "We can turn it up immediately if they mention the plane. How about I go rummage in the kitchen? You need to keep your strength up right now, even if you don't feel like eating. What sounds good to you?" Haley just gave her a vacant stare. Food seemed like a foreign substance right now. Yes, her stomach was empty, and she was hungry, but to sit and eat right now felt almost like being a traitor to Jack. How could she think of herself like that when he could be somewhere barely alive? And if he were dead, how could she just learn of that and pop up suddenly to eat? Sarah seemed to read her mind.

"Haley, listen to me. Jack would want you to take care of yourself. We don't know what the next hour or so holds or even tomorrow. He would want you to not ignore your needs."

"You're right. I am hungry. It just seems so ...." And she began crying again. Sarah sat beside her and just held her for a long time. "We are going to get through this, Haley."

After a bit of time, Haley thanked her for being there. "I guess if the company is right and they say there are no survivors, I have to believe that. But it's all so quick, so shocking. Sarah, I love him so much. I cannot see living life without him."

Chapter 20 ~ Sarah

Sarah felt such weight on her, trying to know the right thing to say, but she didn't. While the loss of Jack impacted her and the entire family, Haley had lost her husband, best friend and lover in a few hours, with no notice. How could anyone deal with this? She felt she needed to call in help from others for Haley, but who? She knew Jessie and Alex next door were very tight with Jack and Haley.

"Look, I am going to see what I can rustle up for us to eat, and I need to make a few phone calls. Will you be alright here while I'm in the kitchen?"

"Yeah, I'm fine. I actually need to pee."

"Do you want me to go with you?"

"No, no. I will be fine to walk. I'll be back on this couch as soon as I'm done, though."

"Okay. And I will be right in the kitchen."

Sarah figured soon, if not already, Evan Mitchell had met with Joe & Sharon. Good lord, what a day this was for everyone. Just goes to show you never know what turn of fate can happen in life that changes the dynamics of everything. She opened the freezer and found some frozen meals that could be heated easily. She almost stopped to ask Haley if it was okay to fix them, but decided not to. It was best to keep her from making what might seem like trivial decisions right now. Sarah intended to simply heat them and get something in Haley's belly.

While the food was heating, she dialed Jason. He picked up right away. "Honey, I am here with Haley and might be here for a while. Are you still with the kids?"

"Yes, what do you know?"

Sarah sighed. "Where are the children right now in the house?"

"They are in the play area, not within ear shot …. Tell me, Sarah. Is my brother alive?"

"They, being the Chadwell company people, say the plane has been located and there are no survivors. I am so sorry, honey. I know he's your twin brother, but it's hitting me, too."

"How in the hell did this happen? Do they know that?"

"Not yet."

Jason was silent, and Sarah could hear him whimpering. "Please don't say anything to the children until I am there with you."

"I won't. I need some time to process this in my mind. What about mom and dad, do they know?"

"If they don't, they will soon. Evan Mitchell, who Jack left in charge, has gone to meet with them. Not the best choice for the company, if you ask me, to break this type of news."

"Why do you say that?"

"Ahh, maybe it's the Porsche he drives or the way he just carries himself. A bit arrogant and not a real empathetic sort."

"Was he rude to Haley?"

"No, no. I'm not saying that. I don't think he was, but it's just a vibe I get from him."

"Well now, I feel like I may need to get to mom and dad's house soon. What should we do, Sarah? I know you don't want to leave her there by herself?"

"I don't think she's eaten for awhile. I'm heating us some dinners she had in the freezer. Let me figure out something and I will try to call back in about thirty minutes or so."

"Okay, I'll be waiting."

"I'm so sorry honey."

"Me too. I can't believe this. My brother ...." He said trailing off. Sarah could hear Jason crying. She wanted to be there for him, to hold on to him. She felt torn because she knew Haley was probably in some type of shock. But Jason was too.

The phone clicked off and Sarah realized she had gone from bringing her kids home from daycare and just being a regular old mom to needing to mother all the adults around her tonight and maybe for some days into the future. She would need help.

Haley had vacillated from lying down on the couch in front of the television to sitting up with her head in her hands and elbows resting on her knees. This woman was going through a type of mental torture that Sarah never wanted to experience. She pushed back tears to try and stay steady for the situation at hand. "Haley, I've got some food here ready."

Haley slowly rose, walking toward the kitchen with her feet sort of shuffling. She looked at the food and said nothing. She sat down and almost seemed catatonic. "Go ahead and eat, honey. I'm worried about you," Sarah told her earnestly.

Sarah watched Haley as she delivered the prepared dishes to the kitchen table. They ate silently together. Finally, Sarah spoke. "Haley, I don't want you to be alone right now. I am going to have to leave soon and go home. You are welcome to come with me. I could help you pack some things. The only other thing I have thought of is that you could either go to our in-laws or perhaps have Jessie come over. Do you think I should call Alex and Jessie next door and tell them what we know so far?"

Haley placed her fork on her plate and looked up at Sarah. "Thank you for being here. Of course, you need to get home. You and Jason have lost Jack too." She looked so defeated. Sarah could tell the reality was sinking in with her now, but she also knew that Haley could not be left alone. Between her struggles with post traumatic stress and this tremendous shock, she needed someone with her.

"Yes, we have all lost Jack. It's like a mountain has collided upon us, but even more so for you, honey. I cannot leave you here alone in good conscience."

"Would you mind being the one to talk to Jessie and Alex? I just don't feel as if I can make that phone call."

"Of course, I will give them a ring in just a minute. But I do need their number."

"Sure, let me grab my cell phone."

Sarah saved Alex and Jessie's numbers to her phone and then dialed Jessie. She got voice mail.

"Hi Jessie. This is Sarah, Haley's sister-in-law. I am at Haley and Jack's house, and I need you to give me a call when you get this message. Haley is okay, but something has happened."

Within moments, Jessie called. "Sarah, hey I'm sorry. I was bringing in groceries. What's going on?"

"A plane that was carrying Jack and his coworkers into the rain forest has crashed."

"What? Oh, my gosh."

"We have been told there are no survivors. I am here with Haley, but I have to get home to my husband and kids soon. Haley is welcome to come with me, but she probably prefers to stay here. Is there any way you could be with her until we figure out what we are going to do next? I can come back at some point, but I don't know exactly when yet."

"Of course, yes. Let me talk to Alex and I will be right over."

Chapter 21 ~ Alex & Jessie

Haley Sarah had just finished cleaning up after their meal when the doorbell rang. "I'll get it," she said. Haley remained in her position on the couch, glued to the television screen for any additional news

Jessie's silhouette could be seen from the cut glass in the front door and Sarah opened it. "Thanks for coming, Jessie."

"No problem at all. What can I do, Sarah? I'm not sure what to do."

"Unfortunately, we can't do much of anything," Sarah looked at Jessie and deliberately opened her eyes very wide, nodding affirmatively to get her attention. "Come to the kitchen and let me get you something to drink."

Jessie took the cue and followed her, first stopping to check on Haley. She sat down beside her on the couch, making sure she was not blocking the view of the television, which Haley seemed entranced by. "Hey. How are you holding up? This is so horrible. I am so sorry, Haley," she said through tearful eyes.

"Haley moved her attention off the television, which was playing another relentless commercial and looked at Jessie. Her eyes were ringed with red from crying. "It just doesn't seem real, and then it does. I feel so angry and devastated at the same time."

"Of course, I am here for you. Let me get something to drink. Do you want anything?"

"No, we just ate and I'm fine. Thank you, though."

Jessie made her way into the kitchen where Sarah made herself look busy but was waiting for her. "Jessie, can I get you something, or do you know where everything is here?"

"I'm good. I'll just grab some water from the refrigerator."

"Again, thank you for coming over. I will know more about what we all plan to do as a family soon, I suppose. She probably could use a hot shower, but I'd stay close by and check on her. This is so shocking; she could pass out or something."

"Yes, you're right. Sarah, I'm sorry for your loss of Jack too. Are they sure he's gone?" Jessie whispered.

"As sure as they can be right now. Haley is holding out hope so she keeps watching for any additional information on the cable news. I don't think we are going to get her to stop doing that."

Just as Sarah spoke the words, they both saw Haley rise from the couch.

"They just said they have some images and information on the plane crash. It should be coming up after these damn commercials," Haley said with bated excitement.

Jessie motioned for Sarah to follow her into the living room. Even though Sarah was leaving, she knew that any information might help both women … and her as well. Plus, images could be hard for Haley to see, especially alone.

Sarah sat to the left of Haley, while Jessie flanked her other side. The relentless commercials finally ended and the newscaster resumed.

"We have exclusive first scene footage that has come in from Brazil on the small plane carrying four employees of Chadwell Pharmaceuticals and the pilot. The aircraft was a King Air 250 small plane for private transportation. The report coming from rescue crews is that there were no survivors. Names of those aboard are being withheld at this time until next of kin are notified. The cause of the crash is under investigation."

Haley sat with the remote and paused live television as the screen changed to show footage of the downed aircraft. Her expression and those of her two companions were ghost white as they saw how crushed the aircraft was — not only from the ground impact, but the large limbs on top of it.

There was total silence in the room as the three sat looking at the frozen screen with the horrific image. Tears came strong now from each of them. Finally, the three stood huddled together, holding each other tightly. Sarah spoke first.

"Haley, honey, this is real and we have to make plans — plans for Jack's service, plans for you. We don't have to do it right this minute, but over the next few days."

Haley nodded her head up and down between more tears as Sarah spoke. Jessie squeezed Haley's hand. She looked at Sarah gratefully for saying what needed to be said.

Today was requiring more courage in Sarah than she perhaps had. But someone had to help.

"Jessie is going to be here with you for now. I've got to get with the rest of our family, but I'll be back in touch soon, okay?"

Haley hesitantly said, "Okay."

After Sarah left, Jessie received a message from Alex:

Hey, just saw it on the news. How is Haley doing? Hell, how are you doing? Can I come over?

"Yes, come on over."

Alex arrived a few moments later, and as Haley saw him and the look of sorrow he wore, she became aware again that the loss of Jack impacted everyone, not just her. She hugged the big former NFL linebacker, hanging onto him with both of them sobbing. Alex did not know what to say as he embraced Haley, except that he was devastated to hear this news and so very sorry. "Do you and Jack have a pastor or clergy person?" he asked.

"Yes, we attend First Christian Church. Reverend McAllister is there. He performed our marriage ceremony and Jack's entire family attends there."

"I'm going to get hold of him, Haley. We all love Jack and are too close to this situation. I think having someone to talk with us right now, pray with us as well, would be beneficial."

Haley nodded her head up and down, saying nothing. He could tell that she almost felt like we were making the circle bigger in a way she didn't want to. Each person who sat with her or confirmed this accident made it more real for her. But real it was, and he felt they needed the wisdom and advice of someone who dealt regularly in such matters.

Alex searched the Internet on his phone for Reverend McAllister's number and found it quickly. He added it to his contacts and pushed talk. The line rang a few times and voice mail came on. Alex found himself pacing and eventually walking into Jack's office off the kitchen to leave the bad news message for the clergyman.

Rev. McAllister phoned Alex back within a minute. "Hello, Alex?"

"Yes, is this Reverend McAllister?"

"It is and I am so sorry to hear about this tragedy. What an untimely incident for Jack, Haley and his family.

I am actually headed over to see Jack's parents now. I am available to come by there as soon as I am finished."

"Actually, I'm going to be trying to talk Haley into coming to our house for the night. We live right next door and have a guest bedroom she could stay in. We don't want her to be alone with this. I don't know if she will agree or not. Can I text you in a bit and let you know exactly the situation?"

"Yes, that sounds good. I'll watch for your message, Alex. Thank you for reaching out to me. I am here to serve however I can."

"Thank you Reverend. Thank you very much!"

Alex joined Jessie in the living room, sitting on the couch beside her. "Where is she?" he inquired of Haley.

"She's taking a hot shower. I asked her to leave the door unlocked, just in case she needed me for anything. She probably needs a little space, even though I don't think she should be alone."

"Reverend McAllister from their church is visiting with Jack's parents now or about to. After that, he can meet with Haley. I think we should try to talk her into staying with us tonight. What do you think?"

"Oh, honey, I'm glad we think alike. Of course, I don't mind staying here with her, but just getting her away from the same bed she and Jack shared might help. It will give a little distance while she absorbs all of this. So much to deal with, Alex. I can't imagine it if I were in her shoes and it was you gone."

"Yeah, I know. It's all hard to believe, but believe it we must," he said.

Jessie wore a look of concern. "I'm going to see if I hear the water running still and check on her status."

"Okay."

Jessie could hear the shower still running from the master bedroom door. She wondered what thoughts were going through Haley's mind. Returning to Alex in the living area, she let him know that as far as she could tell, Haley was still showering.

Lines appeared on Alex's forehead. "We need to have her come over and stay with us for at least a few hours, if not the night. This is not a time for her to be alone."

Chapter 22 ~ Bearer of Bad News

Evan felt emotionally fatigued after the meeting with Jack's parents. Mrs. Foster was inconsolable and his father was angry, demanding to know how the accident had occurred and who was going to the crash site. Evan had some answers, but not enough to placate the man for now. He promised to keep him in the loop and call when he knew anything further.

He had several more visits to try and make quickly, but delicately. As he sped up on the freeway, he realized he was probably falling behind the news cycle. He had spent too much time with Haley, but honestly, he was most worried about her. There was something about that woman that really appealed to him and he wanted to not only stay on her good side, but be there to catch her if she fell emotionally.

While all families had been initially notified of the accident, he was making the in-person visits to represent Chadwell and make sure that any information he gave them was not only what was really known at the present, but stayed with the narrative that needed to play out.

He pulled up to a large condominium complex to meet with Luke Felder, Lance's partner. The complex was well laid out in a town home design. Each unit probably had the bedrooms upstairs and living area in the lower level. He approached the door and noticed how well it was decorated with the colorful autumn wreath and a wooden plague beside the door that said *Grateful*.

Luke opened the door before he could even knock. "Hello Luke". He recognized him from functions Chadwell had sponsored when spouses and partners accompanied the employees.

"Evan, what do you know?" he asked expectantly. "Come in."

Evan entered the small foyer and was directed into the living area. "Please, sit down. Do you need something to drink?"

"No, I'm fine, thank you. I do not have good news. I'm sorry. Let me tell you everything I know so far."

Luke Felder's response was silent with eyes that initially filled with tears and then he sat head down, resting upon his hands. Suddenly, he rose quickly and said, "Evan, we need to know what in the hell happened here."

"Yes, we do, and I know the investigation is already underway to see what caused the crash. It may take them some time to determine things."

He could tell that, like others, Luke needed an emotional punching bag. Unfortunately, as the messenger, that was him.

Evan passed his business card to Luke. "I am so sorry! Lance was one of our most valuable people at Chadwell. He is going to be sorely missed. Call me anytime and go ahead and make arrangements with a funeral director. Once you know where and who that is, I can give the address to Mr. Tellinger."

Luke seemed dumbfounded with words about funeral directors.

"If you have no further questions or anything you want me to know, I will leave for now. I still have to meet with other loved ones."

"Sure, of course. No, I have nothing to say except that this is so bad and unbelievable. I don't know what to say."

"Of course, this is horrific -- something we have never had happen within the company before."

Evan made his way toward the door. "I'll see myself out," he said. "Do call if you need anything."

"Thank you," Luke said.

Evan hurriedly slipped into his car and entered the next address into his GPS. Time was not on his side. He did not want to just pop in at each stop, deliver the bad news and leave. Compassion took more time than he ever realized. Of course, it's not like he made a habit of such a thing. His life philosophy might not work for everyone, but so far, it had worked fine for him.

Chapter 23 ~ Coping

Thursday, December 5, 2019

Sleep was not deep, but fitful and filled with occasional dreams that Haley could not remember. Awakening at Alex and Jessie's contributed to her blurry brain status, wondering where she was at first. Then, she remembered -- plane crash - no survivors - no Jack coming home again. She lay there looking at the beautiful room she had helped Jessie redecorate recently. *Never knew I would end up sleeping here.*

It was kind of Reverend McAllister to come last night, praying with all three of them for guidance and direction. Haley suspected the fact she was hoping Jack had felt no pain was an indicator that she was beginning to accept the fact he was gone. Strangely, she could think that and a few moments later hold hope that this was all some huge mistake … that Jack would call her and everything would be normal. Reverend McAllister had a tough job, but one that he seemed very attuned to.

Slipping out of the bed, she walked into the bathroom to relieve herself. Once finished, she looked in the mirror over the sink. Her face looked so fatigued, and she did feel tired. She had woken so many times last night, crying herself back to sleep once. The disjointed dreams left an invisible residue she felt she couldn't remove. She grabbed the small bag she had packed on the bedroom chair and retrieved her toothbrush and toothpaste. *Time to wake up and face this.*

She thought of Evan Mitchell and wondered if Chadwell knew anything further. She made the bed and slipped out to the kitchen where she found Jessie. "Hey Jess, thanks for letting me stay."

"I'm glad you did. Did you sleep okay?"

"I got some sleep but not enough, woke a lot. I'm going to go on home, get some breakfast, and probably nap some unless something happens."

"Are you expecting anything to happen?"

"No. Just waiting for any more word on the accident, any information at all, I suppose."

Jessie nodded understandingly. She had to allow Haley some space to process things however she could.

"Okay, well I have a couple of appointments today, but I can reschedule them if you want me to hang out with you."

"Oh no. You are my best friend in the world, but I will do some napping today. Honestly, I don't know what I'll do, Jess. I could feel different in an hour."

"Understandable. Just realize I would be upset and disappointed if you needed someone around and you did not call me. Okay?"

"I will Jess. Thank you. I love you."

"I love you too."

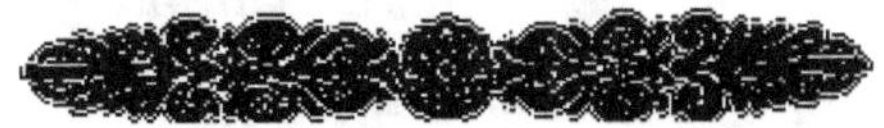

Grabbing a banana, frozen blueberries, and almond milk, Haley made a quick breakfast smoothie, along with oatmeal. She found herself thinking of how Jack had initiated their morning smoothie ritual. After eating, she gravitated to the couch.

Instead of the delight she had felt, it was almost painful now to see the Christmas tree. Regardless, she needed to check the tree basin and see if it had water. The tree stand held barely any liquid. She refilled it and turned the tree lights on. She stood back and admired their tree. Jack had wanted to change her mood, cheer her up, get the holidays going when he spontaneously purchased the tree. He was one of the few men she had known who loved the holidays with such gusto.

Now, it felt like a thousand shards of glass had pierced her heart and mind. Damn, her mind was hazy, cloudy in a fog. She almost felt like she was stuck in a spider's web of a dream that made no sense and she could not escape it. This change, not having Jack, might crush her. How in the world could she be normal? It seemed like her whole life was becoming about losing those important to her. Mom's death, losing their baby, and now Jack. It made her question so many things. It had not been very long since they were married. She thought of their last night together at the house. *Here I am, Jack, and even though you are not here where I can hold and touch you, I feel you inside my heart … tremendously.*

For some reason, the living room and the couch, in particular, felt like a safe zone to Haley. It had become a newfound nesting area of comfort in what felt like a cruel, harsh reality. She wrapped herself in a warm plush throw and made her way back to the couch, laying her head upon one of the throw pillows. She kept her eyes open as long as possible, even though she felt so tired. She kept herself glued to the cable news. At first in case there was some miracle — some tidbit of information that this was all a mistake — wrong plane — wrong people. Not her Jack.

Haley felt catatonic as the cable news stayed on turning into a background noise. Ultimately, the news was nothing but a small negative messaging system that did nothing to move Haley forward into her future, even if that was just an hour from now. But the silence was worse. Haley realized what people meant when they said "deafening silence". No longer would she hear Jack's voice calling to her from another room in the house or whispering softly in her ear. The loneliness was overwhelming. While friends and relatives had gone out of their way to provide her with comfort and company, no one could replace the essence of Jack being right there with her. It had not even been one day and she felt this way. She dozed off wondering how she would cope with these feelings.

Haley awakened as the home phone rang. She quickly grabbed it off the coffee table to answer. "Hello," she said, trying not to sound like she had been sleeping.

"Haley, this is Sharon. How are you doing?"

"Oh," she sighed. "I don't know. I guess the best I can be. But what about you? I'm sorry I have not called."

"Don't be. Jack's father and I are going to get through this and so will you. I already miss my son so much. Scenes of him as a baby, toddler and child are etched upon my brain. How I wish I could go back in time with him, Haley. But the life we are given here is temporary. We forget about that as we go through our day-to-day plans. I want you to know you are part of this family and always will be. We all love you and want you to let us in when you need others around. Okay?"

Haley smiled. "Thank you. That means a lot to me. I haven't called because … well … I don't know. I've just been feeling like this is unbelievable. I've had a difficult time accepting it as fact."

"Yes, I feel the same. Haley, Papa Joe wants to speak with you for a moment."

Jack's father picked up a phone extension.

"Haley, I know Sharon has told you how much we care and we are all in this loss together. I also want you to know I intend to find out what happened with that aircraft — why this happened to begin with. Are you okay? Do you need anything?"

"I'm fine as I can be. I didn't sleep well last night. I stayed next door with Jessie and Alex. Reverend McAllister came to visit us there. He is such a nice man, and it did help, but nothing can bring back Jack, can it?"

"No, nothing can. But I guess we can go on a bit easier knowing what kind of man Jack was and his soul is now with the Lord. I take a great deal of solace in that. This brings up a subject I would rather avoid, but we must address. Evan Mitchell says the passenger remains will be shipped back to the United States and then transported to the funeral home of our choice. In the past, our family has used Shultz Funeral Home. Would you be alright with me authorizing that? Haley, we will pay for any costs involved."

"Yes, I'm fine with that. Remains? I guess we will have a casket still, only closed?"

"I think that is what will be suggested."

"Go ahead. You have my permission and we have savings. I can pay for whatever costs are involved."

"Haley, is there anything we can do for you right now? You know you're welcome to come over if you want … anytime, day or night."

"I'll keep that in mind. Today, I'm going to reach out to my aunt and uncle and let them know what has happened. Jessie notified my work supervisor for me, but I need to check in with them and perhaps take some time off. I'm not sure yet. Sometimes work helps keep my mind off things. But, this is so big. I can't afford to not be focused on my work and perhaps make a mistake or break down crying at the hospital. I think I'll take at least a couple of weeks off. I really have no idea what I'm doing."

Sharon spoke up. "Probably a good idea. We'll let you go for now. We are all hurting, each dealing with it the best we can. But we are all here for you, Haley. Jack loved you so much, and we do too. You are part of us and this family. Call us for anything, honey."

"Thank you, I will. Yes, Jack had such a beautiful essence. He is going to be so missed."

Haley hung up and went to the bathroom to splash some cold water on her hot, tear streaked face. Her eyes and the darkness underneath were grotesque at this point. She wondered if she should contact Evan Mitchell and see if he knew anything more. Seems like he would call her. She decided she would call him first, before calling Aunt Molly and Uncle Mike.

Haley dug Evan's business card out of her purse and dialed his cell phone instead of phoning through the company's line. She desperately hoped he had some information that could ease her mind in some way.

Chapter 24 ~ Malachite Heart

Evan's phone vibrated upon his desk and he looked over to see Jack Foster residence on the caller identification screen. He grabbed it quickly to avoid the call going to voice mail.

"Hello, this is Evan Mitchell," he said, knowing it was probably Haley on the other end. He heard the softness of her voice and it somewhat weakened his hard interior. In his mind, he could see her flowing hair and those gorgeous blue eyes.

"Evan, it's Haley Foster. I was wondering if there were any additional updates."

He hesitated with his response, wanting to choose his words carefully. Yeah, there were some updates — bodies in pieces had been completely retrieved now and preserved for shipment to the United States. They were due to arrive late tonight via special air transport. How could he say this to her without causing too much distress?

"Hello, are you there, Evan?"

"Yes, I'm sorry. I guess my phone cut out there for a moment. At this time, I know that the remains of the passengers are being transported to the United States and will arrive very late tonight. Once a funeral home is chosen, they will contact us for delivery."

"Evan, I don't remember if you told me before. I know you said there were no survivors. Did the plane explode or catch on fire?"

"It's my understanding there was some fire damage, yes."

"I need you to find out if they found a necklace I know Jack was wearing. It was a simple thing really, something I gave him and he told me he would wear it the entire trip. If he told me that, he would."

"What does it look like?"

"It has a leather cord, and it's holding a copper wire wrapped, heart shaped green malachite stone."

"Okay, I will make a couple of calls to be sure people are aware of that," he responded.

"Thanks."

"How are you doing, Haley?"

"To say this is hard would be inadequate. I feel like my world has been ripped or torn and I can't put it back together."

"Of course. How else could you feel? Things are different here in the department with so many valuable members not here. A strange silence. Jack was an amazing scientist and researcher that will be greatly missed," he lied.

"He was my best friend — everything to me, really. He was the father figure I never had when I needed that kind of strength and my playful buddy at times. I don't know how I am going to go on without him."

Evan realized he never had a full understanding of the bond between the two of them. It was hard to tell with people you saw socially or through work. Things could be going downhill in their relationship, but they would put on a happy face for others. Obviously, this was not the case with these two. Again, Evan wondered how much Haley knew about what Jack and the team had been working on. That's something that had to be found out — one way or another from the people close to all the deceased workers.

"Haley, I'm glad you phoned. I will talk to those in charge about the malachite necklace. Call me anytime. I'm here to help."

"Thanks Evan, I will. Goodbye."

Evan wrote an email to J.D. Tellinger:

I received a call today from Jack Foster's wife, Haley. She stated Jack was wearing a necklace. She described it as having a leather cord with a wire wrapped green malachite stone attached to it. I am sure if it was on or near any remains, she would want it returned to her. We should notify the appropriate parties on this. The stone is shaped like a heart.

What are your thoughts on this or any knowledge you may have?

I'll await your reply.

Evan Mitchell

Only what would be considered normal communications in a situation like this should be put into texts or emails. Documenting anything that would truly show the nefarious design behind this incident could bring down everyone. But there were always fixes.

Chadwell - one of the most powerful corporations in the world always had ways to flip things around. The company secretly kept many varied types of people on temporary or permanent payrolls to assist with that. Besides, they had installed an email system that deleted all emails after they were read. Still, Evan decided to walk the line and be cautious with every conversation, email, text message, and move he made. Everything in his world was at stake. The tension was building, and he needed a release.

He quickly put away the files he had on his desk and locked the cabinet. Strolling past Kendra's desk, he placed his hands on one end of her work station. "Kendra, with all that has happened, I've got to get out of here for a little while. I'm going to go to the gym and release some of this stress. So, I will take a longer lunch than usual."

"Sure, I'll be going to the gym myself after work. It's good to do something physical. It helps."

"Call me if anything comes up. Otherwise, I will be back about 1:30 pm."

"I think this place can survive a couple of hours. Go and feel better."

"Thanks!"

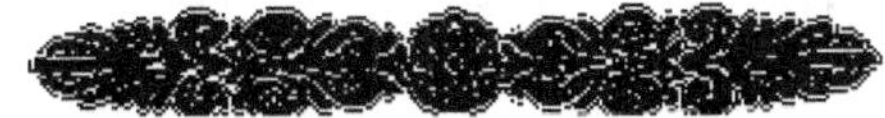

Chadwell maintained an upscale facility for their employees to work out. Evan also had a built-in membership at his condominium complex to the clubhouse gym. He decided to go there instead of the work facility. This would keep people from asking him questions about the crash at Chadwell's gym.

There was a part of him that needed to be at work, but another voice inside urging him to release some steam. He had begun working out in high school and hated it then. It was to appease his father, who saw him as the weak link in the family chain physically. His older brother had broken the school's records in a number of touchdowns and completed passes. He was a star athlete again in college and in the professional world. Most people would recognize his name instantly, but they would never know Evan was his brother.

He had no desire to be like his brother. He only worked out for the physical sweat and release, for the reward of pressing a little. It had nothing to do with trying to be liked by his father. That would never happen. Instead, he had seen Evan's strong suits in academics as being a "pussy".

His brother made a lot of money at pro football and endorsements. Perhaps he would never surpass that, but he was on his way to greater wealth now. Soon, he would be the head of the division at Chadwell, and hopefully, a board member as well.

Chapter 25 ~ Jessie Helps

After speaking with Evan Mitchell, Haley's afternoon had been filled with phone calls to her aunt, uncle, work, and Sarah. The doorbell rang and Haley peeled her body off the couch. Whoa! Her legs were sore now and feet asleep with an annoying tingling sensation. She really needed to walk around a bit, anyway. There was a young woman at the door, probably selling something. Haley hesitated to answer the door and opted to use the intercom system to inquire why she was here.

"Yes, can I help you?" Haley asked.

"Are you Mrs. Foster?"

"Yes."

"Mrs. Foster, I know it seems untimely with the tragedy that has occurred with your husband and his coworkers, but I would really like to talk to you. My name is Megan Adams. I'm an investigative reporter."

"I don't want to speak with reporters or the news."

"Can I leave you my business card on your doorway? I'm not your average newspaper or television reporter. I've been working on an investigative story for a while involving the pharmaceutical companies. If you would like to meet and talk to me at some point, please give me a call. Again, I am very sorry. Please accept my condolences."

"That's fine. You can leave your card, but I doubt I have any information to assist you. It's a very difficult time for me right now, understand?"

"Yes, I do understand. Thank you. Again, I am so sorry about your husband. But, please keep my card. You never know how we may be able to help each other."

This bothered Haley that someone would have the nerve to pound on her like this for information. Just another person wanting to be ahead of the rest of the news. *Hell, I'm lucky to find out anything about Jack myself.*

Once the reporter had driven away, Haley went to the front door and retrieved her card. She stuck it in a drawer in the bathroom where she kept the majority of her cosmetics and proceeded to undress and take a shower. Haley thought about Tuesday morning and how she and Jack had showered together before leaving for the airport. How she wished she had jumped his bones and made him late for the flight. But would it have changed anything? There were so many unknowns. She knew she loved him more than anything. Placing her palms against the walls of the shower, she stood still while hot water pulsated her skin. This space felt so lonely now and she felt her body begin to convulse with grief. Tears, more tears.

There was light knocking, and Haley could see Jessie's silhouette through the lead glass in the front door. She opened it and her friend stepped inside, gently embracing her by the shoulders. "How are you?"

"Doing okay I guess. I've just been hanging out here at home today. I spoke with a few people on the phone."

"Have you eaten?"

"Not since this morning. Are you being my mom right now?" Haley smiled.

Jessie gave her a look that said, don't mess with me. "Oh, Haley! I cannot imagine what you are going through. Alex is picking up take out and bringing it home. Would you like to have dinner with us?"

"I suppose. I know I need to stop isolating, Jessie. More than anything, I just like sleeping. If I can sleep, none of this is real. I'm in another world then."

"Well, speaking of sleep, are you planning on staying here tonight or would you like to stay again at our house? How did the guest room work out for you last night?"

"Oh, it was fine. It felt somewhat familiar since we worked on decorating it together. I had not thought about tonight yet."

"Let's plan on you staying one more night again? You okay with that, Haley?"

"I guess so, Jessie. What am I going to do about sleeping here again? If I lie down in our bed, it's going to send me into such sadness. Do you know what I mean?"

"I think I do. I'm not sure what the solution is yet, honey. But we will work on one. I will tell you something else. We need to go through your closet and find what you will wear to the funeral home. I know that is a touchy subject, but if it is already planned out, it may make things easier. Want to do that while I'm here now?"

"Funeral home?"

"I called Sarah on my way home from my last appointment. She said your father-in-law has taken care of the arrangements. It seems to help him in some way to put him in charge and give him something he feels he can control."

"Yes, I spoke with them this morning. He told me as much and I gave him my permission. I just did not realize everything would be moving along this fast. When are we doing the funeral home?"

"Saturday will be the visitation from three to eight. Sunday, the service will be at two o'clock."

Haley looked at her, confused. "What day is it now?"

"It's Thursday, so if we figure out wardrobe stuff today, we need not worry with it later."

"Okay, I need to call my aunt and uncle tonight and let them know where and when the funeral is. Remind me, Jessie, if I forget. I feel like I could forget a lot of things right now, like the fact that some investigative reporter came to the house today. I forgot to tell you that."

"Really! What did he want?"

"It was a female who said she's been working for awhile on a story about the pharmaceutical companies and wanted to talk with me. I told her I did not have much to talk about in that regard and now was a really hard time for me, anyway."

"Damn, for sure. I can't believe she wouldn't know that."

"Desperate for something to write, I suppose. She left her card at the doorstep. I did not answer the door; just spoke with her on the videoconferencing."

"That's good. Makes it easier to tell her no. Sorry you experienced that, girl." Jessie gave her a look of sadness.

The ladies went into the master suite and headed for the walk-in closet. Jessie knew it might be best for Haley to wait just outside the door while she brought out potential choices for her. At least a third of the stuff in that closet belonged to Jack and could be too much for her to handle the sight of right now. Haley would need two different ensembles. She chose one that was black and a dark navy with a crisp light pink blouse. Haley agreed they would do. She didn't seem to care much. But she did about shoes.

"Make sure you grab my new boots that Jack bought me. They are still in the box and I want to wear them. It was my last gift from him," she said, with tears beginning again.

"Of course," said Jessie. "Just having these out and ready to go will help in the next couple of days. Fewer decisions to make. Okay, let's pack up what you need to come back over to my house for the night."

"I don't need a lot. I still have my basic toiletries in that purple case on the vanity." Haley added, "Oh, I want to bring my tablet with me this time."

Jessie nodded, "Oh, I almost forgot. Sarah needs us to supply the funeral home with photos of Jack you may want included for the service. How do you feel about that?"

Haley was quiet. "Well, I would not want to go through them right now, Jessie. I just can't."

"Do you have them digitally stored?" Jessie asked.

"Yes, I do. Almost all of them are digital. Can I give you access to my account and then you two do what you see fit with them"

Jessie nodded, "That will work."

Haley wrote the web address and password for access. She wondered how many other people had been through this same situation now. These were the things you didn't think about until something bad happened.

Chapter 26 ~ Alex Helps

As Jessie entered her home with Haley, she immediately sniffed the air. "I smell food". Alex had brought home a variety of salads and sub sandwiches. Haley found herself unusually hungry, devouring an entire submarine sandwich loaded with turkey, Swiss cheese, and bacon, plus a salad. The conversation between Jessie and Alex at the table was light, mostly about the upcoming weather forecast and local holiday events. Haley half way listened, focusing more on her food than anything.

"Don't forget to contact your aunt and uncle about the funeral visitation and such," Jessie mentioned.

"Oh, yeah. I'm glad you reminded me. My mind feels blank inside." Haley folded the paper that had surrounded her sub sandwich and threw it in the trash. She took another sip of her water and told Alex how much she appreciated him serving them dinner.

"Ah, it was hard work," he kidded. "No problem. It was pretty good, wasn't it?"

"It was actually very yummy. I didn't know I was so hungry."

Alex smiled at Haley, wondering when she ate last. "I'm glad you liked it."

"Well, I will go back to the guest room and call my aunt and uncle. Then, maybe we should talk about long-term plans for me. I can't have you two adopting me."

Alex and Jessie looked at one another and smiled.

"Why not?" said Jessie.

Haley smiled back. But inside, she felt like she was playing out a very familiar pattern. This is how she felt when her mom died and she went to live with her aunt and uncle. It was almost exactly the same. *Last weekend, I had the most wonderful life and man I could ever want. In a few days, everything has flipped and changed.*

Jack had paid to have a very extensive security system installed in their home. Still, she not only wanted to avoid their bedroom because it reminded her of him, she was also afraid to be there at night alone. Somehow, the daytime felt safer. Yet, actual crimes and break-ins probably happened just as much in the day as they did at night. *I can't live my life here at Jessie's or at Sarah's. I've got to figure something out to get past this.*

Haley thought of the women in her group therapy, many who had sworn by the power of learning self protection. It would be Tuesday before the group met again. Before calling her aunt and uncle, she decided to text her therapist.

"Hey, this is Haley Foster. Something has happened to my husband. He's gone. Can we talk soon?" Haley could not bring herself to type the letters d-e-a-d.

Dr. Miller messaged back within moments.

I can make room for an appointment with you tomorrow at 1pm. Will that work for you? Otherwise, I could do an Internet consult tonight at 8pm.

I have no plans for tomorrow. The sooner the better. Can we talk tonight at 8 instead?

Sure, I will email you a link for us to have a video call.

Thank you so much. Talk to you then.

Haley phoned her family. Aunt Molly answered the phone.

"Hey, it's me Haley. I hope it's not too short notice for you, but I just found out myself late this afternoon. The visitation will be on Saturday from 3 – 8, and the funeral Sunday at 2pm."

"We'll be there. We will get a motel room for Saturday night so we can be there both days. Which funeral home?"

"You can stay with me. In fact, I would feel better if you could stay at our ..ah. the house. I'm actually staying next door with Jessie tonight because I don't want to be alone. They are going to have it at Shultz Funeral Home."

"Oh, Haley. We will be there for you. No problem. Don't feel you have to clean or anything. In fact, if you have things that need to be done at your house, it would give us something to do while we are there. Sonya wants to come with us as well."

"Great, I'm so glad she is coming. I haven't seen my little cousin in quite a while. You've only been here once. Do you remember the way?"

"I think so, but just to be sure, let me write down your address and we will put it in the GPS."

Haley rattled off the address and added, "Well, Jack and I never messed up things too bad at home, so it's no big deal on that end. I look forward to having you. Do you think you will come to the house first and then go to the funeral home or just come later?"

"We'll leave Saturday morning. It's about a two and a half hour drive, so we will come to the house first".

"Great, see you Saturday."

"I'm praying for you, Haley," Aunt Molly said.

Chapter 27 ~ Mayday

It was now 7:00 p.m. Haley slipped out of the overstuffed, but comfortable bed and put her flip-flops on. These were her most worn shoes, as she often used a pair as house slippers. She made her way back to the kitchen, finding the two had reclined in the den and were watching some evening news. Jessie and Alex appeared so relaxed, while Haley felt like a bundle of nervous tension that could be lit by the slightest spark. Aware of the vast differences in their emotional demeanors, she took a deep breath and tried to calm herself a bit before speaking. She slowly approached the den.

"Hey, I hope I'm not interrupting," she uttered rather demurely.

"Not at all," replied Jessie. "Did you speak with your aunt and uncle?"

"I did and they are coming Saturday, early enough to be at the house with me before arrival time at the funeral home. Do you know if I need to be there early?"

The corner of Jessie's mouth lifted and her eyes looked puzzled. "I'm not sure, good question. Check with Jack's parents, to be sure."

"Okay, it's likely I will need to be there ahead of time. Anyway, they are going to bring my cousin Sonya along. I have not seen her since she graduated high school. They will stay with me Saturday night."

"Good! I suppose that will be your first night there, assuming you stay here Friday evening."

"Yeah, I have an online consultation with my therapist at 8 tonight. That woman has been a godsend for me since I was attacked," Haley said, closing her eyes with relief.

Jessie did an air pump with her fist. "Two goods in a row. I wanted to suggest you contact her, but I also didn't want to make you feel … I don't know … like I thought you needed psychological help, I guess. Because I do think you are coping well, Haley. This is so much to go through."

Alex joined in the conversation. "Haley, I want you to know you are always welcome here and you can also call us anytime, day or night, if you feel unsafe. Always!"

"Thanks Alex. You two have become my male and female knights in shining armor. Not to mention the best neighbors and friends anyone could hope for."

"We're all going to get through this loss somehow, although moving forward seems unknown," Jessie added.

Alex previously half muted the sound on the television when Haley had joined them. An image of the downed plane in the Brazilian rain forest appeared on the large screen and he pushed the remote to take it off the mute setting. The newscaster was stating they had something significant to report in the investigation of the crash, along with an audio recording and then broke for a commercial.

Haley sat forward toward the television. They sat silent, waiting for the commercials to finally end. Jessie moved closer to Haley and put her arm around her. Somehow, she intuited this could be upsetting.

The female newscaster continued, "We have obtained the first exclusive of audio from the cockpit of the plane that went down in the Brazilian rain forest on Wednesday of this week."

The screen showed only a still image of the plane on the ground missing wings and portions of the broken fuselage in at least three sections, with some indication of fire. The audio began with the words close captioned on the lower screen.

"Oh, my god. It's Jack!" Haley whispered under her breath. She listened to his words.

"Mayday, mayday! I've got an emergency."

"Air six six three delta whiskey I hear you loud and clear. Do you hear me?"

"Yes, I hear you. The pilot and crew have been drugged or poisoned. I need help up here. I can't wake them up".

"Air six six three delta whiskey uh ... roger ...uh. Are you a pilot?"

"No, I'm not a pilot. I need to get this plane down safely."

"Air six six three delta whiskey roger that. You're in a King Air, correct?"

"Yes, this is a King Air. Who can help me?"

There was a long patch of silence. Finally, a new voice emerged speaking clear English.

"Are you a pilot?"

"No, the pilot is unconscious but breathing."

"Are you in his seat?"

"I moved him over to the co-pilot seat. Yes, I am sitting in his seat now."

"It appears you're at 11,000 one one thousand, but still climbing now. We need to find out if the autopilot is on and if so, get it leveled off. Give me a moment to clear your area."

Jack could hear the ground control rapidly issuing instructions to several other aircraft in his area, telling them to move away from that sector.

"Air six six three delta whiskey, are you able to maintain one two thousand?"

"What do I push or turn off? It looks like it's set at ten thousand. I don't know why it keeps climbing."

"Air six six three delta whiskey, can you tell if the autopilot is on or not?"

"It looks like it is and set at ten thousand. Now I'm at thirteen thousand. How do I shut this off?"

"Air six six three delta whiskey understand that we're trying to find some help with that King Air. Stand by"

"Still climbing fourteen thousand"

"Okay, six six three delta whiskey. When you look at the center console there, do you see anything that would disengage the autopilot?"

"I don't know. I see where the autopilot switch is. I can disengage it if you think I should."

"Six six three delta whiskey, roger that. Disengage the autopilot. We're going to try and help you hand fly the plane."

"Okay, I've disengaged the autopilot. Now what?"

"Six six three delta whiskey, I need you to hold the yoke or steering wheel steady for a moment. Can you do that? Hold the yoke level and steady."

The newscaster resumed, "That is the last heard of King Air Flight six six three. Our deepest condolences go out to all the loved ones of those who perished in this tragic accident. We will bring more coverage as new information becomes available."

Haley's face was a ghastly white, and all three sat with wide eyes, mouths open, looking at the screen. Jessie hugged Haley hard and said, "Jack said they were poisoned or drugged. Did I hear that right?"

Alex chimed in, "That's what it sounded like."

Haley asked with tears streaming down her cheeks, "Alex, can you back up and repeat this on live TV. I want to hear it again."

"I think so, let me see," Alex wielded the remote as one would a surgical instrument to remove a sharp piece of metal from someone's arm. If Haley wanted to hear that recording again, she would. And he wanted to as well. It worked and the recording played again. "Pause it, right there," she said as Jack spoke of the pilot and crew. "Play it one more time."

Haley had to be sure that she was hearing Jack correctly. Poisoned or drugged? Why had Jack not been affected?

Alex allowed the recording to play through once more. "Haley, I think you need to contact someone in law enforcement. This was no freak accident. It sounds like sabotage."

"Yes, Jack clearly says something happened to the pilot and the other passengers. Who should I call?"

"I'm not sure. I wonder if your father-in-law has heard this on the news? Even more, what do the people at Chadwell know?"

Chapter 28 ~ Sabotage

Haley's emotions had traveled from profound grief and sadness to shocked rage, especially after hearing the recording of Jack. She stood up in the den and began walking toward the guest room. She looked back at Jessie and Alex, still sitting there stunned about the news report. "I'm going to give Jack's dad a call right now".

She grabbed her cell phone off the bed and hit her contact list, dialing the Fosters. Her father-in-law answered almost immediately.

"Papa, this is Haley. Listen, I'm at Alex and Jessie's next door spending the night. We were just watching the news on Fox 5 Atlanta and they played a recording between ground control and Jack in the plane. She began crying hysterically.

"Haley, Haley I know. I heard it too," he tried to say in a calm manner. Inside, he was angry as hell.

Haley spoke between sobs. "Alex believes we need to get law enforcement or our own investigators involved.

Jack said the pilot and all passengers were drugged or poisoned. Who would do that? Why would they do that?"

"Who indeed?" Joe Foster replied. He paused for a moment.

"Haley, don't worry with calling anyone unless you know of someone who specializes in such things. I will take care of this as Jack would want me to. I'm not shutting you out, honey, but protecting you as I can. Jack would want that. Let me deal with the investigators and police authorities, even though they still may want to interview you."

"Well, I'm not a suspect."

"No, but anything you could tell them about this trip and Jack, perhaps why he was down there would help anyone investigating."

"Unfortunately, I know very little. But, yes, I would talk to them if it helps."

"I thought I had a head start on investigating this crash. Apparently, the news knows more than I or Chadwell Pharma does. It was hard listening to that recording. I can only imagine what was going through my son's mind in that plane."

"Did Sharon hear it?"

"Yes, it was terribly upsetting to her."

"I will be by tomorrow to see her and you."

"Sounds good. Probably the afternoon would be best. She's moving slow right now in the mornings and not sleeping well."

"I totally understand. See you then."

Haley hung up from the conversation and felt like she had been jabbed with a sharp knife. Imagining what Jack went through as that plane crashed was overpowering her thoughts, and she did not want to think about him being in pain or hurt. Perhaps whatever poison or drug was used just hadn't affected him as quickly as the others. Perhaps he blacked out as the crash occurred.

Haley checked her email on her tablet and saw the conference link her therapist had sent. She looked at the time … 7:59. She clicked the link. As she connected, she found she needed to take herself off mute.

"Hey, sorry about that. Technology! Thanks for doing this," Haley said.

"No problem. You said you lost your husband. What do you mean?"

"Jack's gone — as in passed away. He was in a plane crash."

"Oh my, Haley. I was afraid you were going to tell me that. I heard about the Chadwell employees in a crash in Brazil. I just saw you on Tuesday. When did this occur?"

"On Wednesday. What's worse is we just saw a news report … I say "we" because I am staying next door at Jessie's house. They had audio of Jack in the cockpit talking to the radar control saying that the pilot and passengers had been poisoned or drugged."

"Seriously? That is awful."

"Yes, it was shocking and heartbreaking to hear his panicked voice."

"I cannot imagine how you are feeling. Do you have plenty of people around you right now for support?"

"I do. I have Jack's family, my neighbors here. Plus, my aunt and uncle will arrive Saturday. They will be staying with me Saturday night. I have not actually seen Jack's mom and dad yet, only talked to them on the phone a couple of times. I'm going to visit with them tomorrow afternoon."

"That's good you have people to lean on and be with during this. Of course, I am here for you too. I'm very sorry, Haley. You and Jack had one of the best marriages I've seen in a long time … maybe ever."

"We did. I'll never get over this. Listen, the first reason I wanted to talk to you is that some of the women in the group spoke about self-defense classes. I want to go, try and build some skills. I'm thinking that may help me move out of my fears somewhat."

"That sounds great. I think it may help."

"The second thing is I noticed a pattern today. Here I am at Jessie and Alex's home for the second night in a row. Part of it is because I am afraid of what it will feel like to climb into the same bed where Jack and I slept. I'm worried that the feelings would be so overwhelming I could not cope. I'm also suddenly afraid of being alone there at night. I know I have the security system and all, but I just can't shake it right now. I try to tell myself that if

Jack were still alive and down in Brazil working, I would be mentally prepared to be there by myself. And, I think I would have done fine."

"You said a pattern. Can you elaborate on that?"

"Yes, I feel like I did when my mom died. Just like when I moved in with my aunt and uncle as if I need someone to take care of me. I'm a grown woman now and not a teen. I've got to be able to manage on my own."

"Thanks for clarifying that, and I can see where the similarities could be felt. It's possible that you are feeling like you need to keep and comfort of others in order to cope right now, especially if that was what occurred as a teen. But think about it, you left your aunt and uncle's home as you matured and went to college. You lived on your own at that time and you will again. I think you're being too hard on yourself. Right now, those friends and your family are serving in a way that helps buffer the extreme shock of this situation. It's all okay. Does that make sense?"

"I suppose. I just don't want to be this helpless woman who is afraid of every noise the house makes — someone who can't stand on their own."

"I'll make some calls tomorrow and find the information for those classes and text you. What are the arrangements for Jack?"

"The visitation will be Saturday from 3pm to 8 at Shultz Funeral Home. The funeral is on Sunday at 2pm."

"I will definitely come by."

"Thank you. Just knowing I can talk to you is a tremendous help tonight. I feel like there is so much ahead of me and I don't have a map for it."

"Speaking of help, I'm going to have a script called in for you. Just something light to help you sleep at night, nothing heavy duty. I know you don't like taking anything, but it's there if you need it, okay?"

"Sure, thanks. I don't know at this point, but call it in and I'll pick it up tomorrow just in case."

Haley and Dr. Miller signed off their teleconference. As she walked to the bathroom, her feet shuffled slowly in her flip-flops. Exhaustion had set in from all the emotional conversations. Yet her mind was swirling like a vortex with thoughts about Jack's voice and questions about what happened to him and how it happened. She brushed her teeth and pulled on some sweats to sleep in.

Almost as soon as her head hit the pillow, Haley fell into sleep again, this time dreaming she and Jack were running along the beach together. It felt like flying with their feet barely touching the sand and surf. He was smiling and she felt his happiness touch her inside. There was such love, an indescribable love that was not only playful like friends, but deep as the ocean they wandered beside. The elation and intense emotions in her dream made her wake suddenly, only wanting to stay within the dream. But it was gone, broken like a spell that had cast itself over her and now she was back in the world without Jack.

In her sleep, she could almost will herself to dream about being with him. The stark contrast of real waking life felt abrasive and empty. It was hard to get going each time she woke. The temptation to linger in bed and just sleep was overwhelming, and it was winning. Jack's passing had taken such a toil on her … on many people. Sleep felt like her escape time, her only reprieve.

Chapter 29 ~ Cleanup

Friday, December 6, 2019

Evan sat down at his desk, booted up his laptop and checked his watch for incoming messages. Nothing consequential, and nothing about the crash. Kendra waved as she approached his office. "Tellinger wants you to meet him at his office as soon as you can. His assistant just called me, didn't want to talk on the phone to you, but in person he said."

"Alright, I'll head that way. Thanks."

Evan traveled the halls to the central elevator and took it to the top floor where all the executives and accounting were located. *Money and power all sitting at the top,* he thought. As he exited, he turned right and headed through heavy floor to ceiling glass doors only to come upon Tellinger's male assistant. His heart beat a little faster than usual with a strange anticipation to know what Tellinger had to say and a dread of it at the same time.

"Ah, you must be here to see Mr. Tellinger. He's waiting for you, Mr. Mitchell. Right this way."

Langley, the administrative assistant, had better style in clothing than Evan did. He looked like he stepped out of GQ magazine. They turned a corner and he opened J.D.'s door. "Mr. Evan Mitchell is here, sir."

"Thank you, Langley."

The door closed and Evan approached the sitting area across from Tellinger's desk in the massive space, richly appointed with wood and leather.

"Please have a seat. We might be a minute while we hash out some scenarios. Would you like something to drink?"

Evan felt it would be impolite to not take him up on his offer. Sure, I'll take a bottle of water. The aging CEO sauntered over to a bar area and opened a refrigerator retrieving the drink. Instead of circling back and sitting in his executive seat behind the desk, he sat in the adjoining chair next to Evan. Slightly twisting his body in the chair toward Evan, he handed him the water and looked him in the eye, speaking low. "We have a situation."

Evan looked at him with a solemn expression. "What kind of situation?"

"It seems that everyone on the aircraft partook of the coffee except Jack. He is heard on the radio control replay stating he believes the pilot and passengers were poisoned or drugged. Evidently, he was trying to fly the plane. Obviously, that didn't work out. This brings in some new elements of risk. I wanted to hear your ideas on clean up of the situation?"

"That's crazy. This is something we did not plan for, but should have. It seems like the main problem is who made the coffee and could they be made to talk? It's a loose thread."

"My thoughts, as well."

They were both quiet for a long moment that held the ominous vibe of a next step. Evan placed the top back on the water bottle and squeezed it. "Unfortunately, it sounds as if another tragic accident or disappearance must be put in the works immediately."

"You take care of the logistics, Evan. You will need to act quickly as I'm sure they are already looking for the employee. Think it through."

"Yes sir. Anything else I should know?"

"Regardless, it sounds as if everyone on the plane drank the coffee — except Jack.We have no way of stopping the information on this suspected drugging from leaking out. They are now playing the audio recording of Jack on the news. I've heard it and it sounds damning to someone. It will affect the families greatly and increase the tenacity of all the investigators. I have Shelly Larson looking at framing the narrative on this toward the pilot instead of Chadwell. As I told her, perhaps someone had a vendetta against him."

"That sounds good for shifting suspicion away from Chadwell and toward the pilot. It might work if it is broadcast frequently," Evan added.

"Plans are limited when evidence like that is available. That's why I'm telling you to think everything through carefully when it comes to the person who served the coffee. It will cost us more money, but that's how the cookie crumbles, isn't it?"

"In this scenario, it is, sir."

"One other thing, Evan. Make sure you find a way to gauge how much knowledge any of the family members could have about the experimental drug project the team was working on. As you know, we have to keep Chadwell products that have not been patented, or that will never be patented, top secret."

"I'll find a way to test that without being conspicuous. Jack's team would have been on a tiered need to know basis. Of course, Jack knew it all. So his wife is our largest concern there. She's pretty torn up. Seems they had a close relationship. It might take several meetings with her to determine what she knows, if anything."

"Think about it Evan. People share things they are sworn to secrecy about when they feel they can really trust someone. In a relationship or marriage, that's going to take place primarily as pillow talk. That means we need to go over any and all surveillance we have on Jack."

Evan nodded his head up and down while his eyes glazed over a bit from the large windows overlooking the company grounds. "Yes, you're right."

Tellinger touched his knee with his right forefinger to bring Evan back into the room with him. Obviously, Evan was beginning to feel very anxious. Evan turned and met Tellinger's squinted eyes as the CEO spoke. "The information in the wrong hands could sink this company. They'll have a hell of a time proving Chadwell had anything to do with the plane going down. But, if the potential unpatented drug is known, that gives us problems on a multitude of levels. So, be diligent about getting this information from them if they know it."

He rose from the chair and Evan followed his cue by standing also. He held out his hand to Tellinger, giving him a firm handshake. "I better get to work on this right now."

"No need to report anything to me unless you have a problem or need something. And, I know you are not going to have a problem. Good day!" he said, and turned to go back to his light tan leather executive chair behind his desk.

Evan stepped out of the CEO's executive nest and felt like he was falling through the sky himself. This was a problem - Jack's voice claiming the crew had been poisoned or drugged. He needed to hear the recording himself. He phoned Kendra, who answered on the second ring.

"Yes," she said instantly.

"Kendra, it seems there is a recording being broadcast on the news. It's an audio recording of Jack on the plane before it crashed. Can you find a link to it for me and text it to me?"

"Oh, my gosh! Yes, I'll find it on the web and send it to you."

"Thanks Kendra. I'll be out of the office for a bit meeting with others."

"Oh, here I just found it while we were talking — sending the news video link to you now."

"Thank you so much."

Evan clicked the conversation off and looked at the link. He would need to listen to this someplace private. He left the building and slipped into the quiet solace of his vehicle. Clicking on the news link, he listened to the entire video twice. The weight of worry now upon his shoulders was excruciating. Time to get Ragland on this pronto.

Evan drove to the nearest big box store and picked up another burner phone. Once he had activated it with false information, he drove to a park nearby and phoned Steve Ragland, a former black ops contractor employee who now did private work for corporations.

Ragland, it's Mitchell."

"Oh, yeah. What can I do you for?"

Evan was a little exasperated. "Got a problem. Whoever served the coffee needs to disappear permanently. Hope it wasn't someone on your team."

"Whoa, that wasn't part of this deal."

"One person didn't drink it. There's a recording of the unaffected person on the plane claiming the pilot and passengers were poisoned or drugged."

"Well, that is a situation!"

"So, how much for clean up on aisle three with this?"

Ragland hesitated. "You're asking me to take down someone so young, practically a kid."

"I'm not asking, but insisting, that you clean up spilled coffee."

"Well then, if you insist upon that. It's going to be fifty thousand wired to my account in the Cayman Islands today."

"Can you make it a total disappearance?"

"I can have him taken out and never found ... ever."

"Done!" Evan quickly replied.

He hung up the call, revved up the engine and pulled out on the highway back toward work. On the drive, he wondered what would happen to Haley if she did know something very relevant about Jack's pet project. Would a wire transfer to a dark operator be the end of her as well? Evan felt the stress and burn inside the pit of his stomach. He was playing with fire. It wasn't the first time he felt it, but it was just a smolder in the beginning and now it was growing into a bonfire of problems. He had to put out these fires, and he wanted Haley to be okay, whether she would ever have anything to do with him or not. There was something about her, something he wanted if he could make a way to do so.

Evan pulled back into the parking lot at Chadwell, fast pacing it back to the executive suites and Tellinger's office.

Langley took notice of Evan's demeanor and how out of breath he was. Before he could greet him, Evan blurted out, "Is he in? I had one more thing I needed to mention to him."

"No, he's attending a Board Meeting now. Is it urgent?"

"A bit, yes. Do you have a piece of paper and envelope I could use? Perhaps you could slip this into the meeting."

"Sure," Langley said, handing him a piece of stationary and a Chadwell envelope.

$50K to Ragland's Cayman account today - dispenser disappears - never found

He sealed it in the envelope. "Tell you what, I've got to walk by that meeting room on my way back to my division. I can drop it off. Should I just knock on the door?"

"Yes, knock on the door and just go in."

"Will that piss anyone off?"

"Probably, but they'll get over it," Langley said, with a half smirk on his face.

Chapter 30 ~ The Boardroom

Evan knocked on the etched glass of the entrance to the board room. He didn't wait for an invite, but swung the heavy wood door open. Immediately, he felt the stares of the board members. He ignored this as he hand delivered the envelope to Tellinger. If someone disapproved, they would have to take that up with him later. Time was of the essence and it had to be done. He turned, making his exit from the room and strolled back down the hall toward the elevator.

Inside the elevator, he loosened his tie and ran his fingers through his hair. Right now, Evan sought the solitude of the research facility and his office. He was going to need a little time to just chill and think. As he approached his office, Kendra flagged him down.

"That was devastating to listen to, Evan," she said, in a low hushed voice.

Evan knew she expected his reply. "Yes, it was truly shocking and heartbreaking."

"I cannot imagine why that happened. Who would poison them?"

"Nor can I, Kendra. I heard from Tellinger that it was meant for the pilot. Apparently, it was some kind of vendetta, but I'm not sure of the specifics. Some small plane pilots run contraband and he could have been caught up in something like that."

"Well, to take out the pilot is to kill everyone on the plane," Kendra said, her face showing anger.

"Yep, that's true. Horrible situation. Listen, I've got to make some calls and order flowers for the funeral home. Let me know if anything else pops on this."

"Will do."

Plans always have a way of going awry and this one was spinning its own threads, beginning to make a web that Evan had to make sure no one was caught up in. This included those at Chadwell and the families of the loved ones lost. What would Tellinger and company want done with anyone who knew about the drug Jack had been working on? It would probably not be pretty … another accident or disappearing. This bothered him deeply. He never envisioned a string of deaths occurring one after another. He had some sense of conscience about him, even though he would admit he was power hungry. He really wasn't a killer, or was he?

It especially bothered him about Haley. He knew she had been suspected before. She was pregnant at the time and it was told to him that Tellinger believed she had proprietary knowledge about the project, and perhaps other things too. He had heard about the attack, but had nothing to do with ordering it. But he did order surveillance, before and after the attack when they moved. Without their knowledge, sound surveillance had been placed inside Jack's condominium to try and catch anything that might have slipped from his lips to her ears. After months of surveying, nothing showed up leading the covert team to assume she knew nothing. But that was only an assumption.

Evan used the burner phone to call the surveillance team. He let them know they needed to carefully go over the last two weeks of recordings to check for any mention at all of corporate information.

Evan hung up and grabbed his right wrist with his left hand, gripping it hard. He paced the floor simultaneously. *If Haley did know anything about the drug Jack was developing … well … we will cross that bridge if it happens.* In the meantime, he needed to send flowers to the funeral home. He searched for a local florist online and called the first one with the highest review rating.

"Jacob Hartley Floral Creations, how may I help you?"

"Hello, I have a coworker that passed away and his funeral is on Sunday with visitation on Saturday. Can you deliver something very nice by then?"

"Yes, depending upon what you order, we can," the clerk replied.

"I'm really not sure what to order. Can you put together an arrangement of some sort? I'd like it to be a bit unusual, perhaps even tropical."

"I think we can accommodate that very well. We can create a standing wired easel tropical spray with vivid colored flowers in tribute to your coworker. Those would include orange orchids, red gladioli, orange roses, and Asiatic lilies matched with tropical foliage such as ferns and leaves. The total would be around $210.00 delivered."

"Sounds perfect. Let's do it."

Evan gave his payment method and sympathy message to accompany the floral arrangement. He hung up and wondered if he should send each of the departed co-workers flowers for their funeral or just Jack. He opted to send it only to Jack as he knew Chadwell would already have flowers delivered for the company. Then he changed his mind again. Obviously, he felt apprehension right now about every decision and how anything might look to anyone. His guilty part in this plan was gnawing at him. He phoned the florist again and ordered simpler sprays for each of the four coworkers who had accompanied Jack.

Ultimately, he needed to find a way to build some rapport with Haley so that he could pursue her not just as Jack's potential leak point, but for his own selfish desires. He wasn't sure how to go about it. Evan needed to find or invent something he and Haley shared in common. It should start with him sympathetically soothing her over

Jack. That son of a bitch had thrown a monkey wrench into this plan, but he and others at Chadwell would find a way to grab that tool and ratchet it down until it was nonexistent.

Chapter 31 ~ Anger to Action

Sleep was tempting, as it put Haley out of the real issues she was dealing with. Upon opening her eyes, she felt a renewed sense of action. She could not continue just letting all this happen to her and not take hold of it in a way that made sense and moved her out of her fetal sleeping position. She told her therapist that she wanted to find out about the self defense classes and she would be at therapy on Tuesday. As much as she wanted to hole up and do nothing, it was important that she continued to keep herself moving forward and be around people.

Jack's voice over the radio of the airplane played in her mind again. The anger she felt that her husband and his coworkers had been sabotaged and murdered infuriated her, making her want to seek justice. She had told Papa Foster she would visit today and that was on her agenda. It seemed as if there was something else she was supposed to do, but she couldn't think of it right now. *I hope Jessie still has some coffee left.*

"Hey, good morning," she greeted Jessie in the kitchen. "Alex gone already?"

"Yes, he took off pretty early today. Something about a big meeting at his company he needed time to get ready for."

Haley sipped on the hot beverage and looked a bit anxious. "Listen, I've got a lot going on too."

"You do, like what?"

"I've decided I'm going to take self defense classes for women. My therapist is going to text me the details today. Jessie, I have to become more confident about my safety."

"Agreed, it's a bold move for you but a smart one. Still, we are here for you anytime."

"Any chance you want to go to the classes with me?"

"Yes, I might want to do that. Let me know more when you find out the details."

"I will. I'm going home to grab a shower and I also need to visit with Jack's parents today."

"See you later. Let me know if you need anything before the visitation tomorrow at the funeral home."

Haley hugged her. "I will. Thank you so much."

Jessie smiled and hugged her back. "I'm here for you."

Haley showered quickly, dressed and put a minimal amount of make-up on. She blew out her wet hair, set the house alarm, slipped into her car and backed out of the garage quickly for her in-laws. Ideally, she would have already visited them at this point. She would have to apologize again.

Joe and Sharon had downsized to a large patio home in a golf course community. They both belonged to the country club and played regularly throughout most of the year. The move was a big thing. Like many Americans, they had accumulated so many items over the years. It was a gradual thing as they rid themselves of so many personal possessions collected throughout their married life. The move had been the perfect choice for them as they were getting up in their years.

The rain had lightened to tiny drops as Haley pulled into their drive. She grabbed her purse and ran up to the door. After ringing the bell, Sharon Foster answered. Haley hugged her immediately and said, "I'm so sorry I have not been here before now. Please forgive me."

"Don't even think about it. I know you have been going through a lot. We all are. Glad you could make it now."

"Haley, you're here. That's good we need to talk," Papa Foster said. Even as a retiree, he had a business-like demeanor. He was dressed in his usual khaki trousers and short sleeved golf shirt. She knew he would not be golfing with what was happening now, but it was probably just easy attire for him to grab and put on.

She slipped out of her rain coat and placed it on the hall tree, then removed her shoes before stepping onto their light beige carpet.

"Papa, I'm sorry I have not been here before today."

"No, no, no. Don't worry about it. You needed some time. We understand."

He grabbed her shoulders to hug her and she noticed how tired his face looked. Haley followed them to the kitchen where they sat around the table. Joe Foster had a spread sheet and other papers in front of him.

"Haley, I don't know about you, but after hearing Jack's voice on the television last night, it lit a fire under my butt to find out who is behind this atrocity."

"I'm right there with you. Since last night, I feel angry. I want to know who would do this and why? And, I want to see them punished."

"As you know, my brother, God rest his soul, owned the largest detective agency in Atlanta. My nephews are in charge of it now and they have made it larger and better than before with more precise ways of getting information."

Haley nodded that she was aware of the agency and he continued.

"I've hired them to go to South America and find out anything and everything they can on the ground. This includes who may have drugged or poisoned the pilot and passengers. Anyway, I want you to know I am handling this and working on it."

"What can I do?" she asked, anxiously.

"Probably, just stand by. I may need you at some point, but I don't know how or in what capacity."

"Okay."

"For now, we have Jack's funeral to get ready for and think about. All the arrangements have been made and I am told it will be a closed casket as we talked about before."

Haley looked down at her lap and fumbled with her engagement and wedding rings nervously. "Doesn't feel real to me. I just cannot imagine Jack being gone."

Sharon grabbed her closest arm. "Nor I, my dear. I can see him coming in the door now with his big infectious smile, just like he did since he was a small boy."

Haley reached out and squeezed her hand. "I've promised myself I will be strong throughout this funeral. In fact, I need to be stronger in general and face many of my fears. Ironically, I attended a group counseling session with women who have been abused or violently attacked the same day I took Jack to the airport. A few of them mentioned that a huge part of making strides in their recovery was taking up women's self defense classes. I have been staying at night next door with Jessie and Alex because of several reasons, but mostly my fears of being alone. My cousin, aunt and uncle are arriving tomorrow. Tonight, I'm going to stay by myself."

"You can stay here, Haley, if you want," Sharon offered.

"Thank you. I'm feeling different today. Papa, you're right. Hearing Jack's voice and the extreme situation he was in did something to me inside as well. I guess you could say I'm ready to go on the offense."

"Haley, I think those classes would be great for you. I wish Sharon would have gone to them. Although, I would never want either of you to actually need to employ what you learn there."

Haley nodded in agreement. "Jessie may come with me to the classes. We would welcome you," she said, smiling at her mother-in-law.

"Oh, I don't know. You go and find out how difficult it is. Then, we'll talk," she chuckled.

"Fair enough," Haley said.

Chapter 32 ~ Papa Joe Foster

Joe Foster, retired now, had run a fortune 500 company for eighteen years. Prior to that, he had worked in finance. His career had afforded him the ability to put his family at ease financially and travel the world with them. Now retired, a puzzled problem such as the one that lay before him with his son's death was the perfect thing to rev him up and give him something to bite into. After the report last evening that Jack said they were drugged or poisoned, the old man's suspicions he initially felt were confirmed. Something very sinister had happened with that flight and, who knows, could still be happening.

Joe listened as the funeral director phoned to say they still did not have anything for his son's remains. When he questioned the contact at Chadwell, the employee said they would check on it and get back in touch. Now, he had called back to tell the funeral director they could not identify any remains for Jack.

"Tell me the condition of those you did find. Be specific with me, but not his wife, Haley. I can handle to hear it. What kind of remains did you find of the others?"

"I am told there were actual body torsos of the pilot and three employees. From their appearance and dress, none of them appear to be Jack."

"Interesting," is all that Jack's father would say.

There was momentary silence between the two men. Finally, Joe spoke. "Alright, thanks for letting me know this first. It does produce quite a quandary with his wife and mother. I don't want to lie to either one of them, but I also do not want them holding false hope he is alive."

The grieving father hung up the phone. He then dialed the lead investigator hired the day before. "Matt, here is what I know right now. This is the situation with the body. We have no body. Tell me what you think, but to me this indicates either Jack was able to crawl or walk away from the crash into the forest and has either died from injuries he sustained, or he is alive and we just haven't heard from him."

"Hard to say he is truly gone without the body. It does happen, but it's rare."

"What do you suggest at this point?"

"We already have two men on their way to the crash site. It's remote, so it could be a day or so before I have more information. I will, however, get in touch with them and let them know there is a real possibility Jack could be out there in the forest somewhere. The thing is, I really need them doing investigations at the airport and a couple of other spots as well. Do you want me to put more people on this?"

"I think you better. Put an army on it if you have to, whatever it takes."

Chapter 33 ~ Hiding Place

Evan received the message on the burner phone to meet at their usual location. The team had something interesting. He pulled into the parking lot and the contact walked toward his Porsche.

"Nice ride, dude," the guy with greasy hair said.

"Thanks, tell me what you've got."

He handed an envelope to Evan. "Here, read it for yourself."

Conversation Monday, December 2, 2019

Jack Foster - Haley, I isolated something. Initially, it was a plant we gathered by accident while harvesting. I didn't even know what it was, just a stray plant hanging onto our harvest. It's tricky to cultivate in our climate or the greenhouses. Sercy had success, but we need more of the plant. That's why I have to go back to the rain forest. I can't tell you anything else about the project.

Haley Foster - I understand. Jack, I am so proud of you.

Jack Foster - Baby, you are what pushes me to want better for you, our children we will have, and everyone in this world. This could possibly be such a game changer medically, that this information is on a "need to know" basis only at Chadwell. Nothing is to be known about it outside of the company. Do you understand how secret it must remain? Competitor companies would kill for this information.

Haley Foster - Yes, I will speak of it to no one, Jack.

Jack Foster - Good. I have taken considerable efforts to make sure any information and notes I have on this are hidden within secure files and not emailed or spoken of even on the phone. Everything is backed up in a secret hiding area here in this house. That's how important this is.

Haley Foster - In our house, where?

Jack Foster - Someplace very safe from anyone who might try to get to it. Don't worry yourself with it.

End of conversation.

Evan finished reading through the transcript. "Good work! Guess you guys will get a bonus for this. Keep up the surveillance and let me know if anything else interesting comes across your radar."

"Will do, see you later."

"Later"

Now, Evan needed to get someone into that house to find what Jack had hidden. He decided to keep this information to himself. If he shared it with Tellinger, he'd be willing to eliminate Haley to obtain the files. He dialed a contractor he hadn't spoke to for several months on the burner phone. The man answered quickly.

"Tell me what you want," is how he greeted Evan. But he didn't know it was Evan calling. It could have been anyone.

"It's me, Evan Mitchell. I need something located at a residence and brought to me."

"Is it occupied?"

"Yes."

"Let's meet up somewhere so you can give me the specifics."

"How about that bar over on 10th street where we met before."

"What time?"

"Make it in a couple of hours. I need to try and talk to the resident and get a feel for what's going on there."

"Sounds good, I'll see you about 2:00"

"Okay"

Evan needed a reason to call Haley so he could find out what her plans were. He did not want the guy breaking into her house when she was there. Most people were savvy to someone breaking in while they were at a funeral. Plus, it would be hard to get onto that cul-de-sac in daylight hours. But that was not his problem.

He phoned the personnel at Chadwell in charge of collecting the personal property found at the crash scene of the victims.

"This is Evan Mitchell. I am inquiring whether you have identified any items belonging to Jack Foster in the haul from the crash?"

"Hold on, I believe so, but let me make sure."

"Yes, we have one bag that is tagged with his name."

"Good, I'd like to make sure we get it delivered to the Foster residence. Do you mind if I take it myself?"

"Sure. That's possible. You will need to sign for it."

"Not a problem. I'll be right over to pick it up."

Evan dialed Haley's cell phone.

"Hello, is this Evan?" she answered.

"Yes, Hi Haley. Listen, I hope I'm calling at a good time."

"What do know, anything?" she asked.

"One of Jack's bags has been located and brought back to the United States. I thought I would drop it off to you, if that's okay."

"Actually, I'm not home right now. I'm not sure what I'm doing yet or when I will be there. I've been staying with friends the last two nights. Do you mind if I get it after the funeral, say on Monday?"

"Sure, that's no problem. I could bring it by. I do plan on coming by the funeral home as well, but I can drop it off to you on Monday."

"Sounds good, that would work out better for me. Thank you. Oh, I have a call beeping in, let me let you go."

Evan hung up and felt this was his guy's opportunity to get in there and find the goods.

Chapter 34 ~ The Noise

Friday Night

Tomorrow was the day she would be at the funeral home for many hours. She checked the clothing Jessie had chosen and everything looked in order. She selected a pair of earrings Jack had bought her on a weekend trip. Haley felt conflicted about staying at the house alone, but decided she was making too much of things. She settled in the bedroom and watched television, falling asleep at some point.

She woke abruptly, hearing what she thought was a loud thud on the deck. Her heart raced as she wondered if someone was outside. Grabbing her phone, she reviewed the security footage from the camera. Something showed up in one video, but it was not clear what it was. Haley talked herself down as her heart rate increased exponentially. What if someone is out there? She reviewed the footage. The camera picked up some kind of movement and it didn't appear to be a spider crawling on the lens. You could hear the thud on the replay, but she could not make out anything except a slight shadow. Perhaps it was a raccoon. They were plentiful at night here in the woods.

When she could not stand the fear any longer, she phoned her neighbors. Alex answered, sounding sleepy. "Haley, is that you calling?"

"Yes, Alex, I'm so sorry. I heard a loud thud on the deck and the camera picked up something. I'm scared."

"I'll be right over. Watch for me at your front door."

Alex came with a flashlight to her door, and she quickly disarmed the system and let him in. Haley showed him the footage and he also could not see anything significant. "It was probably an animal out there on the deck. Listen, why don't you grab your phone and whatever you need and come back over to our guest room? I don't want you here by yourself afraid, okay?"

"Sure, yeah, it's probably best for tonight."

Haley set the alarm and followed Alex back to his house. Jessie met them at the door. "Did you guys figure out anything?"

"No, probably an animal," Alex said.

Haley noticed he had a handgun. "Wow, you were prepared."

"I promised Jack we would watch out for you."

"Thanks you guys. I don't know what I would do without friends like you."

"Ahh, we're family now," Jessie teased. "We're going to adopt you."

Haley laughed. "You would be sorry you did."

Evan's burner phone was ringing. He sat up quickly in the bed to answer it. "Yeah," he said.

"What the hell, Mitchell! I couldn't get in. That place is a fortress with every window and door wired. You didn't tell me there were cameras everywhere too, although I guess I should have expected it."

Evan tried to make sense of the guy's words. "Hey, I don't know how extensive things are there."

"Anyway, I gave it a good try, but she was home. And the neighbor came over with a flashlight. I was damn lucky to get out of there without being seen."

"Wow, I'm sorry, man. She told me she wasn't staying there."

"Yes, well, she lied. We will need a Plan B and maybe C on this one."

"I'll call you if I know of any other way."

Evan ended the call and looked at the clock. He was not about to stay up. With the stress he was carrying, he needed more sleep. He tossed and turned, wondering how in the hell he could get Haley to give him a tour around her house. Probably would not happen. Still, he would remain open for any opportunity to get in there.

Chapter 35 ~ Facing Fear

Saturday, December 7, 2019

Waking to another day, Haley tells herself she must accept the loss of Jack. Sleep offers another world, one of fantasy and things not hitting her in the face. She has some sliver of hope he did not die and then she realizes he's not there and won't show up. With each rise of the sun, she experiences deep feelings of loss coupled with disbelief. It felt like passing through a thousand needle torture chamber to wake in this new reality.

Haley began chastising herself for not making it through one night at home on her own. *So many mental things for her to tackle right now.* She packed up the small amount of belongings she had brought with her to Alex and Jessie's and popped into the kitchen to say she was going home now. Jessie was working at the table with orange juice and her laptop. Obviously, she was perusing possible real estate listings for a client.

Jessie glanced up as Haley entered the room. "Hey, how are you?"

"Doing okay. I did get some sleep, finally."

"I'm really glad to hear that. Alex is gone now but we tried to be very quiet to make sure you slept as long as you needed."

"Oh, I'd sleep just about all the time right now if it were feasible. Big day with my family coming and the funeral home visitation."

"Alex and I will both be there. Let me know if you need anything."

"Thanks so much Jessie. I will."

Once at home, Haley prepared a smoothie and toast for breakfast. As she sat eating, she remembered to refill her daily vitamin container and decided to put a reminder on her phone to make sure she was taking them. It was so easy for her to forget the simplest things now. Everything needed to go on her phone calendar with reminders.

She showered and began trying to transform her weak complexion and under eye circles with foundation and concealer. Typically, she would not wear foundation, just a little concealer. Today, she would be talking to people she did not see often. While they probably expected her to appear physically distraught, and she was, there was a part of her that also wanted to be the brave woman. She remembered reading about Jacqueline Kennedy at President Kennedy's funeral. The First Lady had been strong not only for her children, but for an entire nation and world. She wished to channel even a little bit of that now. It would be an act, but one that felt more empowering than the fetal position she had taken up for so many hours on the couch or bed.

Without Jack being here, it was time to enact some changes — especially when it came to her fears and safety. She had to start taking the upper hand and not be afraid of everything. That reminded her — come hell or high water, she would go to the group therapy on Tuesday. Yes, it seemed too soon, but she couldn't wait. There was something freeing about being with the other women as they all talked about their pasts and strides they were making toward better futures. The group energy was empathetic, but upbeat. It could not hurt at this time. Plus, she had to find a way to be independent without excessive fear. Many of the women had sworn by self defense classes and other methods of protection. Once finished with makeup, she donned a pair of sweats to wear until time to leave for the funeral home.

Aunt Molly and Uncle Mike arrived about eleven in the morning with Sonya. They had only been to the house once shortly after she and Jack bought it and were still doing renovations. She would give them a brief tour to see the differences they had made since their visit. There were two spare bedrooms for them to occupy. Haley very much welcomed them being at the house, especially after last night.

Sonya had changed her hair style to something a little more wild with pink streaks. It actually looked very pretty on her light blond hair. "Can I touch it?" Haley asked as she reached out to rub two fingers on Sonya's hair.

"Go for it!" she said. "You like it?"

"I do like it. It suits you."

Aunt Molly and Uncle Mike were dressed in dark conservative clothing, ready for the funeral home. Haley looked down and waved her hand at her sweats. I only have hair and makeup complete. I thought I would wait to put my clothes on I'm wearing today … just in case."

"Just in case?" Aunt Molly asked curiously.

"Oh, you know. Ruining it somehow with a spill or something."

"Gotcha," Aunt Molly replied. "You look amazing Haley, especially considering."

"Thank goodness for correcting cosmetics, huh?" she lightly laughed.

"Well, I'm in need of those every day," Aunt Molly giggled "I'm laughing, but quite serious."

"You both are a feast for sore eyes — and you too Sonya. I'm so glad you are here and happy you will be spending the night here. You can stay as long as you like."

Uncle Mike spoke up, "Sweetheart, we want to be here for you, but we also don't want to impose. Could be you need moments by yourself at times to absorb this." He always knew human reactions to things. Uncle Mike made a study of people and situations.

"Well, you're right about that. Truth be told, I need both -- time alone and time with others. Plus, I'm still suffering bouts of PTSD from my incident. I've been staying with Jessie and Alex next door at night for a couple of reasons."

Uncle Mike looked concerned. "Is anyone bothering you now?"

"No, no. My imagination can go into overdrive though."

"I see. Well, never fear — Uncle Mike is here."

They both laughed and she motioned for them to unload whatever bags they had and walked out to their vehicle to assist. Once inside, they placed them in their appointed rooms and Haley gave them a quick home tour showing the changes she and Jack had made. They loved everything, especially the renovated master bath.

"Oh, look at the time. I better get dressed," Haley said.

"We'll wait in the living area for you, honey," Aunt Molly said, squeezing Haley's hand.

Chapter 36 ~ Closed Casket

Everything seemed surreal as they entered the funeral home. Close family members were directed to the viewing room or visitation area. They were asked to arrive an hour before visitation actually began. Reverend McAllister was present along with Jack's parents, brother, Sarah, the children, and Haley's entourage. At first Haley's gaze was fixated on the closed casket with its copper colored finish. She walked toward it and placed her right hand on top of it, leaving it there for a few moments. It felt like a cold, fancy rectangular box. What was inside? Where was Jack — the real man she knew — his spirit and essence?

Uncle Mike held her lightly by the right arm and stood silent beside her as she traced the gold cross emblazoned on the coffin with her finger. She turned and looked at him. "This just does not seem real. Can we sit down for a moment?"

Uncle Mike, sensing that Haley might even faint, held her more firmly now and directed her to a small couch at the side of the room. He continued to stand in front of her while Sonya and aunt Molly sat with Haley, flanking each of her sides. Haley took her aunt's hand on one side and her cousin's on the other. "I hope this waterproof mascara really works," she half laughed.

"No worries today, Haley. No one expects anything of you."

Haley thought about how important her aunt was to her. She had been with her through so many pivotal things in life. Molly had immediately come to Haley's rescue when her mother had overdosed and died, taking her in as her own. She had shopped for prom and homecoming dresses with her, and filled out college admissions forms alongside her. This woman had been a real rock for her.

"Thank you, you're always here for me Aunt Molly."

Other than greeting and hugging Haley when she arrived, Jack's family had held back giving Haley some space while she stood at the casket and now sat with her birth relatives. Finally, Sarah and Mrs. Foster walked over to approach her. Mrs. Foster spoke first.

"Miss Haley, you are the finest daughter-in-law I could ever have wished for. I am so glad Jack had the good sense to court you and very glad you chose my son. We are all gonna miss him like crazy."

"Oh, Mama Foster. You are everything I could ever want in a mom-in-law. I know you've only met my aunt and uncle once at the wedding. This is my Aunt Molly and Uncle Mike. And this is my cousin, Sonya. Mr. & Mrs. Foster shook hands with them.

Uncle Mike spoke first. "I cannot tell you how sad we are to meet you again on this occasion. Jack was a real blessing." Aunt Molly nodded in agreement.

Joe Foster looked down at the swirly patterned carpet on the floor, then nodded at them thankfully.

"Thank you and we are glad you came. I do remember you from the wedding," Sharon Foster noted.

Haley spoke next, "They are staying with me for the weekend at the house."

Sarah joined the group and she seemed very quiet as compared to her take charge, gregarious self. Normally fiery and directing others, Sarah was in a silent, almost demure mood. Haley wondered what was up. "Hey Sarah, want to go to the ladies room with me?"

"Sure thing."

The two walked out of the large visitation room into the hall, making their way toward the restroom. As the door pushed open, the room was quiet large with a sitting area, including tissues and a vanity with mirrors. It was decorated with high quality silk flower arrangements. Haley pointed, inviting Sarah to sit on the love seat. She looked at Sarah with curiosity once they were seated.

"Okay, what's going on with you? You're being so quiet."

"I'm just trying to be calm for Jack's brother and the kids. Honestly, I took something prior to coming inside. I know it's not fair of me with what you are going through, but I just felt such anxiety."

Haley looked at her with new understanding. "I knew you seemed different — much more laid back. Who knows, Sarah? I may need some of that as well. Actually, I'm feeling so damn angry about all of this, but I'm trying to keep a lid on it by being more proactive. Someone sabotaged that flight and the people on it. They lost their lives over it and I intend to find out who and why."

"Papa Foster is headed down that road with you. I know Jason is not far behind. Yeah, it's no longer an accident. It's murder. I'm so sorry, Haley."

They grabbed each other and cried. "I'm glad I have you, Sarah, and all of my family."

Sarah grabbed the box of tissue and offered it to Haley, taking two tissues for herself. They both took deep breaths and looked at one another.

Sarah smiled. "Okay, we better look in the mirror now and see how much damage we've done."

The ladies freshened up their lipstick and Haley supplied some cotton swabs to pick up any streaked mascara.

As they left, Sarah took Haley's arm and directed her to the floral arrangements and notes of condolence that were on display in the funeral's visitation room.

"Wow, these arrangements from Chadwell Pharmaceuticals and Evan Mitchell are massive and gorgeous," Sarah commented. Haley nodded her head in agreement as she lightly touched both arrangements and glanced at the cards.

"I suppose many people will be arriving today. I'm really not sure how to respond, Sarah. I keep thinking about how the First Lady, Jacqueline Kennedy conducted herself, trying to emulate it in some strange way. Especially now that I know Jack was deliberately taken out, instead of some freak accident."

"Haley, you are doing so well already. Just be you. No one is expecting strength from you now. They are here to show their sorrow and support for the loss of Jack. If anything, they want to give you what strength they have to offer."

"I suppose you're right."

"Haley, there will be photos of Jack, and many of us with him, portrayed on the screen over there," she said, pointing to the far side of the room. "If this is too much, stay at this end of the room closer to the casket and don't look at it. There will be copies made and you can view it later at home if you wish."

"I'm glad you warned me about that. I don't think … no, I absolutely cannot look at that right now. Honestly, just the smell of this place with all these flowers is something I'm trying not to let bother me."

Just then, Jessie and Alex appeared in the room and Sarah and Haley walked over to greet them. They hugged and Haley made introductions to the close family present. Haley walked with Jessie and Alex toward the casket, again tracing the golden cross on top with her fingertips. She murmured in a low tone to both of them, "I wish I could see Jack one last time. I need to know what happened. This just doesn't provide the closure I need."

Jessie squeezed her hand tightly. "Of course, anyone would feel that way."

Alex was dumbfounded, not knowing what to say. This was his friend's funeral, someone he joked with, patted on the back, and shared stories with. And he was gone. The reality of it began to hit him at the funeral home, standing beside Jack's casket. He glanced at the screen display with photographs of Jack from a young boy to the time he had known him. Tears escaped his eyes silently, even though he had told himself he was there to be strong for Haley.

She looked over and noticed him wiping away those tears with the sleeve of his coat. "It's okay to cry, Alex. Jack cared for you too. He cared about everyone."

"Yes, he did. He was the type of person that would go out of his way for anyone. I'm going to miss him like crazy."

Haley realized there would be a lot of this today and tomorrow with everyone having their own stories and experiences of Jack to share. Inside the pain of this loss, it was hard to feel cordial or social. Yet she was resolute that she would find her place, trying to channel her inner Jackie. She longed for sleep, a place now of retreat where she might dream of Jack and felt like she might connect with him even if it was not real. It seemed so authentic in the dream, and that was all that mattered to her now.

Soon, the room would be open to anyone wanting to visit with the family and pay their respects. She had to pull herself together and get through this.

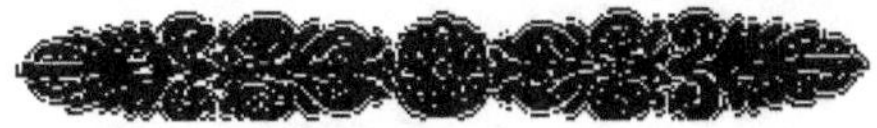

Lance's partner, Luke, tentatively approached Haley as she stood near the closed casket with the memorabilia of Jack. "Haley, I'm very sorry to be meeting you for this type of occasion. Lance really looked up to Jack."

"Come here and give me a hug, Luke!" They embraced and then Haley pulled back with her hands still on Luke's shoulders. "I'm very sorry for your loss too. We could never have imagined this. Honestly, it doesn't seem real at times."

"I know what you mean. The loss is haunting me day and night. I'm sure you are feeling similar."

"Yes, actually everything has moved so quickly. I just sort of feel like I'm floating through life right now. Thank goodness I have family and friends assisting me any way they can. But, what about you? Do you have anyone?"

"I do and thanks for asking. This is a real head trip to go through. Lance and I have many friends in our community and that helps. Both of our families have been there from day one of this ordeal for me. They have really added a lot of strength right now."

"Good, I'm glad to know that. Let me ask you something? Do you think I should attend the services of everyone on the plane on Jack's behalf? He was the head of the department."

"I don't know. I know everyone would love to see you."

"I'll think on it. So far, I've found that staying busy does seem to help in dealing with this, but I'm not sure how I will be at any certain day or time. My state of mind feels in and out, up and down."

"I know what you mean. I've taken time away from work but will have to go back by the end of next week. Listen Haley, if you want to meet for coffee, lunch or just to talk, just say the word. Here's my card."

"Oh, I didn't realize you were in the insurance business."

"Yes. I followed my dad into that profession. He's had his own agency for years."

"I will give you a call because I think we should talk, but somewhere private. Did you hear the news with Jack's voice talking to the radar controllers about poison or drugs?"

"I did hear it … I listened to it over and over again."

"Same here."

"I just did not want to mention it now in case you did not know."

"I appreciate that. Do me a favor, would you? Find out if all the family members of the other work group know about that recording."

"Will do. Jack was an incredible team leader and scientist."

"Yes, he was. Jack was incredible at anything he put his mind to."

Sensing there were others standing around wanting a close conversation with Haley, Luke said his goodbyes for now, promising to talk again soon.

Haley continued to stand near the casket as people came to her with condolences and support. The closed casket was a symbol of her love locked away from her, taken much too soon. More than anything, she realized this was going to be the longest day of her life. Receiving guests as the wife of the deceased seemed to cement Jack being gone. Each person who held her hand and spoke to her was another confirmation. While she appreciated all the love and support, she noticed there was a longing inside her that wanted to avoid it. *God, I need this to be over!*

Chapter 37 ~ Evan Arrives

Evan Mitchell adjusted his tie and slipped into his jacket. Admiringly, he lingered at the mirror and felt his attire might be too formal for visitation day at the funeral home, rather than the actual funeral. He took off the jacket and decided to hang it in his vehicle if he changed his mind once he arrived.

He was feeling more in charge and upbeat today about the fallout surrounding the plane accident. He was taking charge, best he could. The contractor was unable to get into the house last night. Somehow, Evan would make an opportunity. He needed to get closer to Haley, but it had to be done in a natural, gradual way.

He opened the door to his black Porsche and hung the jacket in the small section in the rear. He slipped behind the steering wheel. There was a surge in his loins as he started the engine. Evan felt things would come together on this just as he needed them to. He had already received a text on the burner phone from Ragland that said the problem had been taken care of. He had thrown the phone away into a dumpster at the back of a building on Charter Street.

Evan reminded himself that he needed to be respectful of what people were feeling at the funeral home and elsewhere. Solemn came to mind as his approach. He really could not connect with how they felt losing members of their family. His own family had been so one sided and disjointed, with extreme favoritism going on between him and his brother. Evan had been looked upon as the lackey — not wanting to follow in his father's footsteps as a career football player — a giant in the sports industry. The fact that Evan cherished his brain more than his brawn had been seen as quirky, weird for his family to conceive and understand.

Soon, he would work his way up to becoming not only part of the board of Chadwell Pharmaceuticals, but one of its chief executives. Sometimes having more brain power meant outsmarting your competition to achieve your goals. It was much different than just scoring the next touchdown. It was a different way of winning the final game.

Deep in his gut, Evan looked forward to seeing Haley and dreaded it as well. He had to keep up his sorry appearance about Jack being dead, but he felt elated — a major problem out of the way. He parked outside the funeral home, checking his face and teeth in the rear view mirror. He stepped outside the vehicle and pushed the

FOB to lock it up. A small boy came over, "Wow, that's a really nice car. Is it a Porsche?"'

"Sure is," he said smiling proudly.

The boy's father approached and reached out his hand to shake Evan's. "He's already dreaming of the day he can finally drive."

"Well it's a big milestone in life, now isn't it?"

"Would you like to peek inside the car?" Evan asked the boy.

"Yes!" the boy said, nodding enthusiastically.

Evan unlocked it and opened first the driver's door, then the passenger side.

"Wow, it is slick inside, Dad. Look at the shifter. And all the leather. How long have you had this car?"

"A little over two years. I ordered it exactly as I wanted from the factory."

"You must be rich."

"No, I would not say I am rich, just really wanted one of these cars for years and made it happen. You could do the same when you're older. Study and work hard in school. Get a good job and you can do it too," Evan said, smiling.

"See," his dad said. "What did I tell you about how important your education is? Thanks for letting him take a peek."

"No problem, nice to have someone admire the vehicle."

Evan strolled toward the funeral home entrance and saw that Jack Foster was in Room 2A. He signed the visitor log and proceeded inside the visitation area. Immediately, he spotted Haley, but she did not see him. She was speaking with Lance's partner, Luke, another person who had lost a loved one. He glanced around to see if he recognized anyone and saw Mr. & Mrs. Foster. He could not help noticing Jack's twin brother and this was a bit jarring at first. They looked exactly alike. Evan slowly walked toward them as they huddled together close to the casket area. As he grew near, he reached out to shake Mr. Foster's hand.

"Hello again. Evan Mitchell from Chadwell. I wanted to come by and say again how sorry I am about this tragic time for everyone. It's already not the same around our department without Jack. His brilliance will be sorely missed."

Mr. Foster half smiled to be cordial and shook Evan's hand. There was just something about the guy that was off putting, as if he had an air of importance around him that was unjustified.

"Thank you for coming Evan. Walk with me, please."

Mr. Foster led Evan outside the room into the foyer. "I need to grab some coffee if you don't mind. Not getting a lot of sleep right now."

"I understand," Evan replied.

Evan followed Joe Foster to a room with trays of food and beverages. Evan decided to have a cup along with the gentleman. He sensed there was something the man wanted to say to him.

"Any more word on what caused the crash or belongings found, Evan?"

"Yes, I have some limited information. Some of the belongings found were clearly identifiable. There is one bag I will have delivered to Haley that belonged to Jack, but we are waiting until after the funeral. Some of the items found at the site are mixed together. It was hard to identify what belonged to whom. We will need the close family members to come take a look and assist with that. As far as the crash, we are still waiting on an official report, especially after the claim about possible outside intervention by someone. The initial word is that the pilot may have had a few enemies that wanted him gone. We are guessing he may have shared coffee that had been brought to him prior to take off with the other passengers."

Joe glanced down at his coffee and chuckled slightly. "Makes anyone a bit paranoid now doesn't it?"

Evan also looked at his styrofoam cup. "Yes, I suppose it does."

"Evan, I'm not so sure about that scenario. What I really wonder is whether my son is actually gone. I don't know if you know it or not, but there were no identifiable remains for the funeral home. My wife and Haley do not know this. Only Jack's brother knows, and now you. I do not want you to allow that information to get to his wife or mother. They do not need false hope if that is not the case. Yet, we need to find out if Jack is alive somewhere. Maybe he was able to crawl away from the crash."

This news hit Evan in the pit of his stomach and he worked hard to cover the shocked reaction he felt inside. "Alive?" was all he could say initially.

"Yes, what if he is alive and needing help?"

"You said you did not want me to mention it, certainly not to Haley or Mrs. Foster. For me to try and put together a team to investigate this, I would need to speak with Mr. Tellinger at Chadwell. Do I have your permission to explore this idea with him?"

"Yes, you do. But, I couldn't wait. I have a team on this now. Since I heard the recording of Jack on the news I have had people on the ground trying to find out what happened. Once I spoke with the funeral director about the lack of any remains for my son, I made some calls to expand their assignment."

Evan sat his coffee aside as his nerves were coming up through the surface of his skin now. "Sir, any way we can help, I am sure Chadwell will. I will speak privately with Mr. Tellinger about it today."

"Good! Like I said, I don't want to give my wife, Haley or anyone false hope, but if my son is alive, By God, I will find him."

"Of course, I suppose I should give my condolences to Haley now. But, you have certainly opened up an area that gives me pause."

"Yes, you should do as you planned when you came here. There is a death certificate and the memorial service and funeral are happening for my son. Like I said, if Jack is gone, I don't want them having false hope."

"Got it, sir."

Evan followed Jack's father back to the visitation room trying to regain his composure and intentions he had arrived with. There was a small line of people now waiting to speak with Haley and he joined at the rear of the line. Good, this gave him time to decompress that bit of news. He needed time to think about what Jack's father had said; time to regain his composure and act the part he had set out to do originally. Haley stood to the right of the casket which was adorned with a spread of roses and lilies. There was an older lady speaking to her and Evan was next. As he approached her, he almost felt tearful, not about Jack, but the anxiety holding him captive in this plan that was beginning to show yet another hole in it.

"Haley, I wanted to come by today and once more let you know how sorry I am about the loss of Jack — for you and all of us that worked with him."

"Thank you Evan. As I have told many people, I'm just not sure it feels real all the time for me. Just going through the motions as best I can."

He could tell by her demeanor and tired eyes that it was quite an ordeal for her.

"You asked me about that necklace. Personal items have been recovered from the crash and the malachite necklace you described does not seem to be there. I had a couple of people look carefully, but it was not found."

"It's strange. I know Jack and how he is. If he promised me he would wear it throughout the trip, he would."

Feeling the need to shift the subject matter, Evan volunteered a story about how he and Jack had worked on an innovative project together. He was very complementary about Jack's tenacity and expertise in bioscience and pharmacology.

"Thank you for sharing that with me, Evan. Have you ever lost anyone close to you?"

Sensing the opportunity to create a commonality between them, Evan proceeded to lie to her about his one true love that had been killed by a drunk driver on a fateful night.

"Is that the reason you are still single?" she asked.

"I'm afraid it is. Fear of losing someone I love again, I suppose. But that's me. I am here for you right now, Haley." He squeezed her hand and looked into her eyes. "Call me for anything you might need."

"Thank you, Evan."

They parted company as others were waiting to speak with her. As he walked away she said his name again. "Oh, Evan, I meant to say thank you for the incredible floral arrangement you sent. It's stunning — very tropical. Jack would have loved it."

"You're welcome. I wish I could do more," he said.

Evan walked toward the funeral home's foyer. He had paid his respects to the family involved here and while there were others he could have chatted with from Chadwell, he wanted to get the hell out of this place. Jack alive? The necklace never found had become another intriguing element. Could have been destroyed in the crash along with Jack's body. The word was the scene was beyond tragic in scope. But, what did that mean? And Jack's father — was he just holding onto some type of hope that any man might feel losing his son? Holes … more possible problems to check out and fix.

Chapter 38 ~ Funeral

Sunday, December 8, 2019

A bed full of memories is where Haley awoke on the day of Jack's funeral. Their special place of sharing soft, intimate moments and rousing pleasures hinted of something missing. Instinctively, she reached out for the side Jack slept on, knowing it was empty. She wanted to feel him in some invisible way. Her eyes fell upon three walls of the massive bedroom where something just felt off. It was like walking back into a familiar room but a major piece of furniture was missing.

The knowledge she had gained over the last few days about the crash was shocking. She imagined what thoughts went through his mind, knowing the pilot and passengers were out cold and the plane was going to potentially crash. Red hot anger fueled her legs to move as her feet hit the floor beside the bed and led her into the bathroom. Someone wanted to commit murder that day. Who were they after? Jack, someone on his team, or the pilot as the news had intimated? Regardless, it affected everyone on the plane. They all were murdered. Haley grabbed her robe and made her way out to the kitchen.

Aunt Molly and Uncle Mike were making breakfast and greeted her.

"How did you sleep, honey?" Aunt Molly asked.

"Better than I thought I would. I guess — considering that today's the day I say good bye to Jack. It's not easy with so many unanswered questions about the crash."

Breakfast preparation paused on the part of both her aunt and uncle as they gave her their full attention. Uncle Mike came to her side. "For sure," he said. Aunt Molly came near and they all hugged.

"While we are huddled for a moment here, can we ask for a little divine intervention, as in prayer?" he inquired of Haley.

She sighed and looked directly into Uncle Mike's eyes, "Yes, please do."

Remaining together in their three person circle, Aunt Molly glanced up to see Sonya standing a few feet away in her pajamas watching them. She motioned with her hand for her daughter to join them. Sonya came over and squeezed Haley slightly on her side, letting her know she was inching in to join.

With everyone settled, Uncle Mike spoke aloud, "God, we ask that you guide us all today and going forward in the next few days in knowing what to do or say that will be in the best interest of all. Lord, we thank you for friends and family and those who will bring comfort and support to Haley and others hurting at this time. We ask that you assist us, Lord, with knowing the answers we are allowed to discover in the great scheme of things as to what happened to Jack and the other fine individuals on that plane. Finally, please allow one or two of your comforting angels to walk with Haley today and over the coming days as she navigates through this physical separation from Jack. We pray this in the name of the Father, Son and the Holy Spirit."

"Amen!" was heard unanimously from all and a few tears escaped the eyes of all four.

Haley looked at each of them with gratitude. "It is such a blessing to have you guys here. Thank you for coming."

Molly put her arms around Haley and whispered, "Hungry?"

"I'm just going to have my usual smoothie and skip any solid food this morning."

"Are you sure, I can put something together for you quickly?" Aunt Molly offered.

"Thanks, but I just don't feel like food right now."

Haley grabbed her fruit and almond milk and headed for the blender. Uncle Mike motioned to Aunt Molly not to over mother her right now, but just give her some space. The two had been together long enough that she knew what his hand motions and facial expressions meant.

They arrived an hour and a half prior to the time of the funeral. Haley was quiet, glancing once more at all the flowers. She thought again of all the kind visitors from the previous day. Absolutely everyone seemed to deeply respect and like Jack. This included Mr. Tellinger who hired him on at Chadwell straight out of grad school. Why would anyone want to kill him? It had to be that someone else was the target and perhaps the pilot story was true. It was diabolical and completely evil, no matter who was behind the crash.

Her mind continued to play the heroic, yet panicked, voice of Jack trying to fly a plane he knew nothing about thousands of feet in the air. She was devastated and angry that someone had intentionally sabotaged the people on that plane. If it killed her, she would find out who. Inside, Haley knew she should be feeling something different right now at her husband's funeral … something other than revenge. She snapped herself back into the room mentally as she heard Reverend McAllister's voice, "How are you doing right now, Haley? Is there anything I can do?"

"I'm hanging in there, Reverend. It is a hard day but I'm doing well so far."

"Yes, it is one of the most difficult things any of us ever have to face. We are all here for you and also present to pay tribute to Jack and his life. May I walk you to a seat with other family?"

"Yes, thank you."

Reverend McAllister took her arm and guided her to the front row where she sat beside Jack's mother. Sarah sat on Haley's other side, holding onto a box of tissue to hand out to anyone who might need it.

A few of Jack's favorite songs played softly in the chapel room that looked more like a small church. The casket had been moved to this room along with many of the floral arrangements and photos of Jack. The small crowd that gathered was seated now in the rows of chairs. All were quiet. As the last song ended, Reverend McAllister took to the podium beside the casket and began to speak into the microphone.

"Thank you for coming to observe and celebrate the life of Jack Foster. My name is Reverend McAllister and I have known Jack and his family for many years. At this time, Joe Foster, has requested your audience." Reverend McAllister stepped away from the podium and shook Mr. Foster's hand as he took the clergyman's place.

The bereaved father waited for the reverend to take a seat before proceeding. He spoke tentatively at first, getting comfortable with the microphone on the podium as if he was determining how close or far he needed to be to project his voice.

"Thank you all for being here to remember my son, Jack Foster. I have some things I want to say to you today that could be shocking, but please hear my words and reasoning. Both Jack and his brother grew up camping, hiking, climbing cliffs at first and later mountains. Each of them knew how to take care of themselves in situations many would find challenging. When Jack met Haley, he found a woman who shared his love of the outdoors … so much that they spent their honeymoon in the Brazilian rain forest."

Jack's father paused, clearing his throat and then continued.

"My son has a long list of friends, accomplishments and people he cares for in this room and beyond. I could spend quite awhile here in this chapel that contains an empty casket telling you how great my son was. It would probably drive all of us to tears. There's one problem with all of this. Jack may not be gone."

There were several gasps within the crowd. Sharon Foster put her hand to her mouth and began crying. Haley, sitting next to her laid her palm on her mother-in-law's thigh, as if to steady her. But Haley was also steadying herself as she held onto her leg. Joe Foster allowed the gasps to occur, but then continued.

"I know many of you, if not all of you, have heard the recording of Jack trying to get assistance in flying the plane. You also heard his claim that everyone on board had been poisoned or drugged. If my son survived that crash and he was able to move, he would not stay right there where someone obviously wanted them to die. That is my first point in this matter. He may have survived the crash and was able to move away from it."

"My second reason is that I was told by the funeral home director yesterday there are no remains that could be identified for my son. Folks, we have an empty casket."

Sarah grabbed a couple of tissues from the box and bent over Haley toward Sharon Foster handing them to her. She grabbed them immediately. Haley took a couple and Sarah as well. Throughout the room, quietness prevailed, pierced occasionally with sniffles.

"Finally, when I heard of the crash, I hired people on my own to investigate — feet on the ground in Brazil. When I realized there was horrible sabotage and murder of these fine people and the pilot, I asked for more individuals to be put on the investigation. This brings me to why I waited until this late date to tell you this."

"You see, I knew the casket was empty and there was no body. But, things happen and while I hoped my son might be alive like any father would, I wasn't going to pass that false hope on to his mother or wife. Fifteen minutes before the good reverend was to speak here at what we have been calling Jack's funeral, I received a message with photographs of the well worn and favorite hat my son wore. The hat was found on the ground of the forest and it is positively Jack's. I am told that it was located far enough away from the crash that it could not have blown there in the wind."

Tears streamed so fast from Haley's eyes as she listened to her father in law. But as he continued, hope rose within her and it was an easy find. Whispers could be heard between attendees. J.D. Tellinger and Evan Mitchell made eye contact with one another briefly. Both wore a grim expression. Mr. Foster continued.

"You may hear my words and see me as a grief stricken man who has lost a son. Obviously, that is true. Wherever Jack is right now, he is lost from us in this world or perhaps the next. You may begin to rationalize, as I did, that maybe an animal carried Jack's hat off into the brush away from the crash. Yet, where is Jack's body? With the discovery of his personal clothing article and its location, plus the fact that we still have unanswered questions without physical evidence to back it up, I am officially calling off Jack's funeral for now. While many of you may believe I hope in vain, I can only tell you that hope, tenacity and fortitude to find the truth is what my son would expect from me at this time. Please join me in any way you can to assist with what is now a hunt for our beloved Jack. If alive, it is likely he is injured in some way."

Reverend McAllister rose from his seat, "How can we help?" Many of the attendees chimed in with the clergyman asking, "What can we do?"

"Thank you! What each of you can do that costs nothing is pray. Yet, we also need those who can lend their talents in any form to this investigation and search for a possible survivor." Joe Foster looked at his son Jason. "Jason, can I count on you and Sarah to coordinate tasks that we need and match them to volunteers?"

"You bet, dad. We can do that and more."

"Okay everyone, Jason and Sarah are the people you will want to communicate with on anything to do with the possible reasons for the crash or any talents you may be able to donate in the search for my son."

In the meantime, I will need to meet with my family. Like you, they had no idea I was putting a big pause on this funeral ceremony.

Chapter 39 ~ Aftermath

As guests of the funeral service filed out of the room, some congregated in the foyer while others made way for their vehicles to leave. The Foster family briefly hugged or shook hands with many of them who had encouraging words. Overall, the group mood was upbeat. Joe Foster gathered his family around him, along with Haley's aunt, uncle and cousin.

"I am very sorry to spring this on all of you. I know it's a shock. But if Jack is alive and I believe there is a good possibility of that, we must find him. Let me show you the photos of the hat." He held up his cell phone and showed the photos first to Haley, She grabbed his arm with one hand and put her other hand over her mouth. "That's Jack's hat," she murmured.

He turned his phone to his wife, Sharon. She looked at each photo for a long time. "There is no doubt that is Jack's hat," she said.

One by one, Joe allowed everyone to pass his cell phone around to see the photos.

Jason spoke up, "Dad, did they send you a visual showing how far it was found from the site?"

"Not yet, son. They were just getting back to their accommodations when these photos were sent. As you know, service is very spotty in the rain forest and they had to wait until they were back at the hotel. However, I was told they will get a map to me later, as time allows, showing the difference."

"That's good. I have to admit, Dad, I thought you were losing your mind this morning. God knows the loss of Jack is weighing so heavy on all of us that we could easily go off the deep end. But those photos are definitely convincing. And, you're right, we don't have Jack's body."

"Or the malachite necklace he promised he would wear the entire trip," Haley added.

Joe Foster looked at her. "I didn't know about the necklace."

"I told Evan Mitchell at Chadwell about it. They said it was not found in the wreckage."

"Well, that's one more thing to be on the lookout for and one more reason to think Jack survived that crash."

He looked again at Jason. "Son, we need to find that necklace so have Haley give you exact details on it. Hopefully, we will find it still being worn by your brother."

"Why don't we go have an early dinner and discuss plans going forward? I'll buy," Mr. Foster volunteered.

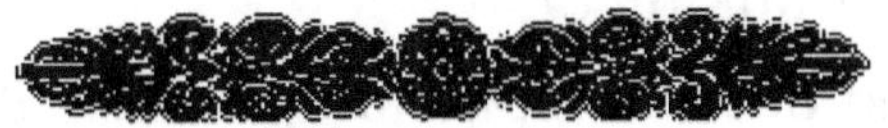

The entire family met at a local buffet style restaurant where they could select whatever they desired. After all were seated with their plates, Haley felt her phone buzz and glanced at it. Jessie was checking on her.

Hey, are you okay?

Yes, fine. At dinner with family. Can I call you later tonight?

No need to call me unless you need to talk. I know it's been a crazy day already.

You can say that again. You and Alex okay?

Yes ma'am. We are fine but just concerned about you.

I actually feel some hope and I won't call it false hope either.

We both feel hopeful as well. Call if you need anything.

Thanks. You guys let me know if you think of anything that could assist us in finding Jack.

Of course, will do.

The restaurant's Sunday after-church crowd had come and gone. Papa Foster chose a table close to the windows on the far side of the restaurant and asked if the staff could expand it by bringing more tables together. They quickly obliged. Before selecting their food, they sat momentarily and Papa Joe brought up something none were probably thinking of.

Joe pulled out a notepad and his executive style pen. He seemed so business like, but this was his take charge way.

"First, we are all family by blood or bond at this table and nothing we say should be uttered to anyone outside of this group. It is possible that the press could get wind of us not acknowledging Jack as being deceased and could begin contacting us. It will be important that we do not talk about things we are doing to investigate Jack's disappearance because someone wanted to murder people on a plane that day and they did. I have hope that Jack has somehow survived it. I do not want to give "someone" a chance to get to Jack from any of the means we are using. Does everyone at this table agree with this?

Unanimously, they agreed.

"Great, just wanted to set the ground rule that all of this is confidential."

He looked at Sharon and asked that she lead the group in prayer.

"Heavenly Father, please bless everyone and keep them safe and well. Please assist each of us individually and as a group in our search for Jack. Lord, we know you do this for us each day if only we listen to the ideas that pop in our minds suddenly or the nudges you give.

Thank you for all the blessings we enjoy each day Lord. Amen"

"Amen!" the group echoed.

Papa Joe Foster stood at the head of the table and motioned, "Please make your way to the buffet and let's eat. We will need our energy going forward."

All fell silent once they were eating. At a certain point, Allison spoke loudly, "What can Elijah and I do to help find Uncle Jack?"

Sarah and Jason's children were so well behaved during the entire funeral scenario that most of the adults had forgotten they were there. This meant they needed to be a bit guarded about the conversation around them.

Joe Foster spoke up first. "Allison, you and Elijah play a very important role in helping us. First, you both have been good as gold during this turmoil our family is going through. That means a lot and helps the grown ups think better and know what to do next. But, second, I believe there is a special role you each could take on. I'm not sure of it exactly yet, but we will determine it and come ask if you can help in that way when we know. Does that sound good?"

Both Allison and Elijah nodded. "Yes, Grandpa," they said in unison.

Sonya made eye contact with the two and smiled at them. "When I was getting my plate, I thought I saw a very tempting ice cream and dessert bar over on the other side of the restaurant. Did you see it?"

Elijah's eyes widened and he turned looking far away toward the other side. "No, I didn't' see it."

Allison smiled, "I know where it is."

"Hey, I have an idea. If it is okay with your parents, we could go to the dessert area together and have our own little sweet eating contest at the table right over there. Would that be okay?"

Jason nodded yes, as well as Sarah. They were happy that Sonya would volunteer to separate the children from the adult table and the dessert party was a great idea.

Still, Sarah put some rules upon it. "As long as you eat most of your healthy food, you both can have a party and indulge with Sonya this one time anyway."

The children each picked up their utensils and began eating more heartily. Once Sarah agreed they had eaten enough, Sonya guided them both to the dessert bar.

Everyone at the table seemed anxious to speak, verbally stumbling upon one another now that the children were gone. Jason spoke to the table. "Hold up everyone. Let me make notes of what each has to offer here so that we can coordinate this hunt for Jack in a cohesive way."

Everyone calmed down as if being called back in for a time out from the baseball field. Jason knew this had to be thought through carefully and even the slightest detail of something could be significant. The group began to discuss solutions and ideas more freely, one at a time. As Jack's wife, Jason motioned for Haley to speak first.

"The day after the plane went down, a lady came to my door. I didn't let her in but spoke to her through the intercom system. She said she was an investigative reporter working on a case about the pharmaceutical industry. Now, I don't want to give the impression I'm pointing my finger at Chadwell, but I also am not letting them off the hook. She left her business card and I'm thinking perhaps I should give her a call."

Joe Foster spoke up quickly, "This sounds like it could be worthwhile. I would be careful about sharing anything. You should be able to get information from her."

"Yes, I know she wants information from me … perhaps something that helps her add more ammunition or information to her investigation. I will be careful, but honestly, Jack never shared a lot of insider information with me. Almost anything I know is public knowledge. But, I also think I should meet with the grieving spouses and families of the lost employees we know are gone. Each of their funerals will happen over the next few days. I think it is important for me to show up at each one and if any of the rest of you would like to attend, please do. While I may not find out anything pertinent at the funerals, I feel so bad for each of them and want to be there for support."

Aunt Molly chimed in with a question for Haley. "I'm sorry if I seem dense about it all, but I was just wondering what this trip to the rain forest was for or about?"

Haley smiled and placed her forefinger on her temple and elbow on the table. "Actually, Aunt Molly, that is an excellent question. I know a little, but not very much. Jack told me they needed to find more of a plant that had been brought in on a previous harvest by accident. Sercy had been cultivating the plant at Chadwell, but they needed more of it. This had been going on since before I met Jack. I know that Jack said he had isolated something from the plant. He said the information was on a "need to know" basis only at Chadwell. It was a top secret kind of thing and often it is with any drug development because of competitor companies."

He also told me that he never spoke about the project on the phone. So, I suppose we should not either, even if we know nothing about it. However, he said that all his notes and information are backed up in a secret hiding place in our home. I asked him where but he would not tell me. I can't imagine really."

Papa Foster looked at Haley's aunt and motioned a thumbs up. "Glad you asked that question, Molly."

Haley tossed her hair back over her shoulder and placed both hands palm toward her forehead rubbing for a moment.

Aunt Molly asked, "Headache?"

"No, just tension."

"One more thing other than the details of the malachite necklace, Luke who was Lance's partner mentioned to me that he thought it might be a good idea for us to get together after the funerals — the immediate family members - perhaps have a lunch or dinner. I think it's a good idea as well. While he did not come right out and say it, I had the feeling that Luke has some suspicions or knows something he did not share with me at the time."

"Jason, the malachite necklace was just like a good luck, safe trip kind of gift I gave Jack. It was not fancy but the stone is beautiful. It's green and in the shape of a heart. The stone is wire wrapped in copper and it is attached by a leather cord."

"That is all I know for now that may help. I only hope it's true that he's alive."

Joe Foster nodded his head and rose. He came over and stood behind Haley. "You had a wealth of information and something tells me that your help will lead to more."

Chapter 40 ~ Evan & Tellinger

The contrast of the bright sun against the low lighting of the funeral home hit Evan right in the eyes as he walked out of the building with Tellinger. Evan thought of how it mirrored the vast difference between someone being alive or dead. He never considered that Joe Foster would annul Jack's death and cancel the funeral. Deftly, he pulled his Ray-Ban aviators from the pocket of his jacket and slipped them over the bridge of his nose.

The two men walked toward their vehicles, neither speaking until they reached Tellinger's black sedan. He opened the driver's door. "Let's meet early tomorrow, Evan, say 7:30 at my office. In the meantime, we can assess what just happened and where we go from here."

Evan nodded in agreement. "I'll be there, sir."

He gave Evan a slight scowl and lowered his voice. "After our meeting in the morning, I have people I will need to report to immediately on this."

Evan nodded his head up and down, letting the executive know he understood the buck did not stop with

Tellinger. He stood as the executive started the engine and drove away.

Once in the safety of his own home, Evan began to feel some emotional relief from the intense revelations of Mr. Foster's speech. He had the rest of Sunday before him and he felt like getting drunk and laid. The need to escape what felt like a slow closing noose around his neck was bursting inside. He removed his Brioni jacket and hung it in his closet.

Perhaps a romp would do him good. He picked up his cell phone and scrolled through his contacts until he came to Becky, a young divorced woman who had the skill to turn him on easily. What did he not like about Becky? She was pretty and had a really nice set of tits, but she was too accommodating. Becky was one of those women who thought sex might lead to something more serious. Deeper commitments rarely happened that way. He deliberated on whether to text or phone her, finally deciding to send a message first.

You busy today?

A few moments went by and Evan went ahead and removed his suit pants, looking them over to see if they needed to be cleaned. They looked fine - only worn three hours, if that. His phone pinged.

Just hanging out watching an old movie. How about you?

I need some company. Do you want to come over and watch a movie with me — or perhaps make one ourselves? LOL

That's what is refreshing about you Evan, you are always so direct. I guess two movie watchers are better than one. I can be there in about an hour.

Sounds good. Can't wait. I'll have your favorite drink ready.

Ciao, she messaged back.

Evan slipped into some casual sweat pants, deliberately not wearing a shirt. He worked hard to maintain his physique and while this expedition to eliminate Jack and his team from Chadwell had taken up quite a bit of his time, he would try to get back to the gym on a more regular schedule this week. He admired himself in the mirror. With his dark hair and olive complexion, Evan always appeared to have a slight tan.

While he didn't keep a ton of food in his kitchen, he managed to put together a platter with prosciutto, salami, two different cheeses, olives and dates. He pulled a chilled bottle of white wine out of the refrigerator and set out two wine goblets. Looking around the living area, he decided music was in order. Evan shuffled through various selections before finding what he felt set the perfect mood. Finally, he pulled the long heavy drapes that covered the tall windows overlooking the outdoor grounds. While this darkened the room considerably, it now had the feeling of a small private theater. Grabbing the remote, he selected an underwater screen saver with all sorts of aquatic animals on the huge plasma television. He could be romantic on demand.

The doorbell chimed and he glided across the floor in his bare feet to answer. Becky stood, trying to be equally provocative it seemed. Her bright fuchsia t-shirt was body fitting and plunged at the neckline showing off her tan bosom. It made him want to reach out and touch her right away. But he would wait. She had changed her hairstyle and it looked good on her. Always, she wore a little too much makeup, especially on her eyes.

"Becky, it's been awhile. Come in."

Becky strode in carrying a white paper bag. "What's in the mystery bag?" Evan inquired, slightly touching her hand.

"A small treat for the two of us. Fresh bread from my bakery. I stopped in to check on things and thought you might need some comfort food."

"You thought right, thanks!" he smiled.

Becky walked further into the living area and kitchen which were open to one another. She noticed how dim the lighting was and that the draperies closed off the nice view outside. She walked toward the kitchen island and saw that Evan had wine and finger food. "I brought you Italian sweet bread and it looks like it will complement the delightful charcuterie waiting to be devoured. Do you have any honey, jam or preserves? I should have brought something from my shop."

"No problem, sweet thing. I have honey and orange marmalade," he replied.

"Evan, you always surprise me. Most men would not have honey in their pantry, perhaps the marmalade."

Facing Becky and trying to focus on her face and not her breasts, he grabbed her around the waist and said, "I'm not most men."

Becky felt his bare chest inches from her torso and smelled his cologne. She rubbed her hand over his left pectoral muscle, lightly moving up to his shoulder and down his arm. "Whatever kind of man you are right now, I like it," she said with lust in her eyes. "But, you are going to at least try and see if one glass a wine will loosen us up a little, huh?" she said with amusement.

"Forgive me for my lack of hosting abilities," he said and proceeded to use the wine key on the bottle. He poured two glasses and joined her in a moment of toasting. "Cheers!" he said. Evan grabbed the honey and marmalade from the cabinet and suddenly had ideas about other ways to use each, but ultimately decided it would be too messy.

Becky tossed her hair and walked seductively with her wine toward the living area. "Mind if I just peek outside?"

"Be my guest."

He watched as she parted a tiny section in the middle of the drapes and stood there momentarily.

"Did I make the wrong move closing the drapes?" he asked.

"No, no, no. I like it Evan. It's just so warm and sunny today. I like to see what people are doing and admire this view you have."

Evan picked up the tray of food and the bottle of wine and brought them to the coffee table in the living area setting them next to the onyx chessboard. He was already forgetting the big shocker of the day. He did not want to think about it for the next few hours. It was all way too real and waiting for him in the morning.

"So, tell me what's new in the bakery business?"

"I have a new cake decorator that is fabulous. She's an older lady with a ton of experience. She's not super fast. But she is very detailed. Her cakes are exquisite."

"What happened to the other decorator you had?"

"She's still with me and they seem to be working well together. My business has really picked up lately and I am glad for that. I cannot tell you what a struggle it was in the beginning. Finally, I am seeing numbers in the black."

"That's great news. Congratulations!"

Becky kicked off her mules and it appeared she was feeling comfortable as she slid into Evan's favorite leather chair. He took a sip of wine, cut her a slice of the bread and drizzled honey upon it. He crouched, straddling her body and offered her a bite of the bread, holding it while she partook. It was a sexy move on his part. He wanted to seduce her soon and slip into another world with this pretty woman where problems were of small consequence to him, even for a short period of time.

Some of the honey dripped down on his chest from the sliced bread and Becky noticed it along with Evan. After taking a bite of the bread and gazing deep into his brown eyes, she raised her torso to meet his chest and licked the honey off slowly with her tongue. This turned Evan on and he felt a surge in his groin. Becky was delectable in her own way — a treat he wanted to devour and dive into. Slow and sweet seduction with food. This was going to be fun.

Tellinger sat behind his desk at the early morning meeting. He tapped his finger and said nothing at first.

Evan sat opposite him and did not know whether to break the silence. Finally, he said, "I'm sure Joe Foster's investigators have tried locating Jack's cell phone. However, they may not have known that he also carried a satellite phone. If he is alive, this could help us locate him before they have a chance to do so."

"You're right. It's one more object that belonged to him that has some tracking capability. Sounds good as a start. I would imagine his wife knows of the satellite phone. What else do you have?"

"Nothing, sir. Absolutely nothing," Evan stated in a defeated manner.

"I think we should increase surveillance to Jack's parents and other close relatives. We need to know what they know. I have a feeling Joe Foster is not going to share that information with us."

"I will look into that right away."

"Keep eyes on Haley, Jack's wife. And not your eyes, Evan," he said, smirking. "I've seen how you stare a little too long at her. She is a looker."

"Didn't realize I was so obvious."

"We probably should put a loose tail on the father. Damn, this is adding up, but it has to be done to protect the company."

"Alright, I'll get started on this right now."

Evan left the meeting feeling like he was on the losing side. But wars were won from many small battles and this was just the battle phase. He had to turn this around and quickly. He debated again whether to let Tellinger know of his plans to have someone break into Jack and Haley's house. The first attempt had been thwarted and it was going to be more complicated to get inside. He was dealing with a professional that claimed he could pull it off. But once inside, could he find the information?

Chapter 41 ~ Sonya Stays

Haley arrived back home with her family and each made their way toward a bathroom or bedroom to change out of their formal clothing. Afterward, they met in the living room. Sonya plugged the cord into the wall to light the beautiful live tree.

"I hope you don't mind me lighting the tree, Haley. It has a nice scent."

"No, I don't mind. Would you like to check the water level too?"

"Sure."

"If it needs water, there is a large pitcher in the cabinet under the sink that I use."

Aunt Molly spoke up commenting how almost everyone at the dinner seemed to have something to contribute toward the search for Jack. Uncle Mike agreed.

"Sadly, we must depart this evening, Haley. Do you feel like you can stay here by yourself?"

Already, Haley had become used to them being there. She knew they would be leaving, but it felt so soon.

She had not been in a mind space with all that had happened to think about how she would feel once they were gone.

"I'm going to have to. I cannot keep being a frightened, paranoid woman."

Sonya walked toward them and said softly, "What if I stayed here with you for awhile and helped on the search for Jack as well? I don't have a job or school right now to be at."

Haley looked at her cute cousin, "Could you really stay longer? I would love that!" She turned her gaze to Mike and Molly for their reactions.

They glanced at each other and nodded. Uncle Mike spoke up, "I think that might be beneficial for each of you."

Sonya and everyone knew what he meant. She'd been floundering in life since her last break up and not serious about moving forward — a clear sign of some depression.

Haley rose and hugged Sonya. "This is great! Thank you for staying."

Aunt Molly chimed in, "But do you have what you need as far as clothing and toiletries?"

"Don't worry about that. I don't mind buying her some things. She's going to be fine. Gives us an excuse to do a little shopping."

"Honestly, I don't need a lot. I brought most essentials with me."

Uncle Mike chimed in, "Sonya, Haley is going to be busy with the search for Jack. You will need to help her on that and not be a hindrance."

"Of course, dad."

"You also are going to be without your car which is needed in an area like this."

Haley generously offered Jack's vehicle.

Sonya shifted in her seat and said, "Oh, no. I would not feel comfortable doing that, worrying I might be in an accident. That's why I drive my little cheap beater."

"Well, what if we go to Valdosta and pick up your car next weekend. We can visit and you would be able to pick up anything else that's important to you?" Haley asked.

"That would be perfect."

"Alright then, I guess we now do the big group hug so you two can get on the road back home."

All four joined in their circle and hugged.

"Thank you so much for being here. Your support has meant so much to me," Haley said.

"What else would we do, Haley? We love you!" Aunt Molly said. "I really don't know what Mike or I can lend to this hunt or investigation to find Jack, but we are open to ideas if anyone has them."

"Yes, I'll keep you both in mind. Sonya and I will be down this Saturday, probably spend the night with you guys if that's okay."

"Sounds like a perfect plan," Uncle Mike said smiling.

Haley watched them gather up their things and as her aunt and uncle waved goodbye from their car, she was aware how much those two had been rocks of strength for her. On the other hand, Sonya was feeling a little giddy about getting rid of her parents and staying at a new place, especially one as beautiful as this one. The two watched them leave the drive, waving as they finally made their way toward the main road. As they entered the house, Haley decided this would be a good time to instruct Sonya on the use of the security system.

"Give me a moment, Sonya. I have to find the book on this darn thing so I can set up a code for you."

Haley retrieved the instruction booklet from a file in Jack's office. The smell of the room hit her as she entered. Aside from his leather chair, it had a masculine scent she supposed from all the time he had spent there just since they moved in.

She walked out toward the main security panel in the kitchen and yelled to Sonya who was in the living room, "Give me a six digit code you know you can remember. "

"Oh, let's see. Try 6-8-9-1-5-7"

Haley entered the numbers in and put Sonya's credentials into the system.

"Okay, let's try it and I'll also give you a lesson on how to use the system. It's really pretty easy."

Sonya sauntered toward her in the kitchen and Haley went through the ins and outs of entering the house, putting the system in stay mode and leave mode as well.

"Right now we will put it in stay mode. If you or I walk outdoors without disarming the system, it will give us thirty seconds to do so. If we don't, it's going to notify the alarm company. Got it?"

"I think so. Do I do everything at this keypad or can the one by the front door be used?"

"Any of them can be accessed to set or unset the system. There are three in total. One in the master and the other two. The big thing to remember is when you come home, you need to disarm right away. Then, set it in stay mode because leave mode activates various motion sensors placed around the house. If the system is in away or leave mode, the sensors pick up any movement larger than a cat. This will immediately trigger the alarm, which is loud by the way. The security company will probably immediately send the police.

"Got it."

"Hey, do you want to join Jessie and me Thursday night? We're going to an introductory women's self defense class."

"Whoa, you ladies are serious about it now, aren't ya?"

"Yes ma'am, we are. How about it? Would not hurt for a young woman like you to know these things. If you decide you want to do it, I'll pay for it."

"That's hard to turn down. Yes, of course. I'd love to check it out."

Chapter 42 ~ Plans

Haley retreated to her bedroom to snag a little time alone. While she loved her family and friends, she also felt like she had done more socializing during these past few days than in a year before. She kicked off her shoes and relaxed on the bed — deliberately on Jack's side. Her fingers stroked the soft duvet cover she and Jack had chosen together for the now lonely marital bed they had shared. Was it really possible that Jack had survived? Would they share this bed again?

She thought about how Sonya had shyly approached her an hour ago, volunteering to stay longer. Haley knew that everyone was aware she felt more comfortable having someone there in the house with her. Sighing deeply, she rose and headed for the master bath to get ready for bed.

As the water poured over her head and shoulders, it seemed to wash away most of the invisible crud she felt like she was carrying. Her deep despair about Jack had been replaced with a hope that was of a medium strength and needed to grow stronger. Jack had to be alive. She had to believe that in her body, all the way to the bone. But, what if it was false hope and not true? Would she have to go through all the grief of the past few days, plus more?

She massaged the conditioner now through her hair. *What would Jack do if I was missing and presumed dead?*

Haley knew he would not give up hope. He would be totally involved, if not leading a search.

He would call in experts to help. He would believe that she would be found.

Haley realized she had to believe the same and feel it with every thought and action.

Her thoughts roamed back to Sonya. Would she be a help or a distraction? Most likely, a little of both. Sonya did not have a job to be back at and needed a breather from her parents anyway, no matter how great they were.

For Haley, having her cousin here was not only soothing to her, she genuinely wanted to help her as well. She seemed to be drifting right now on the ocean of life without a map or plan. While that can be fun for awhile, Sonya also had to think about her future. While Haley did not feel it was her place to direct that future in any way, she did see herself as possibly being helpful. Sonya was still discovering who she was. After all, it was getting away from home that forced Haley to look at life and her future differently.

She loved anatomy and physiology in college and becoming a nurse was a natural choice for her. Sonya was extremely creative, very artful in her approach to dress and her surroundings. Nursing would probably not be her forte, but who knows? It was for Sonya to reveal to herself what her path in life would be.

Haley stepped out of the shower and wrapped her hair and body. She sat down at her vanity and opened the drawer underneath. The reporter's information was at risk of being buried under various skin creams and cosmetics, but there it was. She pulled it out of the drawer and placed it before her. No photo on her business card. It was a simple white background with black lettering. Megan Adams, Investigative Journalist. It was late. Tomorrow, she would contact Megan to see if she could help Haley discover something more in this new quest to find Jack.

"Here's the thing," Sonya said, chewing on a piece of dried mango. "I don't want to get in your way here, Haley. You are going to have to tell me what I can do to help with the search for Jack and anything else around here. You can tell me, I'm a big girl now."

Haley chuckled. "I love that you're at the "adulting" stage now. Thanks for giving me permission to turn you into my slave," she said facetiously.

"Seriously, Haley. I know how nice you are and how you'll try and do everything yourself. Use me while I'm here to help."

"Okay, I will. Actually, I have an idea about putting your artsy skills to work right away."

"Really? Go on."

"You graciously took Jason and Sarah's children off for ice cream while we spoke of ideas and information yesterday. One of the ideas was for me to get together with the survivors of Jack's team. I thought it might be nice to have a dinner for them here. The intention is not only to dine with them, but to get the conversation rolling about the entire incident. I want to try to find out any information I can about who might want to murder that team and why."

Sonya looked puzzled. "Okay, so how does that fit in with me and being artsy?"

"I was thinking an invitation could be sent to them in the mail. Give me your thoughts on it. I was envisioning something that invited them to a private life celebration of our loved ones. What do you think?"

"Sounds like something that has me excited to create. Yes, I like the celebration or perhaps in remembrance aspect of it. In my mind, I'm seeing something that could be classified as casual elegance for the look of the invitation. I may need your assistance with the wording. I can get on it today."

"Great, Sonya! Let me look at the calendar and determine the best date. I'm thinking Friday evening. We're going to be at your house the next day picking up your car. That only gives us four days to have everything ready. Do you think we can pull it off?"

"Glad I brought my laptop. Once I have the design nailed down for you along with the text, we can send these to any office supply store to have printed within minutes or hours, depending how busy they are."

"Wonderful, let me make a note that I will need to get the addresses of each invitee. That will also help me determine how many guests."

Making lists, having things to plan and do was a really good thing for Haley. This was her normal and it kept her focused on finding Jack instead of worrying she never would. And, there was a lot to do. It seemed like each idea or task she began acting upon spawned at least three or four more tasks to take it to completion.

Chapter 43 ~ Details

Monday, December 9, 2019

Haley phoned Kendra, Jack's assistant, and requested the home addresses for the significant others of each team member. Normally, this information would not be given out. With the way that Kendra felt toward Jack and his wife, she had no qualms about giving it to Haley.

Hours later, Sonya surprised Haley with her design for the invitation. It was simple, yet very respectful of someone who is grieving. "Sonya, this is perfect. I suppose if I was trying to visualize something in my mind, this would be it. It's like you just knew and with very little instruction to go on. I love it!"

Sonya beamed, feeling Haley's praise. "I'm glad you like it. Now, I could move this over here, if you think that would look better. What do you think?" she asked, pointing to design elements on the front of the invitation.

Haley thought for a moment, "No, actually it is very eye appealing the way it is. I wouldn't change a thing. Have you thought about going into design as a career?"

Sonya sat down across from her at the table. "Oh, yeah. It's just that those jobs are not paying like they used to and while mom and dad could afford the tuition, they cannot afford room, board, food and all that stuff. That means I would be taking out loans to make it happen and have a lot of debt when I graduated."

"That's never pleasant to have hanging over your head," Haley nodded in agreement.

"Anyway, I'm just not sure I want to do that bad enough to accumulate that much debt. I almost wonder if it would be better to take classes here and there as I can, practice and use it as a side hustle. What do you think about that idea?"

"Well, I know very little about the field you would be working in. I know that if someone is really good at what they do, no one sits around and asks to see a long list of educational credentials. In other words, if I like an artist or creative person who produces certain things, I'm not wondering if they went to school for it," Haley laughed.

"There is no doubt that the education would be fabulous, but I'm wondering if I can find a way to do it at a lower cost. That's all. In the meantime, I've just sort of been drifting and enjoying not having to commit to anything really."

Haley rose from the office chair and looked at Sonya, "Lucky for me you are in that position right now. I really appreciate having you here. You won't be feeling like that forever. At some point, you will know you have to commit to something that feels right for you, whatever it is."

Haley reached out and hugged her cousin. Sitting back down, Haley positioned herself in front of the laptop once more. "Well, let's get this going with the invitation." She pulled a notebook from her purse. "This is short and sweet. Let me know if you think we should change anything. I just need it to be right. The subject matter is delicate. I don't want to hurt or offend anyone."

Sonya read the proposed invitation text. "Hmmm, I really love the words, but I think I would change this one word here. Also, I will need to experiment with finding the right font. Sometimes the actual appearance of the letters can affect how something comes across. Want me to do that now?"

"Absolutely. Why don't you sit in Jack's office and I will begin my next to do on my list."

Sonya slid into Jack's office chair and realized how comfortable it was. She didn't want to say anything to Haley about it. It was Jack's chair. Instead, she worked on perfecting the text for the invitation. Finally, Sonya took care of uploading the visuals and text to the office supply store which indicated they would be ready for pick up by early afternoon.

Haley picked up the phone and dialed Tiger's Eye Martial Arts. She scheduled herself, Jessie and Sonya for an introductory class on self protection and defense.

While Haley imagined this would almost be a fun girl's night out, in reality it was very serious to her. She dialed Sarah on her phone and got voice mail.

"Hey girl, I am finally being more proactive. As I mentioned, I'm looking into self defense classes. I wanted to see if you would like to attend the introductory class. It's free. Sonya and Jessie are going. It will be this Wednesday evening at 7pm at Tiger's Eye Academy in Atlanta. Call me back or send me a text. Just trying to be proactive. Hope you're having a good day. Love you!"

"Hey Sonya, I am assuming the office supply company will have envelopes for the invitations, right?"

"Yes, I told them we would need those as well."

"Great, what time should we go by there?"

"They will have them ready by 2:00. We could stop somewhere and address them, then pop them in the mail today."

"That's perfect. I can't believe how quick you took this from a little idea to completion. Thank you!"

"Haley, I'm really happy to help any way I can."

"And, you are! Next, I need to call this reporter who came by the house and set up a meeting."

Having plans and staying busy with events did keep Haley from falling into dark fits of depression. The loss of Jack was so paramount in her life. Now, she only had two points of interest: finding Jack and discovering who was behind this hideous murder of innocent people.

Chapter 44 ~ A Lucky Meeting

Tuesday, December 10, 2019

Haley failed to get a good look at Megan when she had shown up on her doorstep. But as she entered the small coffee shop, it was easy to pick her out right away. Tall, with a platinum blonde pixie and bright blue reading glasses, she stood out. She was avant garde, yet business like at the same time. Someone was sitting beside her, a companion or coworker perhaps?

The aromas in the shop were downright illegal as the strong scent of java hit her olfactory system. Haley raised a finger to Megan as they made eye contact as if to say hold up one moment. She stepped to the counter and put in an order and watched as the barista prepared her order. The barista approached her job as if she were coffee connoisseur scientist working in a lab. She smiled, wondering if it really might be a bit overly dramatic. Coffee — a substance that led a pilot and at least three others to their deaths. But hopefully, not Jack. *God, please let Jack be alive.* Even if he was injured, Haley didn't care.

The barista completed her order. She tipped her, then made her way toward the back of the shotgun style coffee shop toward Megan, the reporter. The narrow, multi-story building style was typical for establishments in the area. This was the way large buildings were constructed in Atlanta at the turn of the twentieth century. Brick walls were often a staple and she wondered how easy it was for the businesses to adorn the walls with so many photographs or pieces of art that were common.

As she approached the table, Megan rose and her companion did as well.

"Mrs. Foster, thank you for agreeing to meet with me," she said, holding her hand out.

Haley sat her coffee on the table and shook Megan's hand. "Please, call me Haley. Mrs. Foster makes me feel old," she chuckled.

"Haley, this is Ric Hartford who works with me frequently. I know I should have mentioned having someone else here, but Ric has been out of town and I didn't know he was back until he messaged me late last night."

Haley politely shook Ric's hand and the three sat down. She glanced at the booth, placing her purse on the seat between herself and the wall. She was not prepared to talk about details. The fact that one more person had been brought into the mix made her hesitant also.

"Megan, I would like to know more about you and what you do before I commit to anything, even speaking about my husband or the accident. What can you share with me?"

"Please, call me Lucky. I know that seems odd. I was christened with that nickname a while ago. The short story is I had some fortunate breaks in my investigations and skated past a few shifty characters and situations along the way. A federal prosecutor I was working with said, "You know, you're damn lucky and that's what I'm calling you from now on." It just sort of stuck and, to be honest … I like it. It's sort of a positive mantra name each time I hear someone say it aloud. I need a lot of luck with what I'm doing."

Ric interrupted her, "At least he shortened it to lucky instead of damn lucky," he chuckled.

Megan (Lucky) grinned wide showing a beautiful smile and elbowed Rick.

"Where was I?" she asked. "Oh, yes you want to know about me and what I do, so let me tell you that."

Lucky, opened her tablet, quickly accessing a web page displaying a story about Fulastor Pharmaceuticals. "Are you familiar with this drug company debacle?" she asked.

"Yes, I am. They were accused of price gauging consumers by at least a thousand percent, were they not?" Haley replied.

"That's right. The head of the company is a sociopath who had no concern for others. That was my first investigative assignment as a journalist. I feel some satisfaction in helping to expose what was happening and putting a stop to it."

Haley asked, "What happened to Fulastor?"

Lucky rolled her eyes and sighed. Despite her light hair, she had dark brows and red lipstick. Her eye makeup looked like a professional had applied it.

"The price of the drug is now affordable for people and the company was hit with monetary damages. The CEO was shuffled out of the way as a direct decision maker, but he's still on the board at Fulbright."

Lucky took a long sip of coffee, blotted her lips with her napkin and continued. "Just prior to the investigation I am working on now, I completed one in the Eastern United States that became a huge center of controversy around the prescription drug, Madeamur. I'm sure you've heard of it."

"Yes, given it to a few patients. I'm a nurse."

"Interesting. Then you have seen the effects some of these opiod drugs can have on individuals, families, towns and cities."

"Yes, unfortunately I have seen it up close," Haley said.

"That investigation resulted in actual indictments and convictions. Unfortunately, it wasn't the decision makers at the pharmaceutical company. They suffered monetarily, but their henchmen down the food chain will do some time."

"Haven't there been congressional hearings over the matter?" Haley inquired.

"Yes, and a series on television that was pretty good," Ric answered.

Lucky spoke up, "I'm not famous for my work, and I don't want to be. I get things done primarily behind the radar of the average citizen who is busy handling their job and family. My investigations are not revealed until we are at least close to indictments being issued or lawsuits filed. I wait until I think I have enough to go on before I approach law enforcement."

Haley listened intently, but wanted more. "What is this investigation, the one you knocked on my door about?"

"If I were to boil it down into one phrase it would be: Big Pharma is a monster that will devour us all if we don't stop it."

"Really? You truly believe that?"

"Yes. It's not a question of believing it. It's gradually revealing itself to be true."

"But pharmaceutical companies provide us with all kinds of treatments and drugs needed to help a lot of people — from the chronically to critically ill."

Ric and Lucky looked at each other and smiled.

"Sorry," Lucky continued, "Big Pharma brings products to market that help, but they also aggressively push products that hurt. They put profit margins over the number of fatalities, injuries and overall risks to society. That's my take on it."

Haley looked at her and knew she could not argue with at least part of what Lucky said. But she was not sure she agreed with all of it.

Lucky took another sip, blotted her lips once more with her napkin and continued. "What you have to realize is there are at least three overarching personas the pharmaceutical companies have with the public. There is the common persona you hold which puts forth the perception they do more good than bad. This train of thought makes us dismiss much of the negative components. For instance, injuries, side effects and even fatalities are okay and tolerated to a degree.

The second public persona that Big Pharma holds is that of completely sinister corporations that are only about money.

The third persona is one that I hold. Big Pharma needs to be held accountable with more safeguards in place. Yes, we want them to have profit, but not at the expense of human life or societal crises. But they cannot be tied in so tightly with regulating agencies such as the CDC and FDA. They get their approvals because they have their own former employees working in those agencies.

Ric chimed in. "Haley, I'm sure you've heard of the opiate crisis?"

"Of course. Being a nurse, I am well aware of it," she answered. While she did not feel like sharing it, Haley also knew it intimately as her own mother had been addicted.

Ric nodded his head. "Well as a nurse, you do know the risks involved. I worked as a researcher on blowing that situation open and helping to make it public. It wasn't easy. At first, everyone I spoke with was either monetarily compromised and would not be honest, or they were addicted and defending the use of the drug as it had been prescribed and presented to the public. Lucky helped take them down financially. I believe they are in bankruptcy."

Lucky added, "Ric was very instrumental in getting us the information we needed. I say us, because I did not work on that alone. I joined two other investigative reporters who were based in the D.C. area. They contacted me, telling me of their suspicions. At first, it sounded like a conspiracy theory and I didn't see how we could ever help authorities pop it open if it were true. That's when we got lucky," she said, emphasizing the word. "We had a whistle blower come to us from the pharmaceutical company with most of the goods we needed for federal authorities to have some real meat to chew on."

Haley took a sip of coffee and there was a pause. "May I ask, how do you make money or get paid?" She had money and would pay someone to find Jack."

Lucky looked over at Ric and they both chuckled softly. There was another pause. Lucky lowered her reading glasses revealing her brilliant green eyes. Lucky was a good name for her, Haley thought. Overall, she had an air of sleuth about her.

"I have been fortunate enough to sell books to publishers after the investigations and convictions wrapped. We currently have a mini-series being filmed about the opiate take down. But those monies get split five ways. The two D.C. investigators, Ric, me, and we donate a fifth of the monies toward addiction rehabilitation facility that we are knowledgeable of and feel has done a lot of good."

Ric looked at Haley. "We don't make a lot of money, but for us, it's about taking down the evil we see. That's what drives me and I know it drives Lucky too."

"Oh, and we also take hand outs, free lunches and donations when people feel generous."

"Here is what I would like to do," Haley began. "I would like for you to meet with Jack's parents, brother, and those close to us. Right now, we have a pact of secrecy around this situation."

"No problem! We understand and are happy to meet with Jack's other close relatives. In fact, we would want to as part of the investigation regardless," Lucky said assuring her.

Haley nodded, "Thank you for understanding." In the meantime, she felt it was safe to at least throw the dynamic pair a bone. "I will tell you this. My father-in-law does not believe my husband is dead."

They both opened their eyes wide and Lucky said, "Please, tell me why? Didn't you just have the funeral for your husband?"

Haley shared what happened at Jack's funeral and how this has now turned into a search for him. "Anyway, we've made an agreement that before we share information with others, we will clear it with one another. I'm not much into conspiracies, but it is clear to me that someone conspired to take down that plane and the question is why?"

"Before you leave, Haley, could I give you some pointers on dealing with these corporate conglomerate assholes?"

"Sure."

"Meet in obscure places to talk. We have found the homes of many employees are surveilled or bugged."

"We have a security system, how could that happen?"

"I'm not saying they have done that to you. Nor do I want to make you paranoid, just cautious. Often, the employees of these companies are being monitored in some way digitally. We've seen this time and again when the employee hires a bug sweep company."

Ric added, "Yes, vary where you are going each time so there is no pattern. For instance, if we meet every three or four days at this same coffee shop, that is a red flag for them to check into further. If you are being followed and your actions seem random, that makes them slink back and feel safer."

"That makes sense," Haley thought and said out loud. "Perhaps we were being followed by a man the last time Jack and I were out in public." Haley told the two investigators what she experienced with the man showing up in two locations when they were shopping during Thanksgiving weekend.

"You never know. It could have been a coincidence. With everything you have going on Haley, it could have been a tail."

"How can I find out if my house is being monitored?"

Lucky flipped through the contacts on her phone and showed it to Haley.

"Great, can you text me that?"

"Sure, sending it now. They are expensive, but good. Talk with your family and hopefully we can meet. I will be happy to answer their questions and assist in any way I can. I know Ric's on board with this as well, right?" she said, turning her head toward him.

"I'm up for it, boss," he said affectionately.

Chapter 45 ~ Man at the Mall

Haley gulped hard as she made her way out of the coffee shop and back to her Honda. Inside, she felt filled to the brim with something. She didn't know what to call it, but it wasn't coffee. It felt dark, spy-like, and dangerous. The feeling was something she didn't like, but it didn't matter. Whatever she needed to do to find Jack she was willing to try. Some of the things Ric said sounded so conspiratorial. Yet, she did know that many pharmaceutical companies had been caught trying to cover up the addictive nature of their drugs, recommending higher and higher doses for patients. Why had they done this? The answer was simple, profit, as in billions of dollars.

She wanted to have Joe & Sharon meet her somewhere to talk about this, along with Sarah and Jason. While she felt it was unlikely their residences were bugged, she did not want to take any chances. Spooked - that was how she felt. She was now on some kind of high alert, checking her review mirror for signs of vehicles following her as well.

"Hey Siri,"

"Hmmm?"

"Dial Joe Foster's cell phone."

"Connecting now."

The phone rang and it went to voice mail. Haley decided to leave a message. "Papa, I need to speak with you and Sharon soon. Please call me on my cell phone."

"Hey Siri,"

"Yes?"

"Dial Sarah Foster's cell phone."

"Dialing now."

Haley felt relieved when she heard Sarah's voice as she answered.

"What's up honey?"

"Sarah, I'm glad I got you. Listen, I just met with some people that could possibly be a huge help to us, but they also told me some disturbing things that I want to discuss with you, Jason and our in-laws. Here's the thing, I'd like us to meet somewhere public to talk about this."

"Well, we have no plans tonight. I can look into a sitter for Allison and Elijah. What do you suggest?"

"I've been craving pizza and it would be easy for me to bring some home to Sonya when we are finished."

"We could meet at Geraldo's. They have really good stuff."

"That sounds perfect. I left a message on Papa Foster's phone just before I called you. What time would work for you guys?"

"Would six be okay?"

"That works for me. Let's make it definite whether our in-laws can make it or not. Honestly, Sarah, I need to talk to someone."

"Okay, hun. We will see you at six."

Haley didn't want to go all the way back to Alpharetta just yet. Instead, she drove aimlessly for awhile, finally deciding to stop at a mall not too far from the pizza restaurant where they would meet later. Her mission was twofold. She wanted to see if anyone was following her and kill some time with the distractions the mall stores could provide. She drove around the parking lot repeatedly. On her third pass around the main mall entrance, she prayed out loud, "C'mon St. Christopher, help me with a spot where I'll feel safe when I leave." Shortly thereafter, she saw a couple leaving only four cars back from the beginning of the row. *Perfect*, she thought.

Once inside the mall, Haley's eyes became dazzled with various store window displays. The sweet smell of cinnamon drifted through the air from the Cinnabon restaurant. Her heart seemed to beat a little slower and she did not feel as frazzled as she did once she left her meeting with Lucky Adams and her protégé, Ric.

Haley decided to enter Books-A-Million and look around. She loved that they always had such pretty displays for the new releases. Reading wasn't exactly on her mind, though. This was just a spot to kill time. Maybe she'd find something she wanted, maybe not. She wandered toward the medical and health section and tilted her head a bit sideways to read the titles lined up vertically along the shelves. Suddenly, she felt something and looked up to her right. Shivers went down her spine as she locked eyes with a man who had obviously been watching her. He quickly looked away.

Calm down, she thought. Haley remembered some of the suggestions the ladies at the group therapy had mentioned. It's okay if you're wrong and this person is not following you. It's okay to go to the management or security if you want an escort out of the building. *It's also okay for me to snap that guy's picture with my phone,* she thought.

Haley began acting as if she was ignoring the man and continued looking at book titles. She picked up a book, not out of interest, but just to look busy as if she were shopping. She carried it with her, walking the opposite direction from him down the aisle. She grabbed her phone out of her pocket and pushed the camera setting on. She did a semi-circle around the front of the store and positioned herself at the beginning of another aisle. The man appeared aloof and not really shopping for books. *At least he could do a better acting job,* she thought.

Haley turned her back to him temporarily and thumbed through a book of historical photos from World War II sitting on a table in the middle of the store along with coffee table selections. She saw him move away a bit and assumed it was to cover for his being disinterested in watching her. But, it was the perfect time to snap a couple of photos of him as he was not looking at her directly. While she would have preferred to get him from the front, there was no way she could do that without being obvious.

She placed her phone back into the pocket of her jacket and closed the historical photo book. She laid the medical book down beside it and exited the store, heading now for someplace more difficult for him to look like a normal shopper.

Her phone vibrated in her pocket as she exited the store. Papa Foster's name appeared on the screen. "Papa, I'm so glad you called me back. I would like to meet with you and Sharon this evening to discuss some things I found out today. I think we should meet someplace neutral and not at our homes."

"Okay, what time and where?"

"I spoke with Sarah earlier and she and Jason are meeting with us too. She suggested Geraldo's for pizza at six. Could you two make that?"

"Let's see, it's 4:30 now. I think so, but let me check with Sharon and call you right back."

"Sounds good, Papa."

Haley's bladder was screaming with the coffee she had consumed. Surely a guy would not follow her into the ladies restroom. She made her way inside and took care of business, checking herself in the mirror while washing her hands. She looked tired, but fluorescent lights never did anyone any favors. She exited and looked for another store to enter and test whether the man was on her tail or not. Would he follow her into a lingerie store?

Haley entered the pink, red and black store and headed for the fragrance area toward the back. She spotted a sign "Buy 2 Get 1 Free" on their gift sets. That was a pretty good value. She dabbled, sampling a couple of scents on her skin. She positioned herself so that she could see the front entrance and know whether the man was entering the store.

"Hi, how are you today?" a friendly store associate inquired of Haley. Young as they tended to be in this store, she had a beautiful head full of dark curls that flowed down her back and shoulders.

Haley smiled, "Oh, doing okay. I was just trying to find a scent I thought would be a good gift for several women I know."

"Have you found one you like yet?"

"Not really. I am also a bit concerned that if I like it, they might not. You know what I mean?"

"I do. Have you tried Bombshell?" she asked holding up the demonstrator bottle?

"No, not yet."

"This is our best selling fragrance right now. A lot of people like it. Would you like to sample it?"

She handed a test bottle to Haley. She moved her jacket sleeve out of the way and gave a quick spray. The salesperson continued, "This has purple passion fruit, Shangri-La peony and vanilla orchid as top notes in the formulation."

"Mmmm. That is nice. I could purchase six sets, but what if all my friends smell alike?"

The girl chuckled, "Is there anything else I can help you with?

"Let me have three of this gift set and three of your second most popular scent. That should work."

She accompanied Haley to the check out area and Haley noticed how accommodating the store personnel were. Too bad it was not like that everywhere.

As she headed out of the store, she glanced each direction to see if she saw the same man. He was nowhere in sight. She stopped at a kiosk selling calendars and knew that was always handy to have for the new year and as gifts. While looking through numerous selections, she made her way around each side of the kiosk. Some of the calendars looked more appealing to her than others. Rounding the corner, she saw him, shopping for calendars now or watching her. Which was it?

Her heart sped up and Haley told herself to stay calm and breathe. She positioned herself within three feet of him and continued looking at calendars. She was too distracted with his presence and decided not to purchase anything. She walked away quickly, breaking the feeling of being in close proximity to the man.

He was probably in his late thirties, perhaps early forties. Light brown hair and a small goatee that made him look a little devilish to her. He was not the same man she believed was following her and Jack on their shopping trip together.

Initially, Haley walked at a fast pace, then decided to slow down and just appear to be window shopping. She would wait and see if he followed her. She came upon a seating area in the middle of the aisle and decided to rest for a moment here and appear as if she was checking phone messages. She scrolled through several of her past messages, coming across the one Lucky Adams had sent. It was at the top, her most recent message with the information for the Clean Sweeps Security Company. It would be wise, she thought, to wait until she spoke with the family this evening prior to scheduling them. They may have another suggestion.

Her screen changed in front of her in an instant and it was Papa Foster calling.

"Yes, Papa. I'm here."

"We can be there at six. I look forward to it and I'll fill you in on some things on this side."

"Sounds great. See you there."

Haley looked at the time, 5:15 now. Geraldo's was not far from here. Perhaps she should go ahead and leave the mall. Fortunately, the devilish looking guy had not made another appearance. She was sure of that because he would have passed her and she was on high alert for the asshole to show up again.

She gathered her rather obvious shopping bag from Victoria's Secret and began walking back the way she had originally entered the mall. She passed the enticing Cinnabon store's aromas and the familiar stores she saw before. Just as she was approaching the final store where all this began, she spotted him. *Damn,* she thought. *I cannot believe it.*

He stood close to the window facing the mall, with a book in his hands. He was reading a book about murder. Yes, it was fiction, but was he trying to send a message? He had not made visual contact with Haley and she quickly looked away, picked up her walking pace and strode out of the building. Shaking. She was shaking.

Just get to the car ... you're going to be fine. It's daylight and there are people around you. You can scream, kick and make a hell of a scene if he comes near you. Don't look back, keep your eyes on your car. Damn, she had to look behind her. No sight of him. Perhaps he had not seen her leave while he was reading the book. But the way he held it. It was like he was sending a message by holding it up in that manner so the cover was obvious to anyone passing by.

Haley pressed the FOB and quickly slid into the driver's seat and locked the vehicle. She started it and immediately began backing out of the space. Naturally, another driver had pulled into the parking aisle and was coveting that parking space. She backed out in such a way that they could go ahead and pull in. As they did so, she saw him exit the same doors she had exited. He looked at her vehicle and then quickly glanced down at his phone.

"Get the hell out of here girl," she said aloud to herself.

Haley turned her vehicle out of the aisle and semi-sped toward the main mall parking lot exit. There was a traffic light ahead with waiting cars, but the right lane was clear. While she needed to go left, she intuitively knew she would have a slim chance of losing him if she waited in traffic. She turned right and made her way down a couple of blocks and then found a place to turn around to go the opposite direction. She felt herself sweating and still shaking a bit, but not as bad as before. *You've got to handle this and be more assertive*

Finally, she pulled into the pizza restaurant's parking lot and found the closest space she could to the entrance door. Checking the time, it was now 5:40. She would go ahead and get a table for everyone. And, if possible, one where she could constantly see who was entering the building.

Chapter 46 ~ Geraldo's

The click of her boot's chunky heels rang solid on the slate entrance to Geraldo's Pizzeria. Haley approached the hostess area which was unattended and caught eye of the sign which said, **Temporarily Away, Please Seat Yourself**. In her mind, this was much easier than trying to explain that she needed a five or six top with a good view of the entrance door. This sounded like she was part of the mafia or a gang. Haley half chuckled even though she felt grim about her quest to disappear from the man at the mall.

The restaurant was plush with overstuffed furnishings. The lighting was dim with electric candles at each table. A classic rock song played softly in the background. Glancing around, Haley spotted the perfect place on the far wall which held a table for four and a two top that could be brought together. She sat at the four top with her back to the wall. A waiter arrived beside her and introduced himself. He handed her a menu and asked if she would like a drink.

"Thank you, yes I would. Do you have bottled water?"

"We have still, sparking or tap," he replied, and pointed to the beverage section on the menu with several selections.

"I'd love to try the Acqua Panna from Italy. Also, I am expecting four more people. Could we join these two tables?"

"Of course, I will take care of it. Let me do that now should they arrive and then I will be out with your water."

"Thank you so much," and she meant it. It felt safe to sit here with her back against the wall and be waited on by this young man who seemed very mannerly. She watched as he and someone else from the restaurant joined the tables and set it with menus, silverware and napkins. "I'll be right back," he said smiling.

She wiped her forehead with the back of her hand and removed her sunglasses which were on top of her head, placing them inside her purse. Haley wanted to use the restroom so bad, but she would wait for someone else to arrive and make sure the table was not taken by other incoming guests. This day had been stressful and scary. She opened her photos on her phone and saw the two shots she had taken of the man she believed was following her. The door to the restaurant opened and it was Jason and Sarah. *Thank goodness,* she thought. She waved to them and they approached the table.

"I am so glad you two are here," Haley said, not smiling but with what seemed like real relief.

"What's going on Haley? You seem pretty uptight," Jason said.

Haley shook her head back and forth. "I have so much to tell you. You may already know but Papa Foster and Sharon are meeting with us too. First, I need to go to the restroom. But before I leave, I want to show you something. Haley held up her phone for them to look at the two photos. "I truly believe this man was following me at the mall this afternoon." She saw the look of surprise on their faces and they glanced at one another.

"I know, you're thinking I am paranoid. I really don't think I am."

Jason interceded, "Actually, Haley, we're just surprised you were able to get photos of this man. Whether he is following you or not, that is really helpful."

Haley smiled, "Well, that is some relief. I don't want you to think I'm overly paranoid," she said hesitating, "Although I certainly could be. I need people like you around to ground me and help me sort things out at times. I'll be right back. Please, at least one of you watch the front door to see if a man meeting that description enters."

She made her way toward the front of the restaurant to the ladies' room. Sarah and Jason sat against the wall and kept their eyes peeled. Haley returned momentarily and Sarah motioned for her to sit beside her.

As she slid into her seat, Sarah grabbed her hand in a warm embrace. "Haley, as much as you have been through, anyone would be on guard all the time. It's all good and I'm proud that you did this on your own. You were alone at the mall, right?"

"Yes, just killing some time before heading here."

Jason peered down toward Haley from his seat, "Hey, can you send those photos to me? I want the investigative team to look into them and see if they have an identity on this guy."

"Sure, sending it now," Haley replied.

The restaurant was beginning to fill with patrons and it appeared that the hostess station was now being occupied by a lady wearing a tea length cranberry red dress with a black shawl around her shoulders. Each time the solid wooden double doors opened in the dim establishment, a blast of daylight came in with the patrons. Jason thought to alert the hostess that they were expecting two more and gave her their names. Soon, the hostess was seating Joe and Sharon Foster across from their children.

"So glad to see you both. It's been a strange day. Let me tell you about it," Haley said.

Jason suggested, "Tell them about the man at the mall first, Haley, if you don't mind. That way, all of us will be up to date on things."

Haley did as he requested and Jason showed his parents the two photographs as she spoke. She went into detail about the three places she noticed him, both times at the bookstore and once at the calendar kiosk close to Victoria's Secret.

Sarah chimed in, "Well, men do go into Victoria's Secret, but perhaps he knew he would immediately have a sales associate on his spying ass if he entered."

"Yes, that was my thinking. I just needed to find a place to lose him and then hope he would not keep turning up like a bad penny."

The elder Foster was quiet and Jason caught his attention.

"Dad, I think we should let the investigative team see if they can get an ID on him."

"Yep, we should do that." He looked at Haley quizzically, "This happened after you had invited us here, right? Tell us what else happened today."

Haley sighed visibly and said, "Oh boy!" She leaned back in her chair and tilted her head backward for a moment and then returned to her normal position. At that moment, the waiter arrived and offered to take drink orders for the new arrivals. Each guest ordered and he took off to comply with their requests. All eyes turned back to Haley, waiting for her to spill the beans.

"Maybe I should wait until we put the food order in before I go into that. Not to keep you in suspense," she smiled, "just so the waiter will not be interrupting."

Sarah nudged her gently. "Okay, keep us waiting and biting our fingernails."

Haley laughed.

"I promise to tell as soon as he leaves with the food order."

With that, they each rapidly looked over their menu. The waiter returned with drinks and the food order was placed. Again, all eyes were on Haley.

"Thanks for waiting. This afternoon I met with the investigative reporter and her sidekick. Her name is Megan Adams, but she insists on being called her nickname which is Lucky. I met with each of them to see what, if anything, they may have to offer in the way of information. It might be quite a bit. I'm not sure yet.

Lucky and her researcher Ric helped bring down two different pharmaceutical companies. They were instrumental in getting company whistle blowers to participate. Lucky indicated she has more ongoing investigations into Big Pharma, a name we've all heard and even used. I had the impression she has a bit of a vendetta with them or something. But that's not the point. During her investigations, she told me that many employees of the corporations she has investigated are spied upon. Ric confirmed this also, saying often the employee's home is monitored."

"Whoa!" said Jason.

Papa Foster raised his eyebrows and nodded. "Doesn't surprise me, the sons of bitches."

Haley went on, "I don't see how our home could be bugged. We have such a tight security system.

Nevertheless, she gave me the name of a company that does sweeps for this and I think it would be worth finding out for sure."

Papa Foster inquired, "What is the company's name?"

"Would you like me to send their contact info to your phone?"

"Yes, that would be great. Send it to all of us."

Haley sent the text to all at the table.

Jason looked at her puzzled. "What does Lucky know about Jack's predicament — anything?"

"I asked what she is working on now and she said to sum it up, Big Pharma is a monster that will devour us all if we don't stop it."

Everyone at the table laughed.

"Well now, we all know they do shady stuff, but they help a lot of people and animals too," Sharon Foster interjected.

"That was pretty much my response to Lucky and her view does seem a bit extreme. I'm not sure what she is working on, but she indicated that life as we know it is not going to continue if we don't get a handle on these companies."

Papa Foster asked, "Did she happen to say whether or not she experienced issues with being followed, monitored or threatened?"

"While I did not ask her that directly, I know her nickname stuck because a federal prosecutor considered her "damn lucky" in some case they were working on," she answered.

Haley turned to look down the table at her brother-in-law who had the same exact features as her Jack. "Let me get back to your question, Jason. I don't think she knows much about Jack's accident, but she wants to help, most likely because the victims were employees of a large pharmaceutical company. I did not reveal anything except that we believed Jack may still be alive. That is or will be public knowledge soon. They both seemed surprised about it and even more intrigued to help."

Sharon Foster asked, "Anything else from the meeting you think we need to know?"

"Yes, Ric emphasized that we should vary the locations where we meet each other or individuals involved in the investigation. He said that if someone is following us around town, the more varied our stops are so that they appear to be of a personal nature only, the better."

"That makes sense. But, we are family so it's not unusual for us to get together," Sarah said.

Haley nodded in agreement. "Exactly, which makes it easier for us to have a reason to be together and work on finding out where Jack is and what happened."

"Before I contact the bug sweep company, I wanted to make sure I should call them. I thought perhaps you might know someone that you recommended, Papa?" she said, looking his way across the table. "I do want to find out if the house is bugged quickly. Sonya is helping me host a dinner for surviving spouses and partners of those on the plane. I am sure some talk could occur at the dinner, and we don't want it monitored."

"I cannot say I know of anyone who does that type of work, but let me run this by the investigators and see what they recommend. I'll have an answer for you tomorrow morning at the latest."

"Sounds good."

"Haley, do you think we should bring these independent investigators into our search for Jack and who is behind the murders?" asked Papa Foster.

"Yes, but we may want them to sign a non-disclosure agreement to keep things quiet on their end."

Jason spoke up, "Dad, I think we should all just text each other with meeting times and places until we know everyone is clear on the electronic monitoring. The only way they can see those texts is if they hacked our phones or obtained a court order."

"Good idea — texting it is. Sharon and I have a little information to share. I had a Skype call with the wife and daughter of the pilot earlier today."

"Really? How did you make that happen?" Sarah inquired.

"I didn't. Sharon has been working behind the scenes. She found out the information for his family and contacted them, letting them know she was in the same predicament and could we all talk. So, all four of us were on the call."

Sharon spoke up, "We approached it delicately for the sake of everyone concerned. His wife shared a lot about her husband. We learned about his background as a pilot, along with how he was viewed in his community. They do not know of anyone who would want to harm him, much less kill him."

Haley spoke next. "That goes against what the news is reporting. Do they know something that his family doesn't?"

Jason spoke, "I doubt it. I would say that the information being reported on CNN and all the major outlets is just a regurgitation of what has been fed to them by Shelly Larson. After all, that's what she does — handle the media for Chadwell. Until this happened, I never really noticed how many commercials there are for drugs that Chadwell manufacturers on the news programs. It's a ton."

Papa Foster spoke again, "At the very least, it requires us to take a harder look at Chadwell and perhaps why they would want to kill off their own employees."

Haley looked down at her lap.

"I hope I didn't upset you, Haley," he said sympathetically.

"It's not you. The whole thing is very upsetting for all of us. I hope we find Jack and he is alive."

"That's the goal. I have to believe we will. Let's all keep doing our part and check in by texting with each other for now."

Chapter 47 ~ Notifying Sonya

Haley pushed the garage door opener and pulled in next to Jack's lonely vehicle. There was a strange satisfaction just having their cars in the garage together. She wanted to talk to Sonya about the bug sweep that would be happening and the man at the mall. She entered and disarmed the alarm system and was pleased that her cousin had the system armed.

"Hey there! Have you eaten? I brought home pizza."

Sonya was stretched out in front of the television watching a situation comedy. "You must be reading my mind ... or it's a coincidence. I am craving pizza," she said, strolling into the kitchen. "Plus, I have probably seen at least three commercials for pizza in the last thirty minutes."

"No doubt," Haley said chuckling. "I already ate. It's kind of a long story that I want to tell you. First, you must eat."

Sonya grinned and made her way to the sink to wash up. She grabbed a plate and plopped two pieces of pizza on it.

"While you were gone, I found the vacuum and ran it for you and I also cleaned the hall bath. I don't want you to think I just lie around watching television all day."

"No, I didn't think anything of the sort. How are you feeling, bored? Would you like to get out of the house for an hour or so?"

"Yes, kind of, but you did just get home."

"That's okay. There's this little shop I want to visit in downtown Alpharetta if it's still open. I know you're going to like it."

Sonya finished gobbling her second slice of pizza. She held up her finger while chewing to signal to Haley to hold just a moment. After swallowing she said, "Let me grab my shoes and jacket."

Once on the highway, Haley indicated that she would stop at the special store first since they may close early. Then, they would go sit down someplace to talk about her trip out today.

Haley parked her car in a well lit area fairly close to the shop she and Jack had bought the gemstones in. Sonya excitedly leapt out of the Honda like a teen who had been cooped up too long. Haley pushed the FOB, locking the vehicle.

"This way," she said, leading Sonya.

The business district of Alpharetta had been carefully planned and its appeal was becoming known to all who passed by the Greater Atlanta area. Charming buildings bordered older, established businesses. It had a very hometown atmosphere, but was becoming modernized with new additions everywhere.

"Here we are!" Haley said excitedly as she pushed open the shop's door, hearing the familiar tinkling of chimes. Immediately, the smell of perfumed incense hit Sonya's nose. Calm music played in the background at a low decibel level.

"Oh wow, I didn't know you shopped at a place like this," she teased Haley.

"It was a curiosity stop that Jack and I indulged in the last weekend we were together."

"Oh, sorry," Sonya felt like she had opened up a sore wound.

"No, don't be. I hope the lady that waited on us is here. Do you want to look around while I see if she is available?"

"Sure, this place is fairly small so I don't think we have to worry about getting lost from each other."

Haley walked toward the register or checkout area and rang a silver bell on the counter. Beaded curtains parted and the same older lady she had met before emerged. She was happy to see her again.

"Hello!" said Haley.

"Welcome again," the lady answered.

"You remember me?" Haley inquired.

"Of course. You bought the carnelian for fertility and I placed it on a belly chain for you."

Haley was astonished. Either this woman had a fantastic memory or not that many customers.

"You do remember. Listen, something happened to my husband. He was in a plane crash but we believe there's a chance he's alive. I saw the sign that you do readings. Are you really psychic? Can you help me?"

"Did your husband have the malachite and amethyst on him when he traveled?"

"Yes, I am sure that he had the malachite at least. I placed it on a leather cord necklace and he promised to wear it the entire trip."

The woman answered firmly, "Then he is alive."

"How can you be so sure?"

"It's just the way it works. The intentions are held in the stones. Would you like me to try and find out more through a reading?"

"Yes, I would."

"I will have to schedule it with you as my assistant has already left and I cannot leave the store unattended."

Haley paused, looking her in the eyes. "You think a reading could help me find out more about my husband?"

"It's entirely possible," she said, with aged confidence

"Let me make an appointment then."

"My name is Gesta and yours is?"

"Haley — my name is Haley."

"Would the day after tomorrow work for you?"

"No, we have something planned then. Are you open Monday? I'm sorry I seem so anxious."

"It's perfectly understandable with the situation."

"I have an opening at 2:00 on Tuesday. Would that work for you?"

"Perfect, I will see you then. Let me check on my cousin who is probably becoming quite attached to your wares."

Haley turned and saw Sonya bent down looking at a case of turquoise stones. Gesta moved toward the area to see if she was interested in looking at any of the pieces close up.

"Hello, is there something you would like to take a closer look at?" she asked Sonya.

"Oh, yes. It's just hard to decide," Sonya said looking up at the older woman and noticing the large turquoise stones in her earrings. "I love your earrings!"

"Thank you. The turquoise stone is a wonderful choice. Do you know much about it?"

"Not really, only that it is often associated with Native Americans and the west."

"Some of the most beautiful specimens are found in Arizona. It is said that turquoise was actually discovered by the crusaders in Turkey a long time ago. So it is distributed throughout the world like many gemstones."

"Interesting, what is it used for."

"It's one of the best overall psychic protection stones, but it has many great physical properties for health as well. I try to wear some each day as it helps with buildup of inflammation and boosting energy levels."

"I like the idea of having it placed in earrings," Sonya said pointing to a pair in the case. "Could I see those?"

Gesta opened the case and removed the earrings. "These are rough cut stones set in silver. Would you like to see polished ones beside it for comparison?"

"Yes, please."

Gesta hummed as she fiddled around finding earrings with polished turquoise stones. She placed them beside the rough cut specimens. "Which do you like?"

"Oh, they are both really cool. I'm not sure."

Haley who had stood silently beside Sonya spoke up, "May I purchase them for you as an early Christmas gift?"

"Oh, that's okay. You don't have to do that, Haley."

"Do you like them both?"

"Of course, but I could get one pair and wait on the other."

"Suit yourself," Haley said, "but my offer is take it or leave it now."

"You save your money for now. You're always doing stuff for me."

Sonya picked up the rough cut turquoise earrings and handed them to Gesta. "I'll take these …. for now," she said.

Gesta smiled at her and rang up the purchase. Sonya handed her money to Gesta and asked, "Can I wear them now instead of you packaging them?"

"Yes, but allow me to give you this which tells you how to properly take care of your stones."

Haley nodded at Gesta and said, "See you at our appointment."

Gesta bowed her head toward the two women. "I look forward to it."

Sonya had securely placed the earrings on her ears as the chimes tingled upon their exit. Haley looked around at the street. She had developed a new habit recently, watching for strange men alone or loitering about. She saw only couples and families who had spent the evening picking up finds perhaps for Christmas.

She motioned for Sonya to follow her and they walked toward Kilwins on Market where she hoped to be able to catch Sonya up on what had happened today. As they approached the entrance with its white columns and ornate black railing, you could not help but feel you might be in the French Quarter. Once inside, there was no doubt you had entered a world of desserts. Inside the leaded glass door entry, the interior made your eyes pop even before you glanced at a single item they had to offer. From floor to ceiling, black and white identical tiles lined the walls with matching flooring throughout. The rows of homemade ice cream, along with the smell of fresh baked waffle cones, were calling out to each of the ladies.

"Haley, you are going to kill my girly figure."

"You can just order coffee or tea, hon," she said facetiously.

"No, I can't. Smell this place. I could sleep here and be happy just with the scent alone."

Haley laughed. "C'mon, what are you in the mood for? Jack and I had chocolates and coffee when we were here last. But we could do ice cream if you want."

Sonya strolled toward the ice cream area, her eyes reading the delicious choices. She ordered toasted coconut ice cream in a waffle cone and Haley ordered the cheesecake ice cream, but in a cup. "You might have to give me a smidgeon of your waffle cone," she said, looking at Sonya.

"I don't know, let me taste it and then I will decide," she said, smirking.

Kilwin's was not as crowded as usual and they were able to find a table, but it was right in front of a window. They sat and Haley spoke quickly, but thoroughly about the day's events. Sonya paused licking her ice cream cone at particular points as Haley told about the possible surveillance and the man at the mall. "Let me send you the two photos I have of him instead of holding my phone up here in this window." She sent them to Sonya and then folded her arms and leaned back in her chair for a moment.

"What this means is I am going to have someone come into the house and check for surveillance. I am really hoping they do not find any, but if they do, I want them to find all of it." Sonya shook her head in agreement. "Right now, we need to watch everything we do and say inside the house and perhaps my car as well. Obviously, if people are following me, they somehow know where I'm headed. We all agreed at dinner tonight to communicate only by text on anything related to Jack and the plane crash. Jason said the only way someone could get the texts was by hacking or court order for the phone provider to release it."

"That makes sense," Sonya said, looking somewhat sad.

"I hope this didn't ruin your ice cream experience, Sonya. I needed to share this with you away from home just in case someone is listening. You know, Jessie is my best friend and I trust her and Alex. But I'm starting to feel like some of the things I am learning I cannot share with them."

"Why is that?"

"While I trust them, they could inadvertently speak to someone else about it or reveal some element we don't want anyone knowing. Whoever is doing this, the following and the murderous plane crash, needs to be kept in the dark about what knowledge we are obtaining."

"Damn, Haley! Your life is starting to sound like a spy series."

"I know, right? Let's get home. Hopefully, I will hear from Jack's father soon on whether to call that company or have someone else check the house.

Chapter 48 ~ Self Defense

Wednesday, December 11, 2019

Haley felt inexperienced and doubtful as they entered the building. The reception area contained a wall of windows that provided a view of two separate work out rooms. They were massive in size. Sparring or some sort of martial arts was happening in the one on the right. Sonya acted giddy like a school girl going to dance class for the first time. Perhaps that is the way Haley needed to think of it too. Jessie was quiet which was unlike her. Haley knew she felt a bit intimidated.

Checking in at the front desk, they were greeted by a dark haired woman with beautiful large hazel eyes framed with thick dark lashes. "Hello ladies, are you here for the introductory class on self defense?"

"That would be us," Haley replied.

"Great, so happy to have you. Would you each please sign in with your name and favorite way to be contacted? If you have a nickname you prefer, please feel free to add that. We do not ask for any other personal information at this time. Once you are signed in, please go to the room on your left and have a seat. We are beginning the session in ten minutes," she said, pointing in that direction.

Each of the ladies followed her instruction, signing in and walking toward the room on the left. Inside, they could see quite a few other women waiting. Some chatted with one another. Others sat silent. The chairs were arranged in a circle around several mats on the floor. There were four chairs open together. Haley took advantage of that.

Sarah had concerns about Haley. This is the main reason she came to the class. It had only been two weeks since the plane crashed and here was Haley taking on self defense classes. But now that she was here, she could see how beneficial this might be for her. More than anything, Haley needed to keep family and friends around her while they all tried to figure out if Jack was still alive and possibly who wanted that plane down.

"Welcome everyone!" said the young woman who had taken their registration information at the front desk. "Allow me to introduce your humble, yet also esteemed, sensei or teacher, Dan Whitlow." The woman clapped, then bowed to the older gentleman and the ladies present joined in applause. He wore traditional martial arts clothing. He bowed four times as he rotated his body in a circle to the ladies in their chairs. His gi fit snug, as opposed to many she had seen photographs of that were loose. His hair was graying at the temples and he had a well trimmed moustache.

He continued to rotate in a circle as he asked the women, "How many of you believe you are good at being aware of your surroundings?" Almost all of the women raised their hand and he smiled broadly.

"Please, would each of you close your eyes for a moment? Keep them closed. Now, tell me by raising your hand and showing the numbers with your fingers, "How many exits are there right from where you sit to the outside world?"

The women paused, still sitting with their eyes closed. The room was quiet and you could almost hear the mental calculations going on. One by one, each woman began to raise her hand and most indicated two exits by the number of fingers they held up.

"Please now, open your eyes and look around again. Many of you only saw two exits or you imagined that would be a safe guess in a business place like this. But, what if there is only one exit? You need to know that when you go someplace new. Only one of you held up three fingers and that is correct," he said, looking directly at Sarah. She blushed a bit and put up both hands palms up, shrugging her shoulders as if she didn't know how she got this right.

"Don't be shy about this. You are correct. There are three exits. Did you know this or guess?"

"I knew it. I suffer from claustrophobia and I am always looking for a way I can leave if I need to."

"Excellent! You have an underlying need to find safety in certain conditions or circumstances. This is what protecting ourselves is about. It is not about hurting others unless we have to in defense. Yes, sometimes we have to do that to keep from being hurt. However, much of self defense is awareness of your surroundings. By knowing what and who is around, you then have options to choose from in conditions or circumstances that are unfavorable. Does that make sense?" The women audibly said, "Yes."

"Ideally, we want you to be able to avoid using the physical techniques we teach here. Still, it is invaluable to know them. In your training, you will learn to be more aware of everything around you. Not like a frightened mouse listening for the next noise, but as a trained observer of your surroundings. This not only heightens your ability to protect yourself, it also raises your enjoyment of simple pleasures you were not noticing before."

"On the physical instruction, we will teach you successful techniques borrowed from judo, Brazilian Jiu-Jitsu and even street fighting moves in order to overcome aggressors. Please note that we will only teach you. In order to be adept at using physical moves, you must train with practice." He verbally held out the word *practice* emphasizing its importance to the group.

"When you need to utilize the physical moves you have trained for, it is in order to get away from the situation to safety. It is not to beat up your aggressor and win the fight. Often, the wisest solution is to surprise them, shock them with your action, hurt them enough to buy time, and get away. Does that make sense?"

The crowd nodded in agreement.

"Many men attempt to strangle a woman first — not always, but often. I will teach you want to do in order to get free of the hold. If you have been taken hostage in a vehicle or trunk of a vehicle, I will assist you in what to do in that situation. Anytime you are being taken to a second location, you must fight for your very life at that point. We shall talk about that during the course along with things you can use for weapons when you have none."

"Often when people enter training into martial arts, they desire the ability to overcome an aggressor physically. Of course, this is one of the main goals. Yet, in order to do it, you must realize it takes a certain mindset that you either already have and tweak — or is non-existent or weak and must be developed in your training."

"This mental attitude you will adopt during training will help you in many situations in your life, making you more adaptable to stress in a calm, unfettered way. We have heard the term, "ruffle his feathers". If you are dedicated, you will learn to respond to situations without being easily provoked or frightened. You will learn to face your darkest fears and turn the tables on them. Who here is ready to do that?"

All of the ladies raised their hands.

"Okay, I am now going to have my assistant and one of her sparring partners show you some basic self protection moves. You will also partner up and practice three of these moves at your first full class should you decide to enroll."

The dark haired girl centered herself on the mat and began explaining a scenario that could happen in real life. As she did so, the sparring partner came up behind her and she quickly thwarted her attack and took her to the ground. She went through three more maneuvers, each appeared fast, but Haley felt they must be complex.

Regardless, all the women signed up for their first session which would begin in a week.

Sarah joked as they left the center, "Guess I'll be asking Santa for sparring clothing for Christmas."

Haley quickly chimed in, "Santa fulfills all kinds of strange requests!"

Chapter 49 ~ Bug Sweep

Thursday, December 12, 2019

Haley awoke early, feeling a bit pressured with the increasing paranoia she was experiencing. Was she being listened to and watched at home. Had this been happening for quite awhile? There was only one way to find out. She checked her messages.

Glancing outside, it had rained overnight and the skies were still gray with a mixture of dark and light puffy clouds. She slipped into a pair of flip flops, disarmed the alarm and headed out the front door to use her phone outside. Accessing the contact phone number of the bug sweepers, she pushed the icon to call them right away.

A man answered, "Jackson Security, how can I help you?"

"Hello, I was referred to you by someone and would like to have my home checked out."

"Alright, are you in a secure location now where you can give me some background or details, or do you need time to locate the right spot to talk?"

"I'm standing out in my front yard. I suppose this area could be bugged, but I doubt it."

"What kind of area do you live in — city, apartments or house?"

"We are in a suburban area of Alpharetta, just northeast of Atlanta. We have a house spaced somewhat far from the one other neighbor on this street."

"Okay, go on."

"My name is Haley Foster and the address is 710 Cherokee Court."

"Is this phone number on my caller ID the best way to reach you?"

"Yes, it is and you may text me at that number as well."

"Approximately how much square footage does your home have, including any basement and covered porch areas, plus any garages?"

"Oh, wow, I'm not sure. I would say at least 3500 square feet."

"For a full comprehensive sweep, we charge $1.00 per square foot."

"I didn't realize it could be that much."

"Is this something you want to pursue?"

Haley paused for a moment. *Damn, this could be an expensive day.* "Yes, I need it. How quickly can you come and do this? I have an upcoming dinner with guests and I will need this accomplished prior to that time."

"Hold on one moment and let me see if we have anything this afternoon. Would that be too soon?"

"No, that would be perfect actually."

Haley waited on hold listening to Christmas music until the gentleman came back on the line. I can have a two man crew there at two o'clock. When they arrive, please meet them outside initially. They will need your credit card details or you may also pay by check. We will pull your square footage of the home from the county assessor's online portal records and go by those measurements. I promise you if anything is there monitoring you, we will find it. We're the best in this area and use TSCM or technical surveillance counter measures."

"Great, I'll be ready when your crew arrives this afternoon."

"We will see you then. Thank you for choosing us."

Haley wandered back in the house and found Sonya awake. She held up her phone and texted her.

Bug sweepers coming this afternoon at 2pm.

Sonya looked down at her phone, reading the message. She looked at Haley and nodded. She texted back,

"OK, what should I do?"

Haley said aloud, "Nothing, just be your cute self."

Promptly at two, a white van with no outer markings or logos pulled into the drive. Haley met the men out front and Sonya stayed in the foyer area, watching as they spoke. They presented her with an invoice and she wrote out a check for the service to be performed. If you're ready, we will get started Mrs. Foster.

"I have a question. If you do find any devices that are monitoring us, is there any way to find out where that information is going … in other words who is behind it?"

"On rare occasions that is possible, but most of the time not."

"If you find something and remove it, will the other side know?"

"Yes, they will either assume the device stopped working or that it has been discovered."

"Okay, that gives me a little more of an idea about this."

The men proceeded to bring in a trunk filled with equipment. As they opened it, Haley was amazed at the vast array of devices inside.

"We will need to shut down your WIFI for awhile. Otherwise, we will get too many false feedbacks. Will that be a problem?"

Haley looked at Sonya who shrugged her shoulders. "Should be fine. The modem and router are in a room off the kitchen."

She lead them to Jack's office and said, "I'll be in the kitchen if you need anything," joining Sonya in that same space. It felt like the safe room to be in for some reason right now.

"Ma'am, we will be unplugging items in each room as well. Once we are finished with an area, we will plug everything up again."

"Okay, good to know. Do you need us to do anything?"

"Not now, but if we find anything, we'll notify you right away."

Sonya and Haley watched through the open doorway as the men unplugged everything in the room. Once that was accomplished, they proceeded to grab their electronic devices and scan the room slowly. Something was putting off a signal as they went around the walls and ceiling. One of the men scanned Jack's desk, including under it and every drawer. The other man continued looking at the walls with a thermal imaging camera.

Turning toward the credenza on the wall behind the desk chair, the device beeped louder.

"Found it!" he exclaimed lifting up what looked like a plug in phone charger. He held it up to show Haley and

Sonya. It looked like nothing more than a black phone plug-in unit for your usb and cord for your phone.

"These perform double duty as you can actually charge many devices with them. However, if you look closely right here," he said using the tip of a tiny screwdriver to point, "you can see a miniscule lens that may be recording us right now. These are fairly inexpensive and becoming more common with usage. It looks like this one also has an SD card increasing the storage capacity probably to about 128 gigabytes."

Haley and Sonya stood silent for a moment. Haley rounded the desk and sat in Jack's chair.

"So, this thing has been plugged in right behind this chair in the credenza area. Jack's been using it to charge things and had no idea it was spying on him?"

Sonya looked at her, "Do you know when he got it?"

"No, I have no idea."

The security man spoke up. "Often, these are given to employees. Could that be a possibility?"

"Yes, it sure could be," Haley said, shaking her head.

The man who seemed in charge continued, "We are going to totally darken this room and shine a couple of lights around to see if there is anything else that could be present."

Sonya and Haley moved into the kitchen and waited while the men carefully went over the darkened office.

"Nothing, we're going to call this room all clear," said the older security man.

Room by room, the two men worked their way checking every outlet, light switch, smoke detector and much more. The more experienced gentleman educated Haley and Sonya on what to look for. He explained that some devices worked temporarily with no permanent energy source, but on battery alone. Other devices were more reliable for spying because they did not have to be replenished or recharged. This was the case with the USB spy device as it was most likely plugged into the victim's home charging itself constantly.

Unless someone was coming into the house on a regular basis to collect devices and place new ones, whoever was spying on the household would want to have something hardwired. In the master bedroom, they found such a device, hardwired into the light switch.

Haley placed her hands over her face and sighed. "Oh my god, I cannot believe this. Someone could have been watching everything in this room?"

The older gentleman felt her embarrassment and pain. "No, not with this device, it only picks up audio."

Haley felt somewhat relieved, but not really. At least they had not been able to watch her making love with Jack or getting dressed.

"How could someone have placed this here?" she asked.

"Have you had any electricians here or other laborers?"

"Yes, but prior to us moving in. Jack hired people to renovate this room and the master bath."

The older gentleman looked at his partner. "Okay, let's keep going over this room and then we'll start on the bath."

The men completed their sweep of the master suite and bath and found nothing further.

Haley looked at Sonya as they made their way to her room and said, "I'm horrified about this, but I'm glad I know now."

She hugged Haley. "We're going to catch these bastards."

In Haley's mind, she went over and over trying to remember things she and Jack had spoken of in the bedroom. Of course, there were sounds of lovemaking and sweet things they said to each other that were now not private, but shared with whom?

There were no further devices found either in the main floor, basement or garage. The deck on the back of the house was checked with nothing discovered. However, Haley and Jack's vehicles had magnetic trackers attached to the chassis of the vehicles. The older gentleman showed them to Haley. "These must be recharged periodically. Typically they last anywhere from one to three weeks depending on what mode they are set in. They allow someone to track you utilizing GPS. They are pretty accurate. Have these vehicles been out recently?"

"I drive the Honda and was out yesterday. The Jeep belongs to my husband and it has not moved for awhile as he is out of town on business," she half lied.

"Well, let us know if you need us to explain to him what we found here."

"Thank you, I will probably explain to him myself."

"With these GPS trackers, someone would have to replace it periodically with a charged unit in order to provide them with long term continuous monitoring. So, that's something to keep in mind. They would have to get access to the exterior of your vehicle. There are units that can be plugged into the vehicle's computer system to receive a constant charge. If you will unlock the vehicles, we will check for that."

"Yes, of course. Let me grab the keys."

Haley went into the kitchen and pressed the FOB's for each vehicle as she reentered the garage. After a search, nothing was found on the interior of their cars.

Both gentlemen proceeded to pack up the thermal imaging camera and other devices they had used throughout the property. "Let us put our gear back in the van and I will go over things in a final report for you."

Haley nodded her head. She felt tired of having the two of them go over every inch of the house. The entire process was emotionally draining as well to know that real surveillance had been going on for at least awhile, but how long? She longed to just lie down and rest and wondered if she would ever be able to go anywhere without feeling as if someone could know what she was doing.

Snap out of it, she told herself. *This is all part of finding Jack and making sure you are safer today than you were yesterday. It's a process.* She knew this was not the time to become emotional about the circumstances.

As the men reentered, she asked, "Is it possible you did not find something?"

Again, the older one replied. "Yes, it is. However, we do have state of the art equipment to try and find it all. We've spent hours going over every area. But, there could be something new that is hard to detect or that we do not have access to. In this situation, it looks like opportunistic spying."

"Explain that, please."

"The only thing we found hardwired was in one light switch of the master bedroom which had undergone a renovation. It was probably placed there at that time. The USB device was probably given to your husband by someone. Perhaps you can ask him who and that will help you solve who may be behind this. The GPS trackers were likely placed on the vehicles when they were parked somewhere other than here. If they've been changed out periodically due to battery loss, the person spying would know where the vehicle is parked and could easily accomplish that."

The other man spoke up. "We've seen this sort of activity with corporations spying on employees. You don't have to tell me anything about what you or your husband do. In fact, we would rather not know. But, this is what it looks like. Now, I need to ask you if your employer, or your husband's, has supplied you with a cell phone, tablet or computer of any type?"

"Yes, my husband's laptop and cell phone were supplied by his employer."

"Okay, anything he wants to keep confidential from his employer should not be typed, shared or spoken on those devices. They could be compromised as well."

"Good to know. They're not here. He took them with him for work. I'll make him aware of it. I have another question. Those GPS trackers — if I wanted to fool the person spying about my whereabouts, could I keep them for awhile and do that?"

"Yes, you can keep any of these devices going, although we would have to hardwire the one in the bedroom back in place."

He handed her Mylar zip bags marked with each device and where it had been found.

"Okay, well I'll think on that. Thank you so much for what you've done here today. It's disturbing, but at least we know now."

"You're very welcome. Thank you for using our service. One last thing … I want to show you a picture of something that may help you." He pulled out a piece of paper printed with a handheld device on it.

"Most of the devices that people use to spy on each other are easily available on Amazon or other online sites. However, you can also purchase this handheld unit which can pick up frequencies emanating from these devices. It will not work as extensively as the equipment we use, but it could give you additional peace of mind as people come and go from your home. Just thought I would mention it."

"Oh, I'm glad you did. Can I keep this?"

"Yes, it's a print-out for you to keep. We'll be on our way now, ma'am. Call us if you have any questions at all or further issues. Your WIFI and security system are up and running. You should be good to go."

Haley saw the gentlemen to the front door and closed it behind them. She engaged the security system, looked at Sonya standing there and said, "Holy double "o" seven, can you believe this?"

Sonya cracked up laughing, "No, I can't. But here we are."

It was critical that Haley let her family members know what devices had been found at her home. She sent a group text, then sent a separate text to Lucky Adams thanking her and letting her know "stuff was found". She imagined Papa Foster and Jason were already making appointments with the bug sweep company.

Chapter 50 ~ Dinner

Friday, December13, 2019

Haley straightened up the house, going room to room with dusting and vacuuming. Sonya took over in the kitchen, sweeping and mopping the tile flooring. Haley then set the dining room table for the guests. The entire day was really built around tonight as they each busied themselves with preparations for tonight's dinner. The menu was simple to prepare ahead so that Haley could easily be present for the guests. They prepared a meat lasagna along with a vegetarian version just in case. They cut and sliced vegetables for a salad bar the guests could build anyway they chose. While there were plenty of salad dressings, Haley worried if she had exactly what the guests would want or like. Sonya told her she was over thinking and to let it go. "They have seven to choose from. I think it will be fine."

"You're right. I just want them to be content."

"I hope these wine selections will work for them," Haley went on.

Sonya stopped slicing cucumber and placed her hand on her hip. "Will you stop now?" she said chuckling.

"Okay, okay."

In the last week, Haley had attended three funerals for Jack's coworkers. The people closest to those men would be here tonight. She felt odd about the gathering because it was so soon, but time was ticking away. Most likely, all of them were feeling a huge hole in their lives, just like she was. It was worse for each because they knew their loved one was not coming back. Haley had hope, but nothing huge to go on.

Sonya saw her worrying. "Look, what you need to focus on is being a calm hostess and having a chance to speak with these people together and alone. I know we threw this together to honor their loved ones, but also to try and see if any of them know why someone would want to down that plane."

Haley smiled and took a deep breath. "You're right. I'm getting too caught up in worrying what everyone will think. I'm sure the food and drink selections will be fine. Do you need more slicing and dicing for the salad?"

"I think I've got this, but thanks."

"Okay, then I'm going to freshen up my hair and makeup, change and put some laid back Christmas music on real low."

"Great idea, you go get you ready," Sonya said. "I'll tie up any loose ends here."

Sonya had been helpful in so many ways and Haley needed to make sure she told her how much she appreciated her. The Christmas tree would be brown instead of green if Sonya was not watering it regularly. Haley wondered if Sonya was this helpful at home with her aunt and uncle. Often, young people will change things up in a newer environment. She would have to ask Aunt Molly.

Luke Felder, Lance's partner, arrived first. He seemed a bit nervous. Haley attempted to put him at ease. She noticed Sonya was missing and assumed she was freshening up. Haley guided Lance toward the drink area she had prepared in the kitchen. She pointed to the selection, "We have cabernet, merlot, a white moscato and chardonnay. We also have lemonade, sweet tea or bottled water. What shall it be?"

"Hmm, I think I will have a glass of wine — the merlot if you don't mind."

"Of course," Haley said, grabbing a wine glass by the stem and pouring. "Enjoy — I think I will have a little of the same."

"Your home is so beautiful."

"Oh, thank you. It's a nice change and I love Alpharetta. It truly feels like home to me."

"How did you guys find this place? It's remote, but not too far."

"Yes, that is one of the things we liked about the area. It actually turned out to be a shorter drive to Chadwell for Jack, but a longer one for me at Mercy Hospital."

Luke took another sip of wine and swallowed. "I haven't been back to work since this happened," he said with a lot of hurt in his facial features and eyes.

"I haven't been back to the hospital. I may take a leave of absence. I don't know yet. Part of me wants to stay busy to keep my mind off things, but it seems I have been busier lately with the aftermath than I would be if I were going to my job."

"Since Lance and I were legally married, Chadwell will be sending me death benefits. I suppose they are doing this with everyone. I'm kind of curious about that."

"I am as well. I am hoping we can share some information tonight that will assist all of us."

The door bell rang and Haley said, "Excuse me."

Two women she recognized were at the door. It was Sercy's wife, Petunia, and Ethan's wife, Carla. Haley smiled big to make them feel welcome. Sonya joined her in the foyer as well. "Ladies, this is my cousin, Sonya. She has been staying with me for a few days. Can we take your jackets?"

strands. The mood in the room lifted. Sonya looked at Haley, "I think we better get the lasagna out of the oven."

"We will be right back," Haley told them.

With the food ready, Sonya invited everyone into the kitchen to serve the food onto their plates buffet style. In the meantime, Haley placed butter on the table and refilled their glasses.

Luke commented, "I didn't know anyone made homemade lasagna these days. This smells and looks fabulous."

Haley laughed, "I hope you like it. I can tell you that Jack and I both loved to cook, and he was better at it than I am, but this is one recipe he really seemed to like. We have the meat version and the vegetarian. Feel free to try both."

"Lance loved to grill mostly, and he was damn good at it. I did most of the cooking in the kitchen."

"I'll bet you are really good at it," Haley said.

"I try," Luke said shyly.

The dinner proceeded well with the guests enjoying the food and each other. As they neared the end, a dessert of chocolate cake and spumoni were served to each guest.

"Anyone want coffee or is it too late?"

Luke spoke up, "I wouldn't mind for the drive back to have a little coffee."

Petunia agreed and while she had been relatively low key and quiet, suddenly spoke up. "I was hoping we could all try and speculate why the plane crashed, basically who is behind this."

Haley immediately agreed. "Yes, I was hoping the same. The official story that Shelly Larson at Chadwell is stating is that it ..." she held her fingers up in air quotes "... appears to be someone with a vendetta against the pilot." But I ask myself why that particular flight on that particular day?"

"Exactly!" Luke chimed in.

"Does anyone know what the team was working on?" Haley inquired

"I've been wondering the same," said Carla. "Ethan wouldn't talk about it no matter how much I asked him prior to the trip."

Luke wiped his forehead and appeared a bit nervous, "I don't know what the details were, just that it was something important."

Haley asked him further, "Did it involve a particular plant that he may have given the name of?"

"He did, but not being familiar with Latin, I have no idea what it was. No memory of its name. I do know it was an accidental discovery."

"Petunia, do you know anything?"

"No, I know nothing," she said firmly. But Haley had the impression she knew something that she wasn't sharing.

Haley took her turn. "My knowledge is also very limited. Jack called it a game changer at one point. He told me he had to be very hush hush on the project, like he did with anything he was working on. I also know the plant was collected by accident, a straggler that came in on another plant they harvested by the river. I think Sercy had been propagating it at Chadwell. But they needed more of it and to study the replication conditions better. That's all I know. It sounds like a mouthful, but it isn't enough."

Sonya spoke up, "Haley, don't forget to tell them about the bugs."

"Oh, my gosh, I can't believe I didn't tell you this right away. We are talking bugs -- as in spy devices." The ears of all three perked up.

"On a recommendation of someone who has dealt with large corporations, they advised me to have the house swept for electronic spying devices. They said that often corporate employees are spied upon in various ways by their employers. First, allow me to say that if your loved one used a computer, phone or tablet from Chadwell, it was probably monitored in various ways, especially through various work groups that log into their system."

"Isn't that illegal?" Petunia asked.

"I'm not sure. I think it's different from state to state. It's their equipment technically, their software and systems. I could see where it could be argued they have the right to monitor communications and such. However, the four devices the bug sweep company found in our home were … well, let me get them and I will show you."

Haley left, momentarily returning with the four Mylar bags. "These are illegal!" she said, passing them around the table.

Luke held the USB charger with a look of amazement. "This is a spy device?"

"Yes, it can take sound and video. Look closely on the front and you will see the tiny lens."

He shook his head, "I cannot believe this. We have one of these in our house."

"Do you know where it came from?" Haley asked somewhat anxiously.

"Ours came from Chadwell. It was given to Lance in a welcome packet when he joined the company."

"Wow, that's helpful to know. This is not looking good for them. It's really good to find out the source. Of course, you need to verify that once you get home. It could just be a USB charger," Petunia said, but didn't believe.

Haley nodded in agreement. "The bug sweep company explained to me that they are common in use as spy devices and can actually be used to charge devices as well. Now, the one that Carla is holding was hardwired into our light switch plate in the master bedroom. It has no lens and only picks up audio."

Petunia shook her head, "That is so crazy. You cannot believe how this is making me worry about our place."

"Yes, I can," said Luke. "How much is the bug sweep company?"

"It's expensive, but I'm glad I did it. Oh, and they gave me this piece of paper showing a handheld device you can order that is not too much money. I can't claim how well it works, but I've already ordered one," Haley passed the paper to Carla.

"The other two devices were on Jack's vehicle and mine. Basically, they track your location and they work off a battery so they would need to be replaced with new units every so often."

Luke asked, "This handheld unit you ordered, would it pick up those tracking devices?"

"Probably … I think so. This evening, we have been able to speak freely here because I had the place swept. However, my family and anyone involved in investigating this are only texting each other right now. It's not foolproof but a lot harder for anyone to monitor."

Petunia suddenly felt brave and offered, "Now, I remember something Sercy said. He said this potential drug could eliminate many deadly viruses that remain tough pathogens."

"Interesting," Haley said. "Just that little bit of information begins to narrow things. Thank you, Petunia."

Carla interjected, "What do you think we should do, Haley?"

"I would consider not speaking to anyone about this unless they are a real investigator working on the mystery of this plane crash. Be very cautious and use texting to communicate with each other, me or something connected to this. At the very least, buy that gizmo on the paperwork. If you really want to know, have the bug sweep people come in. They carry a lot more state of the art equipment."

"I know you each have loved ones that had their remains returned and buried. Unfortunately, I did not. Jack's family and I are hopeful he is alive somewhere in Brazil. I know it sounds like a shot in the dark but it's all we have to hold onto. Any information you find out could be helpful in us finding the killer, Jack or both."

Everyone made sure they had the cell phone numbers of each and Luke departed first. Carla hugged Haley as she made her way to the front door. "I hope you find your husband and he is okay."

"Me too, Carla. I'm so sorry about the loss of Ethan. I don't know if I'll see my husband again or not. I have to keep trying to find out what happened."

Petunia popped up with her jacket now on. "You know today is Friday the 13th, but I think we've had a little luck here this evening with our information sharing, don't you?"

"Yes, I do. Thank you so much for coming — both of you."

"Thanks for having us. It was a delicious dinner."

Sonya and Haley looked at each other as they left. There was a hollow feeling to the end of the dinner that only their loved ones had the power to fill.

"We did it, Sonya. Now what?"

"Rest, Haley. You need to rest."

Chapter 51 ~ No Surveillance

Evan answered the burner phone when it vibrated in his pocket. "Hello."

"Hey, we have a little problem. We are not picking up anything inside the house, and it looks like she has driven nowhere. We're thinking the devices have been discovered."

"How long has that pattern been going on?" Evan inquired.

"Just a few days. But we do have something that might interest you."

"Go on," Evan said.

"A day or so before we stopped getting any sound, we clearly received an entry code. Seems she gave a code to someone there at the house and it was said out loud."

"Give me the code," Evan demanded.

"Okay, ready? It's 6-8-9-1-5-7"

Evan repeated it back to be sure. "Great, thanks for getting me that. I'll be back in touch. Anything on anyone else assigned to you?"

"Nothing of consequence," his contact replied.

Evan punched in the number for the contractor.

"Yep, it's me," he answered.

"Got something that may help you get in."

"Good, that's a tough spot to crack into. What do you have?"

"Security pass code. Ready for it?"

"Hold on, I will be. Just a second. Okay, shoot."

Evan gave him the numbers, "6-8-9-1-5-7".

"That may do the trick. I'll give it another try and be in touch."

"Counting on you, man."

"I'll do my best. It's too secluded there to get in easily. My best bet is when the house is empty and the neighbor is gone. We missed the boat on this. The day of the funeral would have worked well. It's likely the neighbors would have been there, too."

"Yeah, well, the funeral happened, but it didn't. Long story. Anyway, I've got my fingers crossed for you. I need whatever is hidden in that house."

"Dad, I just couldn't stand it out there in the world without you," she humored him in return.

Sonya slipped past him into the house as he said, "Uh huh, I bet."

"Haley, welcome back to the little ranch. Been awhile since you've visited Valdosta."

She hugged Mike and he lowered his voice to almost a whisper, "You doing okay?"

"Yes and it is really good to be back here, but I'm afraid it will be a short visit. You would not believe what we have discovered. Sonya and I will catch you both up. Anyway, I've got things scheduled already for Monday, so we'll only be here one night this time."

"I can't wait to hear about this," he said, closing the door. "Your aunt's in the kitchen."

Haley made her way to the sunny kitchen she had not seen for awhile. It was a large country kitchen with the dining area separate, but open to the room.

"Welcome back, Haley. How are you?"

"Doing well, Aunt Molly. I'm really enjoying having Sonya live with me for now. Sorry to steal her away."

"I'll admit, it's been a little lonely without her, but I have a feeling you will be a good influence for her. Perhaps you can help her find some direction."

"We'll see. So far, she's been a great help to me and we have a lot of things to catch you up on that have happened."

"Give me a hand and open that oven door while I put this casserole in," Molly requested.

"You got it," Haley said opening the door. Hot air poured from the wall oven.

Molly set the timer for 35 minutes. "Well, you've got enough time before dinner to find your old room and get settled."

"Great, I'm starving. I miss your homemade meals."

Haley ran her hand over a beautiful seed catalog Molly had sitting on the counter. She knew how Molly's mind operated, constantly dreaming of new things to plant for the next gardening season. Aunt Molly loved preserving her own food. She taught both of the girls how to can food, saying you may really need to know this one day. Almost all of the food she preserved was grown right there on their land. They also traded with the neighbors at the next neighboring farm bumper crops each family might have.

"This seed catalog is gorgeous. They really go all out to sell seeds now, don't they?" Haley said.

"Oh, I love that company. I order from them each year and their customer service is the best. They always send me a couple of freebies too."

Sonya poked her head in the kitchen. "Hey, I brought your stuff in along with mine, but guess what?"

"What?" Haley said.

"You get to help me carry it upstairs."

Haley smiled. "Sorry, I got distracted with your mom's seed catalog." She turned to her aunt. "We'll be back in a bit."

"Make yourselves comfortable."

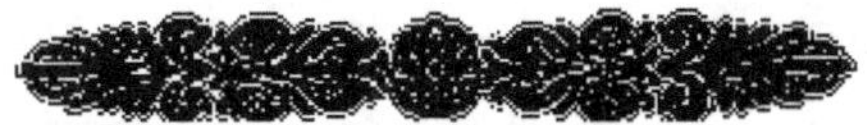

They each grabbed their bags and Haley looked at Sonya. "I think I over packed. I do this each time I go somewhere." Sonya chimed in, "I must have inherited that trait from you." They both laughed as they made their way up to their former bedrooms. Each bedroom had a vaulted ceiling in the middle and was located opposite of one another at each respective end of the upstairs.

When Haley first came to live at the farm, Mike and Molly had gone to some expense and trouble to make her room a happy place for her to be … and it was. As soon as she opened the door, her eyes fell upon the soft yellow hues and warm red tones of the bedspread and pillows. The large queen size bed with its feminine design in the iron headboard seemed to be waiting for her. She had forgotten about the farm style chandelier hanging from the ceiling. Sonya with her artistic flair had helped Haley paint white stenciled lace in a beautiful pattern against one accent wall. What caught her eye the most as she sat her bags down at the foot of the bed was the remembrance wreath hanging above it on the wall. It had been gifted to her anonymously and a bit mysteriously a few days after her mom's funeral. It was a grapevine wreath adorned with sprigs of rosemary and interspersed with dried pink roses. *I can't believe I left that here*, she thought. The room was clean and dust free, but looked like it had been trapped in a time capsule from her younger days. She walked down the hall toward Sonya's room, finding her door open.

"Wow," Haley said as she peered inside. "The last time I saw your room it was more girly girl. You've gone space bohemian."

Sonya smiled, "You like it?"

"I love it. Now, it's not my style but it fits you perfectly."

"Mom and dad would not let me paint what I wanted on the walls. One by one, I ordered these tapestries with the planets and space. Then, I got a ladder and began tacking them up to the ceiling. I wanted to do my own art work, but they were not having it."

"There is a budding Michelangelo in you wanting to paint ceilings," Haley teased.

"Watch this," Sonya said. She flipped the switch on a strip at the side of her desk. The entire room was filled with tiny white lights which gave a star like effect against the space backdrop tapestries.

"That is so awesome!"

Haley walked around the room and noticed other small artistic details Sonya had added. As strange as the ideas she had could sound, she had a way of making everything come together magically.

"Sonya, you have a real flair for visual things. I am so impressed with your abilities."

Sonya blushed. "Not really, I wish I could do more."

"Then find a space and do it. You are a creator and you need to create things."

"Thanks, Haley."

"I'm going to freshen up. I think the casserole your mom put in the oven should be just about finished baking."

"I'll meet you down there."

At dinner, Haley shared with Mike and Molly everything that had transpired since they left, letting them know this was all secret and not to let anyone know anything. They understood and Mike laughed, "We don't get out much so you need not worry about us saying anything." Both her aunt and uncle were shocked about the surveillance devices found.

"Do you think Chadwell Pharmaceuticals placed them there?"

"I can't prove it except for one device possibly." She told them about the dinner party they had for the spouses of the other victims and one saying they had a USB drive like that and it had been given in his husband's welcome packet when he started at Chadwell."

"Boy, oh boy. They start right away spying on the employees, huh?" Mike commented.

"I know they have to keep many secrets about what they are working on. I'm sure the company worries about possible spies coming to work at Chadwell to steal company secrets. But to think they've been listening to what goes on in our bedroom really pisses me off."

"They would be bored here if they tried that," Aunt Molly chimed in. Everyone laughed.

Haley continued, "And following us everywhere or at least knowing where we are at any given time. The man at the bug sweep company said that's illegal."

"So is murder," Uncle Mike interjected firmly.

Sonya broke the momentary silence that fell over everyone at the table at the word "murder". "Mom, let me help you clean up. Dinner was delish as usual."

"Yes, thank you Aunt Molly. Dinner was fantastic as I expected it would be."

"I am truly glad you girls are here with us tonight. Even one night is better than none."

The three reminisced while cleaning the kitchen and putting leftovers away. Once finished, Sonya declared, "I call first dibs on the shower," she said looking at Haley.

"Go for it," she replied.

Haley sat down at the table and Molly continued fooling with things in her kitchen. Haley watched her aunt, noticing for the umpteenth time how much she resembled her sister, Haley's mother. They were both beautiful women. Had her mother not had a drug problem, she would have aged well. "Whatcha thinking about?" Molly asked noticing Haley staring at her as she moved about the kitchen.

"You caught me. I was thinking about how pretty you are and how young you still look," she admitted.

"Well, you share some of those genes too. In fact, someone must have given you a double dose because you're as gorgeous as a movie star."

Haley blushed. "Lot of good it does when the only man I want is dead or missing."

Molly placed her dish towel beside the sink and made her way over to the table. "Sugar, you've got to keep your hope alive constantly on this. Of course, I don't want it to be in vain, but what else have you got right now? Let's think of it this way. Jack Foster did not just vanish without a trace. He is somewhere, hopefully alive. And if he isn't, don't you still want to bring his body home?"

Haley broke into tears, "Yes, yes I do."

"Okay, then let's hope we get that lively version of Jack that you know so well back in one piece. Agreed?"

"Agreed," Haley said with tearful conviction.

A part of her wanted to go back to the safety she felt living here after her mom passed. It had been at the height of summer when she found herself a sudden new member of the clan here. Mike and Molly had welcomed her as if she were their natural born child. Sonya, an only child who had spent a lot of hours alone, was anxious for Haley to serve as her surrogate big sister. The two of them would walk the land and gather ripe peaches from the grove. Those peaches were so delicious and fresh. Their juicy taste could not compare with store bought. Yes, there was a part of her that longed to be sheltered away from things. But she also knew that no matter what, she had to help find Jack and perhaps, the devil behind this fiasco. Haley's phone vibrated. It was a message from Jason:

Sarah said you and Sonya are in Valdosta and will be back Sunday. Any chance you can meet with us Sunday evening for dinner?

Sure, let me know where and I'll be there. Should I bring Sonya — she's staying with me for awhile?

Yes, bring her. I'll let you know where we will meet.

"Something important?" Molly asked.

"Could be. Jason wants us to meet for dinner Sunday night. It's starting to become a weekly thing."

"I'm praying for all of you," Molly said.

"Thank you …. I've been having quite a few moments in prayer myself."

Chapter 53 ~ Morning at the Farm

Sunday, December 15, 2019

The light from the sun cast a gold hue upon Haley's old room. She woke, briefly questioning where she was. She and Sonya stayed up late, almost slumber party style. They talked for a couple of hours about life, death, and what lies beyond. Inspiration for the discussion spawned from Sonya's tapestry images of space covering her walls and ceiling. Both agreed there was a great creative God force behind all of this celestial and earthly majesty. The conversation was deep for slumber party talk, but Sonya was reaching some decision points in her life. Haley was trying to navigate each day, living on hope.

The smell of bacon drifted up the stairs and Haley stretched her limbs, reflecting on the last time she had fried some for Jack. He loved bacon and the smell of it. She didn't like how the odor could linger in the house, but if it made him happy who would care. Haley plopped out of the bed and made her way quickly to the bathroom. She had to pee like a race horse.

As she reentered her old, familiar room, she lie down again gazing at the ceiling. She wondered about her aunt Molly who was selfless to a fault, always wanting to please her family. *As soon as things are settled, I want to do something nice for her, a pampering experience of some kind.* She could hear Sonya in the bathroom now and decided to just lie there until she was finished. Then, she would brush her teeth and try to make herself presentable.

Sonya was taking quite awhile. Finally, Haley heard her open the bathroom door and emerge. She rushed to greet her. "I enjoyed our talk last night, even if it was more on the serious side of life."

"Me too. I think we both needed it."

Haley looked at the duffle bag in Sonya's hands.

"I need more toiletries than I had available at your house. I've got them all packed."

"Great, take your time and go through your stuff. I want you to feel at home there and comfortable."

"First, I'm going to check out that breakfast I've been smelling," Sonya said.

Haley laughed, "Yeah, let me brush my teeth and hair and I'm right behind you."

Mike and Molly were churchgoers and that is where one would normally find them on Sunday mornings. But with company, they were happy to host a big country breakfast. As Haley entered, Mike was frying the last of the bacon. She looked at the stack of perfect waffles Molly had made.

"You guys don't eat like this every day, do you?"

"Lord no, we would die from the fat and cholesterol. We usually have some fruit and oatmeal, sometimes scrambled eggs and toast. But today, we have our girls here and we wanted to make it special," Molly said.

Everyone pitched in, setting the table and grabbing utensils. Molly placed the waffles in the middle of the table along with homemade raspberry syrup and maple for those that were more traditional with their selections. Mike carried the platter of bacon to the table and began prancing, singing a song of how he can bring home the bacon and cook it up in a pan. Haley and Sonya giggled at his antics.

"Good to hear everyone happy," he said.

"Miss Haley, you have a lot to deal with right now. You know, laughter is God's natural medicine."

"You are so right!" Haley said.

They all sat down and Molly led them in prayer.

After breakfast, Haley walked with Uncle Mike to see how the grove of peach trees had grown in size while Sonya finished packing and saying goodbye for now to her home. She packed her car and spent a few alone minutes with her mom.

Later, as the girls drove away in their respective vehicles, Mike and Molly realized how much they were going to miss the two of them. Molly teared up as they walked back into the house. Mike assured her they were less than three hours away.

"You know, we're going to need to be more social, Mike. Perhaps I could invite some women over once a month for Bunco, knitting or something."

"You're right. I need to reach out and plan something as well. I'm just not sure what."

"Well, you're pretty good at woodworking and have all the equipment for it in the barn. What if you taught a class on it over the winter? We could put the portable heater in the barn so it would be more comfortable."

"Yes, and so the carpenter's glue could dry," Mike laughed.

"We didn't talk to them about Christmas which is only ten days away now," Molly said, looking worried.

"I know."

"I felt awkward mentioning it with Haley focused on finding Jack. Lord, please bring that man back to her swiftly," she said.

"Amen," Mike said.

Chapter 54 ~ Dinner with Lucky

Sonya and Haley rode together to the restaurant to meet Jack's family. Arriving about five minutes late, everyone was there waiting but this time in a private room.

"Sorry to be late!" Haley said without making any excuses.

"No problem, honey," said Sharon. "Come give me a big hug," she said, stretching out her arms. "You too Sonya."

She hugged each of them and they sat down. Haley noticed everyone seemed to be in an upbeat mood.

The food server came into the room and took a drink order from Haley and Sonya. Once the door to the room was closed, Jason, spoke up first. "We got a ping on Jack's satellite phone."

Haley's eyes enlarged. "Really?"

Papa Foster spoke next, "Yes, but that's not all. Our team on the ground said there are rumors a man was picked up not too far from the crash site. But they are not sure what happened to him after that."

"Picked up by whom?" Haley inquired.

"We don't know. Could be someone nefarious who wanted to make sure there were no survivors. Or, my hope it was locals native to the area. If so, they could have led Jack to medical help or assisted him in some way."

"Jack's whereabouts are still a mystery, but at least we're getting some information. I feel hopeful with this news," Haley said.

"Me too," Sarah spoke up.

"It's good news, nothing bad so far," Sharon chimed in.

Jason spoke next, "I'm leaving for Brazil in the morning to join the team and hopefully find my brother." Sarah squeezed Jason's hand.

"That's great, Jason. With both of you being twins, perhaps you will sense where he is and have more luck than the team is having. Although, I must say I feel very encouraged by this news. Can you tell me more about the satellite phone detection?" Haley asked.

"The satellite phone may be dead now because they are not picking up anything. Or, it could be in a dense canopy area of the rain forest which could make for a weak, intermittent signal. But a few days ago they received a ping on it and that at least gets us to a location. The team may be there now."

"We have one more person coming to dinner -- Lucky Adams. She could not be here at the top, but will be joining us," Papa Joe said.

A server arrived to refill drinks. After they finished topping off the drinks, Joe Foster continued, "On the spy front, we were in the clear. We decided to go ahead and order the recommended detector just in case something happens in the near future with our vehicles being tracked. I'm going to guess they just haven't reached out this far to us, only you and Jack. But as I said, that could change."

The hostess opened the door to the private dining room and escorted Lucky inside. She was all smiles and dressed in business-like attire. A navy blue blazer with matching trousers and a crisp red shirt that set off her skin tone. Lucky was very tall, trim and carried an air about her that made one think she could handle herself anywhere.

Haley rose to introduce her. "Everyone, this is the lady I've been talking about, Megan, also known as Lucky Adams."

The group said hello. Lucky stood and nodded her head once and then looked questioningly at Haley for direction.

Haley took the cue. "Looks like we saved you a seat at the head of the table." Haley motioned for her to select that place and Jason rose and pulled out her chair for her.

"Oh, my. Now I can see that you're a southern gentleman. Who is your mama? I want to commend her," Lucky said, with a twinkle in her green eyes.

Jason chuckled and Sharon proudly waved her hand and said, "That would be me."

"So many men have not been raised with manners. Thank you," she said, looking first at Sharon and then Jason. "I suppose you're spoken for by that beautiful redhead sitting next to you?" she questioned.

"Yes ma'am. This is my wife, Sarah."

"I am very pleased to meet you. So you are Jack Foster's brother and sister-in-law, right?"

"Yes, I am his twin brother."

"Identical twins?"

"Yes."

The familiar food server arrived and took Lucky's drink order. She hesitated, then asked the group, "Would you like to go ahead and order. I'm just having a salad with a bit of chicken added to it, so I know what I want. I didn't mean to keep you waiting so long."

Haley looked down the table and the group signaled they were ready. "I think we're ready to order," she said to the server. They placed their food orders and the server again left the room.

In a good way, Lucky had an ability to melt everyone at the table. She conversed with each, asking them questions as if she were meeting them at a garden party. In reality, she was filing this information in that head of hers. By the time she was finished, each felt they were going to be long time buddies with her.

Haley noticed her technique and realized it wasn't really to deceive anyone, but to truly get a good handle on the family dynamics and the situation overall. Lucky was sharp and a smooth operator. Haley was thankful the investigative reporter was going to be on their side.

After all the introductions and information she gathered, including practically what color of socks they wore, she asked the question that set things in motion going forward with the investigation in the United States. "Tell me, who at Chadwell Pharma could or would directly benefit from Jack and his team being gone?"

Everyone looked around for who would speak first. Ultimately, they looked to Haley. "It's simple. Evan Mitchell is the only person I know of that coveted Jack's position at Chadwell. Jack was distraught and angry a few times at some of the shenanigans Evan tried to pull."

"What is Evan's position, do you know?"

"Now, he has taken over Jack's role and title. But prior to that, he was an assistant developmental scientist."

"Do you know how much someone in that type of assistant position would make annually?"

"I don't, but I'm going to guess around $100,000 per year," Haley answered.

"Has anyone seen or spoke to him since this happened?"

They all shook their heads affirmatively. "Oh yes, he's been around," Haley answered. "He was at the funeral home and the first to notify me that something went wrong with the plane."

Sarah spoke up next, "Lucky, I've met him and I thought he came off a little aloof and strange. It's hard to put into words, but I did not get a good feeling from him."

"Well, I think your judgment about people is something we should take seriously. Intuition about others is often very reliable until we have facts. What do you think of him, Haley?"

She tilted her head back and thought for a moment. "When I think of him, he seems opportunistic. He's definitely been flirtatious with me over the time we've known him."

"Is he someone that you and Jack had a close friendship with?"

"Oh no, not at all. We did see him socially through some of the events Chadwell put together."

"I see," Lucky answered.

"Well, I wondered where I should start this corporate investigation and it sounds like it is with Evan Mitchell. I'll need to find out everything I can on him and quickly."

She looked at Haley directly, "Can you think of anyone else at Chadwell that would want Jack out of the way?"

Haley hesitated and then spoke, "No, not at all. Jack's work was valuable to the company, He helped them with several successful drugs. If what he was doing was good for Chadwell, why would they want him gone?"

"I'll start with this Evan character. Anything any of you remember or know about him could be helpful. My partner that I often use, Ric, is in the hiring process at Chadwell. It's a low level position, but it gets him into the company. Hopefully, he will be starting there soon."

Two food servers arrived with trays of entrees for the dinner guests. Once everyone had their entree, Haley nudged Sonya sitting next to her. "You've been really quiet."

"I'm not sure what to say or add to the situation."

Haley briefly told Lucky and her family more details from her surveillance inspection.

Lucky commented, "I'm glad I passed that information on to you. Corporate espionage is on the rise. I'm also glad you guys have ordered the electronic bug finder. I practically carry one of those in my purse now."

Everyone at the table laughed.

"Truly, I'm always finding some little way someone is trying to find out what I know and what I'm doing."

Joe and Sharon Foster proceeded to relay the information they had about the sat phone ping to Lucky. Jason relayed that he was leaving the next day for Brazil.

Haley asked everyone at the table, "With Jason in Brazil, Lucky and Ric working behind the scenes, how should we get together if we have more to share?"

Joe Foster spoke up, "These Sunday dinners are typical for many families to engage in. Lucky, one of us will send you a text of a restaurant and time before next Sunday. For now, this is the only way I can think of that is not too risky for us to get together and talk."

Lucky spoke up, "It's actually almost perfect. As you said, it would be normal for families to meet on Sundays."

Everyone finished their meal and Haley insisted on picking up the check this time. Papa Foster would not allow it and gave the waiter his card before the bill was delivered to the table.

"Well, thank you, Papa. But, I can't have you paying for everything. I feel like I should share in this."

"No worries, Haley, I want to take care of it."

She smiled and felt somewhat child-like when he did this, but accepted his wishes. "I have two more things I want to bring up before we leave," Haley said, and she looked at Jason.

"I want to thank you, Jason, for making this trip. I, along with the others, will be praying that you're able to find Jack."

Jason nodded his head. "I'm gonna try my best, Haley."

"I know you will."

The next thing I wanted to talk about is my best friend, Jessie and her husband, Alex, next door. Jessie called once and messaged me a couple of times. I have not said anything to her about our private information we are sharing. But, I feel like I am shutting her out because there is so much I cannot say. How does everyone feel about me talking to her about what's going on?

Postures stiffened around the table and Lucky picked up on it right away. "May I make a suggestion?" she asked.

"Yes, please."

"Tell your friend the truth … what you just told us. Tell her you have been avoiding her because you are involved in an investigation where things have to be kept super secret and you're afraid you may give something away. Be sure and let her know it is not because you don't trust her. You do. However, once she has information, that could be stressful on her."

"That's a good idea, Lucky. That is what I will do."

Chapter 55 ~ Tracking Evan

Monday, December 16, 2019

It wasn't hard for Lucky to locate where Evan Mitchell lived and what vehicle he drove. She knew he was thirty-six years old and a Scorpio. *Hmmm*, she said to herself.

Lucky had three modes of transportation and she switched them often. Her non-descript white cargo van was perfect when she needed to take on a disguise. She utilized a variety of magnetic signs that she could simply place on the side panels of the vehicle. She had posed as a house painter, a wallpaper hanger, and a delivery person.

She also drove a silver Mazda 280Z mostly for pleasure, but work too. It just depended upon the situation.

Her most covert ride, even though it was a louder one, was her Kawasaki Ninja ZX – 10R. Once she donned her helmet, a tight leather jacket and pants, no one would really know who she was zooming in and out or making a quick pass by. While she had purchased all of her various means of transportation used, she paid cash and had them licensed to a shell corporation making it a tad more difficult to know who they belonged to.

Lucky drove her Mazda to the condominium complex where Evan Mitchell lived. Thankfully, it was not gated with security, so that was one less thing to hassle with today. She drove to the common building in the center of the complex where the swimming pool was located. It was closed this time of year, but the building adjoining it looked busy with people coming and going. She decided to go inside and check things out.

The entrance had a secure door with an area to scan a card in order to enter the building. Damn! Just then, the door opened with someone coming out. "Forget your key card?" a lady in workout gear asked, holding the door for her. "Yes, thank you," Lucky said, sliding past the door and into the building.

The gym inside was busy with people on machines and televisions broadcasting sports channels. She gazed into the equipment room, not knowing if Evan Mitchell was there or not. While she had seen a couple of small photos of him online, she had not been able to find significant visuals on any social media. She kicked herself for not checking Linked-in. That's probably where he would reveal his face a little easier.

Behind her, someone called out, "Are you here for the instructor position?"

Lucky turned and a man in gym shorts and t-shirt stood with a clipboard and towel around his neck."

"Me?" she asked, as if he could be speaking to anyone else.

"Yes, are you here for the yoga/Pilates instructor job?"

"Yes, yes I am."

He was professional, yet curt and handed the clipboard to her. "Please fill out this application and bring it to me when you are finished. I will be in the weight training area over there," he pointed.

Lucky took the clipboard with pen attached and sat down at a bench style seat in the reception area. By now, these little — and sometimes big — lies came natural to her. When an opportunity arose for her to be in a better position to gather information, she was going to take it.

Lucky sometimes wondered how fortunate she could be. She simply followed the opportunities that presented. Today, she was almost giggling in her mind about the good fortune here. *Yes, she knew yoga and Pilates and practiced them. Could she teach it? Well, that was another question.*

Quickly, she began to go over things in her mind … like her name. Just as she kept three vehicles for transport, she had fake credentials for undercover information gathering. Lucky should have been an official spy, but if she were that would mean she would have to answer to the big guys. Being an unofficial spy meant she could target the big guys if the situated warranted it. She finished the paperwork noticing it asked for a form of identification such as a driver's license at the end. She shuffled through her purse and pulled out the driver's license for Chelsea Roberts.

She stood, spotting the gentleman speaking to a gym member who was lying down getting ready to press who knew how many pounds. She noticed his chest first, and then his legs. He was an Adonis with golden curls adorning his head, a strong jaw and dimpled chin. *Now, I know I want to work here.*

Trent saw her approaching and told the man who looked like a Greek god that he would be back. He took the clipboard and license from her and said, "Follow me."

They walked back toward the entrance of the facility and he opened a door. "Right this way," he said, leading her down a hall with individual offices. "My name is Trent by the way. You will be interviewing with Linda Abrams."

Trent dropped her off in front of Linda's door after he knocked on it. "Hi Linda, your interview is here for the instructor position."

"What was your name?" he inquired.

"Chelsea Roberts," Lucky said.

Linda stood from behind her desk. She was older than Lucky by a couple of decades but looked fit and competent to be involved in operating a gym. "Nice to meet you Chelsea," she said, holding out her hand. They shook.

"Please, have a seat and tell me about yourself."

Lucky (Chelsea) smiled big and thought, *here we go*. Along with fake identities came fake backgrounds. Could she remember everything that had been assigned to her Chelsea identity, including fake social media profiles?

The interview seemed to be going fine and Linda asked if she had any questions for her.

"Yes, I was wondering what time the classes will be that you need me to teach?"

"Oh, I should have told you that up front. I think it was on the job posting, but perhaps not. This will be an evening and weekend class schedule. Does that work for you?"

"Yes, it works perfect for me."

"Most of the classes have women attendees, however, more men have been signing up for yoga."

Lucky (Chelsea) nodded her head up and down with an expression that indicated she knew this was common.

"I suppose my next question is, when will you make a decision?"

"Well, if your background check can be cleared in a couple of days, you could start immediately, if you're available."

"My evenings and weekends are clear right now, so I can start right away," Lucky said.

"Perfect," Linda said, rising from her chair. Lucky took the cue that the interview was over and she stood as well.

She shook Linda's hand and said, "I look forward to this," as if she already had the position. *Never hurts to act and speak confidently.*

If Lucky was hired, she would now have an actual excuse for being in the area and finding a way to bump into Evan Mitchell. In the meantime, she decided to go home and start planning out itineraries for classes she was likely to teach. *Perhaps that bench pressing Adonis also likes yoga.*

Chapter 56 ~ Assuring Jessie

Tuesday, December 17, 2019

Awakening earlier than usual, Haley grabbed her robe and made her way to the kitchen for coffee. She sat, sipping slowly, while she tried to remember. She had seen Jack in her dream, but what setting was he in? What exactly was happening in the dream? She wished she could remember the details.

She thought about how fleeting moments together can be when looked back upon. If she had known she would lose Jack this early in their marriage, she would have spent each day of their life together differently. She crossed her arms over her midriff and bent over the bathroom vanity sobbing. *God, please help me. I'm literally living on a prayer that Jack is alive and will be with me again.*

Haley felt so alone without him, no matter who was around. With Jack gone, there was a permanency in the air that she feared. *I can't give up hope on him being alive,* she thought.

She messaged her therapist, Laura, and let her know she was fine, but would not make it today for her appointment. She also canceled the group therapy set for later in the afternoon. Feeling somewhat restricted in what she could be transparent about concerning Jack would be a problem at therapy. *Best to just take a breather, maybe for a few weeks.* She'd think about that.

Haley emerged from the shower and dressed warmly for the day. It would not get above the high forties but she would venture out. She had questions and hoped Gesta had some answers. Inside, Haley knew she was vulnerable to this woman. She could be a complete charlatan and not know a thing about Jack. It sort of irked her that she had agreed to the reading. But then again, what if she did know something that could help her? She was beginning to understand that this is what happens to people in desperate situations — like those with missing children. Now, she had a missing husband. Perhaps this woman was not the right psychic to go to. Maybe she needed to find a tried and true psychic detective like she had seen stories of on television. But were they real?

Once her hair was blown out, she placed her finishing make up touches with her lipstick and made her way to the living area. Sonya was in the kitchen looking over a recipe book.

"Hey, I'm thinking of making Chicken Parmesan for dinner. I think we have all the ingredients."

"Sounds wonderful. I'm going out for a few errands today. Text me if you need anything and I'll stop and get it. I should be back by 4pm. First, I'll be stopping next door at Jessie and Alex's to see if they are home so I can explain why it seems like I've been ghosting them."

Haley declined to tell Sonya about her appointment with Gesta. She wasn't sure why, except that some people definitely would not think it was very Christian. Haley wasn't sure how she felt about it. She admitted she was desperate for information, leads, or anything that could solve the dark riddle her life had become. She glanced at the Mylar bags with the devices on the kitchen counter.

She picked up the one marked in black marker Honda Tracker. "I think I'll leave this here for now. Let them think I'm still here at home."

Sonya smiled at her and tilted her head, raising her eyebrow, "Outsmart them at their own game, Haley."

Haley smiled back and exited through the garage. "Later, gator."

"After while, crocodile."

Haley backed out of the garage and hit the opener to close the door. She pulled in front of Alex and Jessie's and went up to the door. Alex answered almost immediately as he probably heard her pull up out front. "What brings you over to visit?" he asked, smiling. Alex always had the most engaging smile and his eyes twinkled each time he showed his pearly whites. It was as if he already knew the answer to any question he asked.

"Oh, I just need to speak to both of you, in person. I'm so glad you're here and not at work."

"Going in a little late today, if at all. I had a bad stomach ache last night and didn't sleep well."

"I'm really sorry. Anything a nurse like me could do?"

"No, but if it gets any worse, I'll have to see someone. Come in, we're just sitting around the kitchen table."

Haley followed the familiar path to the kitchen and found Jessie there in her robe. Her makeup was done and she had hot air rollers in her hair.

"Ahh, now I know the secret to your gorgeous wavy curls. All this time, I thought it was natural," she teased.

"Haley, this morning I decided the only thing happening to me that is natural is aging. I've got to get on this anti-aging regimen I've read so much about."

"Oh, you're being way too hard on yourself this morning. You are still so young and always beautiful."

"I need you to come and tell me that each day, honey."

Haley laughed, "And vice versa, huh?"

They elbow bumped.

"I stopped by unannounced for another reason. You two know that I consider you our closest friends, almost family really. I know I have been vague this week and a bit unapproachable and I want to let you know why. Since we have determined that we are assuming Jack could be alive and just missing, it has become super important to keep information that I'm finding out here and there very private. You both know how distraught I've been and I was worried each time I spoke to you Jessie that I might inadvertently say something I shouldn't. Not that I don't trust you … I do. But that's a huge responsibility to put upon you to keep investigative secrets. Does that make sense? Am I explaining what I'm trying to?"

"Yes, and I am glad you shared that with us, Haley. I thought perhaps you were miffed at me about something."

"No, not at all. Lord, no! Here is what I can share. My house and car were bugged. Not sure by whom. But I feel better knowing and getting the devices removed. Right now, I am communicating primarily by text so you two have my number."

Alex's eyes were huge, "Bugged? What the hell?"

"Yes, there were two devices inside the house plus my vehicle and Jack's were being GPS tracked."

"Jeez!" Jessie stated, with amazement.

"Listen, I'm going into town. I've got some errands to run. Are you working today, Jess?"

"Yes ma'am. I'm taking a couple to see four different prospective homes. I'm really hopeful they will choose something today and write an offer. We've looked at a lot of properties and they have lost two already. Maybe today will be the day they find one they love enough and stop hesitating. It's a hot market with these low rates."

"Well, good luck with the house hunt. Alex, I hope you get to feeling much better soon. Take it easy on that stomach."

"Will do nurse Haley. We'll see you, well, whenever."

Haley waved goodbye and made her way to her Honda, headed for downtown Alpharetta.

Chapter 57 ~ The Reading

Although the sun made a grand appearance, the air in early December was chilly. She decided to explore more shops in the quaint business district. There was time to kill between now and her appointment with Gesta. Despite what was going on, Christmas was still going to occur. She did not feel ready for it. Haley drove slowly through downtown Alpharetta, looking for new places to check out. As she slowly moved down Milton Avenue toward Main, a shop on the right with some of its wares out front caught her eye — Sis' n Moon. It was a cute name for the establishment and probably had a story behind it. She was able to grab a parking spot near the shop. Today, she felt it was unlikely anyone would be stalking or tailing her activities. But she would keep an eye out. It would probably be like that the rest of her life, a little paranoid and on guard.

Sis' n Moon looked playful and a bit eclectic. She entered under the black canopy that covered the exterior door of the brick building. A light acoustic guitar instrumental sounded from the shop's speakers. She was greeted by a young woman at the counter who appeared to be going over some paperwork. "Hello, how are you?"

"Doing well. This is my first time here. Just checking out the store."

"Great, let me know if you have any questions or if I can assist you."

"Will do."

Inside, she found beautifully displayed wares from pop art, fine art pieces, jewelry, clothing, and household items. Items ranged in style from the recent farmhouse trend to funky or formal. Many were traditional with a new, up cycled flair. Haley thought of how Sonya would love this place. She saw a sign about art parties and classes. She noticed a brochure detailing the costs and, while it seemed reasonable, it was perhaps more than she wanted to spend for a Christmas gift to Sonya. She made a mental note to tell her of the unique shop and the art classes when she returned home.

There were many items Haley found appealing, not only for gifts but herself as well. She settled on a stylish fedora for her sister-in-law, Sarah. Brown wool, it would be perfect for the winter months and everyone knew Sarah was a hat person. She would look gorgeous with her copper curls cascading from it. The girl at the counter packaged the hat in a box for her — not a well structured hat box, but one that would suffice for now. Haley paid and thanked her making a mental note that she needed to get sizes and a wish list from Sarah for her niece and nephew. And, then there was Jason. Jack always knew the perfect gift for his twin brother and his father as well. She walked back to her car suddenly feeling very alone about Christmas.

Haley drove, crossing Main and turning right on Market. She spotted Spirited Boutique, another shop geared toward women. This one she was familiar with as she had visited another location a couple of years ago. *I suppose I am in an eclectic shopping mood today. What else could I be given that I will be seeing a psychic a short time from now?*

The combined scents of the soaps, lotions and other elixirs called to her from one side of the shop. Haley found some hand crafted herbal soaps and purchased two for Sharon Foster who she knew loved them — one in lavender sage and the other in rose petals. Her fingers slid over the wide selection of kimonos the store offered. Her hand lingered on one in an aqua blue and yellow. The colors were happy and she wanted to purchase it for herself, but ultimately decided to say no to her desires. That was a problem she had. Haley would go shopping for others and find things she wanted for herself. Noticing the time, she paid for the soaps and decided she would walk from this location around the corner on Commerce to Gesta Gems.

The familiar door chimes rang as she entered the shop. Haley observed Gesta and another lady weighing a stone.

Gesta glanced over and gestured that she would be right with her.

Haley looked to see if the earrings that Sonya did not purchase were still available. She remembered the exact area of the turquoise case where they were. Gesta joined her at the counter.

"Are those the earrings the girl that was with me did not purchase? I'm thinking those are the ones."

"I believe they are, yes."

"I would like to get those as a gift for her."

"Wonderful, do you want to just add this onto your reading charge at the end?"

"Yes, I suppose I should have asked but how much is a reading?"

"It's fifty dollars per half hour."

"Okay, well let's see what I can find out in thirty minutes?" Haley said questioningly.

"Come this way."

Gesta led Haley behind the payment counter into a hall that split into two rooms. She noticed the heavy perfumed smell emanating from the one on the right which is where the older woman led her. While the walls were painted a deep blue that made the room a little dark, there were prints of various bright flowers adorning much of the wall space. With their white frames and backgrounds, they stood out. Haley noticed a trail of smoke rising from two incense burners and Gesta saw her looking at them. "You're not allergic to scents are you?"

"No, not at all. Just taking it all in. I've never had a reading before."

"Well then, let's make this one extra special. Do you mind if I play some relaxing background music?"

"Go ahead."

She watched as Gesta used a remote to conjure sound in the room and her mind darted to stories from the past of mediums and psychics using electricity and other tools to fool their patrons. She felt skeptical, yet hopeful, that she could learn something about Jack — mostly was he really gone or not?

"Please, be comfortable," Gesta said as she motioned for Haley to sit in a chair on one side of a medium size wooden table. Gesta situated herself in the chair across from Haley and she struck a match, lighting a white candle to her left. She turned retrieving three different boxes of what appeared to be tarot cards. "I use these as a divination tool to guide us on the main concern you have. However, I also hear those in the spirit realm who have messages for us. First, I would like you to choose one of these decks for your reading. Just look at the art work and go with the one you are most drawn to."

Haley looked over the three decks finding them all unique. She chose an oracle card set with beautiful images. She felt attracted to the colors used in the deck.

Gesta took the box of cards from her and placed the other two behind her again. "I shall begin by briefly shuffling these cards while meditating. During that time, I would like for you to write down on this small piece of paper what concerns you most and what questions you have surrounding it. Then, fold the paper up several times and place it on the table."

The woman began shuffling the deck with her eyes closed and the serene music sounding in the background. Haley took the pen and small piece of paper and wrote, *I need to know where my Jack is*. She folded it several times as instructed and placed it on the table. Gesta continued shuffling. She appeared very relaxed. Haley felt a bit tense, not knowing what to expect. Gesta must have sensed this as she opened her eyes and laid the cards down in a pile in front of her.

"Next, please shuffle these cards however you want. You don't have to be fancy like you're at a casino. We just want your vibration or energy to be on the cards for the most accurate results."

Haley picked up the deck and proceeded to lightly shuffle at first watching her hands, knowing where the cards were in relation to the rest of her body. She closed her eyes and tried to take slow deep breaths, noticing it was already helping to ease tension and relax her shoulders. After she had shuffled for awhile, she opened her eyes and looked at Gesta who gestured to set them on the table.

"Now, cut the cards if you wish and I will begin laying them out in your reading spread."

Haley picked up the deck and let a portion of the cards fall where it felt natural for them to do so."

The music switched to a new song and it seemed to intensify her feelings of relaxation and euphoria in a strange way. She watched as Gesta pulled the cards and placed them in a pattern in front of Haley. Once all the cards seemed to be in place, Gesta picked up one of them and said to Haley, "This card represents you — your feelings or concerns at this time." Gesta picked up a card that had lain across that one. "This card represents whatever helps or hinders you."

"The first card tells me you are dealing with love, whether it is loss of love or some sort of grief. The card crossing you represents the energy of the sun which is life giving, affirming, and full of hope."

Haley listened intently as she watched Gesta's soft eyes look into hers as she spoke. Gesta closed her eyes, sitting up straight, her chin slightly lifted upward and said, "Someone is here to speak with you from spirit. It's a female energy." Haley's interest was immediately engaged. "She is saying that she is sorry and that one day you will understand everything she could not share with you while alive."

"Is this my mom?" Haley whispered.

Gesta remained in her position eyes closed and quiet for a moment that seemed longer than it actually was. "I know its a female energy. Can you give me a name please? Who you are? She's showing me a tree blowing in the wind. Windy — Wendy. Was your mother's name Wendy?"

"Yes," Haley said, tears beginning to form. "Tell her I love her so much!"

"She hears you. Let's see if she has anything else to say. She says, don't ever give up. Everything is going to be fine."

A single tear rolled down Haley's cheek as she said aloud, "I won't, mom. I've never given up since you left. I love you."

"Okay, I'm losing the connection now. Let's go back to your card spread."

Haley wiped her face and looked to Gesta for guidance with the cards and their meanings.

"In your present and near future, there is a battle of sorts being played out. You are surrounded by deceit and some with bad intentions. Am I reading this correctly? Are you experiencing this?"

"Yes, it seems I am. Can you tell if my husband is alive or not?"

"What is his first name?"

"Jack."

Gesta closed her eyes again and tilted her head back sitting erect. "I'm not hearing, seeing or feeling anything with that name in the world of spirit. It's no guarantee though. Sometimes when a person is newly deceased, they will enter a tranquil time of soul healing, especially if they made an abrupt departure from earth."

Gesta looked back down at the table. "Let me go back to the cards and see if anything shows here. As we look at these final cards in the reading, I see what we call the happy family, but I also see some strife leading up to it. Do you believe your husband is alive?"

Haley was momentarily quiet with this question put to her by the psychic. "I want to believe — very much so."

"Of course, dear. Who wouldn't? I'm sorry I cannot say for certain. Spirit is not giving me any clues about it. But with the happy family card in your near future, I would say that he could be, and you will be reunited with him. Do you have children?"

"No. We want or wanted children."

"You definitely have a child around you either in spirit or coming to you soon. Any chance you could be pregnant?"

"I'm not sure. I guess there is a chance."

"I am predicting things will work out for you, but you must be diligent about overcoming these deceitful, in fact evil adversaries you have. I assume you know who that is?" she said, looking questioningly of Haley.

"Well, I'm still determining who it is exactly. But you believe I will have a family — as in husband and child?"

"That's what the potential outcome is at this moment in time."

"How soon could this happen?"

"Very soon, I would say within weeks or a few months."

Haley smiled and shook her head from side to side. "I hope you're right. Thank you!"

Haley began to gather her jacket and purse as she sensed the reading was over. Gesta placed the cards away and stood, leaving the candle burning.

Likewise, Haley stood and looked at the woman's lined face and kind eyes. "Thank you again."

"You're welcome. Oh, one more thing I'm hearing. Splurge on the art lessons — whatever that means."

Haley smiled, and accompanied her back to the store. Gesta walked over to a counter that held nothing but black stones. She picked up a shiny metallic black stone and handed it to Haley. "Please, have this for protection and keep it on you as much as you can for now."

"Thank you, Gesta. What stone is it?"

"This is hematite."

Haley placed the stone in her pants pocket and paid Gesta for the reading and Sonya's earrings. As she went out the door toward her car, she decided to go back to Sis' n Moon and purchase the art lessons as a Christmas gift for Sonya. *How in the world could Gesta know she was considering such a thing?* The other information she gave could perhaps be chalked up to wishful thinking, wanting Jack alive. But, this last piece of information gave considerable credibility to the entire reading. *Could she be pregnant? Did her mom watch over her from heaven?*

Haley had so many questions, but also felt a peaceful lightness that had not been present in her for months, if not years.

Chapter 58 ~ Faith Tested

Wednesday, December 18, 2019

Haley felt somewhat somber as she looked at the calendar. Today marked exactly two weeks since the small plane went down killing the pilot, the Chadwell team, and possibly, Jack. Christmas day was one week from now, also on a Wednesday. Unless Jason or someone else were able to locate Jack, it would be a holiday without him.

Haley walked to the mirror in the bathroom and looked closely at her eyes. *Are you delusional? If Jack were alive, you would have heard from him. You can't believe a fortune teller!*

But she wanted to believe. What else did she have left but this hope? The same was true of Jack's parents and brother. If you love someone and you're told they're dead but you have no body or even remains, how can you be so sure?

Haley knew if Jack was not found she would be set up for an even more intense grieving than the first week. Truly, life had become an emotional roller coaster since this started. Look how she had changed and was still changing. She had not even thought about going back to work. She needed to communicate with the hospital her intentions going forward. Perhaps she should go back to maintain some sort of normalcy.

Instead, it felt as if she were living in a spy novel. Tonight, she would return to the self defense class. Actually, it would be her first class where they would participate in learning techniques and moves. She looked forward to seeing Jessie and Sarah and having Sonya come along too. She was feeling every woman should learn self defense techniques in today's world.

Sonya had grown up fairly isolated in Valdosta. This was all so new for her. While Haley truly loved Mike and Molly's mini farm, the area outside of the larger cities did not provide quite the view of the world that getting out in a major metro area like Atlanta had done for her.

When Haley left the farm and came to Atlanta for college, her view of things opened considerably. When you're young, you believe you're invincible and nothing can stop or hurt you. I suppose a part of you knows something could, but it was like she had ignored that and forged a life for herself that included friends from university and later those she chummed with at work. Sonya could benefit from some new friends. At the very least, the art class might open some possibilities for meeting like-minded people.

Haley dressed and made her way to the kitchen where she found Sonya watching videos on self-defense moves.

"Good morning! Is there anything you don't do well, Sonya?"

She looked up from her laptop. "What are you talking about?"

"Your chicken parmesan last night. That was out of this world good."

"I'm really glad you liked it. Hey, I just followed the recipe I found on Pinterest."

"Well, it was a winner. I see you're getting psyched up for our class tonight."

Sonya giggled. "Yep, I'm gonna learn how to kick some ass if anyone fools with me or you."

"Why don't we leave early this afternoon and perhaps grab lunch a couple of hours before the class? The last time we barely made it in time with the traffic in Atlanta at drive time. What do you think?"

"Sounds fun and yes, that traffic was a nightmare. I'm not used to that at all. Made me super nervous."

"It was like that for me when I first moved to Atlanta. While most everything I did was centered around the university campus, I still was subjected to traffic at times. You get used to it and figure out ways to try and avoid it. Before long, you'll be a pro at navigating Atlanta."

"I haven't seen Jessie since we attended the introductory class last week. I really miss her, but I have to say that we have been busy each day."

Sonya nodded in agreement. "Did you talk with her yet about why you had sort of avoided her?"

"Yes, and it went well. I'm glad I did it in person. Both she and Alex really seemed to understand."

"Mind if I invite her to ride with us today?"

"No, not at all."

Haley sent a message to Jessie:

Sonya and I are leaving early for the class — catch some lunch in Atlanta first and show her around a bit. It's just a way to avoid the traffic like we ran into last week. We would love for you to join us.

Good idea. I would love to but I am on standby if my buyers get a counter-offer from the sellers. I'm just going to have to wing it with traffic this evening.

As Haley and Sarah hung out at home, they realized this is the first time they could take a few moments and really relax. Both of them, especially Haley, had been nothing but busy since Jack left for Brazil.

"I realized this morning that Christmas is only a week from today. Sarah was planning on hosting, but with Jason gone, it might be a bit much for her with the children. I know with your help we could plan a nice dinner and gift exchange here if she wanted to relent and let us do it this year. What do you think, Sonya?"

"I'd love it if we had it here. I'm up for the Christmas dinner challenge."

Haley messaged Sarah.

Hey Sarah, thinking about Christmas day. Do you still want to do it? I know it might be harder without Jason there to help. Sonya and I would be happy to host here if you want. It's your decision .... Let me know at class tonight.

Sarah messaged immediately.

Are you reading my mind Haley? Yes, I would love to dump Christmas festivities on you but ONLY if you feel up for it. Could be an emotional time.

I think I will be fine. It helps to stay busy.

Okay, then it's all yours, hon. Thank you so much. Now I only have to play Santa on Christmas Eve and have some yummy breakfast planned for the next morning.

I want pictures ... and video of that!

"Sonya, we have a whole new gathering to put together. Call your mom and dad and see if they want to come up here Christmas eve, spend the night and Christmas day with all of us."

"Good idea. I don't know if they will, but I'll call now."

Haley had to make a decision about work. One thing was sure. She was not going to go back before Christmas. She would check in with the human resources department and see if she could take another week or two off and when she did go back, work the minimum hours to have full benefits including medical insurance. Without Jack and his position at Chadwell, she could not rely on anything financially right now except herself and what they had saved together.

Sonya emerged and was skipping around like a young fragile fairy. Haley looked at her with a quizzical expression.

"They said they will come for Christmas."

"You must really miss them."

"It's not that so much. I have never not been with them at Christmas and it actually felt really good to invite them to spend the holiday with us."

"That's great. I'm glad they are coming. We'll have the extra bedroom ready for them."

"Whoa, we have a lot to plan, Haley."

"Let's start making a list on our phones that we can share and head out soon for lunch in Atlanta."

Haley drove toward the interstate and headed south to Atlanta and Sonya watched her. "I love your car, by the way. Don't know if I mentioned it before."

"Well thank you. I love it too. So far in life, I've only driven a Honda … except for rare occasions driving Jack's jeep."

"That's right. Your first car you bought was a silver Honda Civic."

"I loved that car so much. To me, it represented a freedom I had never experienced before. Without having saved the money at my job, plus the loan your parents gave me, I would never have had it. Once I graduated from Georgia State and was working steadily as a nurse, I took out a loan and bought this one. Getting that degree really changed my financial world."

"I need to figure out something. I don't know what's wrong with me, just unexcited about going to classes I suppose."

"I would say it means you don't love what you're learning or have the potential to study. You are a very creative individual and there is certainly an excitement you seem to have about projects you take on," Haley offered.

"Yes, but that's the real world day to day stuff. At school, it's more subjective," Sonya said.

"True, I know what you mean. It was like me practicing on mechanized dummies in nursing school before they let me around real people, right?"

Sonya laughed, "Oh the visual image I have in my mind just now."

"Hey now, don't go there," Haley said, laughing. "Let's get off at this exit. I'll take you on a drive around my old alma mater. It's a huge campus with suburban offshoots as well."

Haley took the Decatur Street exit and turned on Piedmont Avenue. She slowed the vehicle. "This is the health care education area but it also includes real clinics and hospitals in service to the community," Haley pointed to the left. "And that is the Byrdine F. Lewis School of Nursing where I attended. Of course, this campus is huge so I also had classes at other locations and a few online."

She picked up speed on Piedmont and made a loop around most of the huge downtown campus area.

"It's funny, when I see the campus it makes me want to enroll. But, I'm just afraid I'll regret it six weeks into the first semester," Sonya said.

"With the high cost of tuition, I would wait until you feel certain. College can be really challenging, but it will help boost your income long term. What sounds good to eat?" Haley asked.

"I'm thinking of something light for lunch but with protein since I will be slamming bodies to the ground in a few hours."

Haley cracked up laughing. "Okay, keto lunch somewhere close by."

Haley made a sudden lane change and turn. We're headed over to Peachtree Street to a Korean restaurant I think you will like called Blossom Tree.

Although the restaurant was small, the food was mighty in selection and taste.

"You must secretly be a foodie, Haley. You seem to know where to find the good stuff. How do you stay so trim?"

"Luck, I suppose. I do like to eat and often what is not great for me. This was pretty light in calories, don't you agree?"

"Yes, but your favorite stop in Alpharetta wasn't."

Haley chuckled, "Agreed. C'mon, let's go down the road a bit. I want to show you something … a different type of college. It's actually toward the Buckhead area where our class is."

Haley pointed to the front of the large campus building visible from the highway. Sonya saw it immediately.

"Oh wow!" she said staring and sitting more upright. "I've heard of that college but I thought it was in Savannah."

"It is, but they also have one in Atlanta. Want to check it out?"

"Sure, let's do that."

While not sprawling for blocks like Georgia State, the Savannah College of Art & Design was beautiful and large enough for those pursuing creative work. Sonya joined Haley as they walked the lushly landscaped grounds and made their way toward Ruskin Hall. Inside, they found the college's welcome center with leveled off logs for seats in front of computer terminals on one side of the room. The place somewhat resembled a playground for adults. Sonya felt instantly comfortable and like she fit in with students who passed her by. Haley could tell that Sonya would really love going to this school, but it was very costly, more than her parents or Haley could help her with. Still, it seemed to begin to light some desire within Sonya to move toward utilizing her talents and capitalizing upon them.

Chapter 59 ~ Lucky Spies

Lucky received a call from Trent, saying her background check was clear and asking when she could begin teaching the classes at the gym. Enthusiastically, she told him evenings and weekends were clear and she could begin right away. She dropped by the condominium's facility and worked with the director, Linda Abrams, on creating a schedule and notices to the residents about the newly available classes she would be facilitating. Lucky almost slipped up with her identity. She had to remember she was now Chelsea Roberts.

During her visit to the condominium recreation center, she deliberately parked near Evan Mitchell's unit. It wasn't where she was supposed to park, but an investigative reporter didn't get anywhere if not willing to break a few rules, especially the small, inconsequential ones. Evan wasn't home, but she knew this increased the chance she might get sight of him if he arrived. Perhaps this would put her in a position to strike up a conversation. But on this date, she didn't see him at all.

Lucky needed to get a tracer on his vehicle so she knew more about him. Two could play that game. She would return this evening, bringing her favorite yoga mat and blocks for the class. Hopefully, she would spot his Porsche and be able to get a device placed securely on it.

As planned, Lucky arrived at 6:30 pm to, hopefully, put her scheme into motion. She spotted Evan's slick vehicle and parked a few spots down from it. This was risky as residents would be coming home at this hour and she may be in someone's spot. The device had a full charge on it and she carried a large tote bag overflowing with items that could easily spill out. Walking past the Porsche, she purposely dropped several items and had to get down on the ground to collect all of them. In case anyone was watching, this gave her an excuse to look under the car like she had lost something there.

She held the small magnetic device in her hand and it click to the underside of the vehicle easily. The question was, would it stay in place? She quickly acted like she had retrieved something and placed the items in her bag. Walking around the complex building where Evan resided, she was now looking at the condominium workout center. She quickly made her way into the building with the new key card she had been assigned earlier in the day. Making a left, she loved that her classroom had a glass wall overlooking the reception area. This way, she could easily see who was coming and going. She turned on the lights in the room and scoped out how many students she could comfortably fit into a class. She left her mat and blocks and made her way back to her car, leaving the area.

As Lucky drove away, she cranked on some heavy metal and gave a fist punch in the air. "You did it!" she said aloud. Now, her next task was to collect information on where Evan Mitchell goes.

Chapter 60 ~ The Call

Christmas Eve always had a special feeling to it. But this holiday was one they would remember as the most outstanding in their memories. When the boys were young and at home, both he and Sharon would have been busy preparing for Christmas morning. Now, as grandparents, the pace was slower and less hectic. Sometimes, the quiet was not so welcome against the sounds of laughter and sometimes fighting they had heard between the twin boys.

On this evening, Sharon busied herself with the two dishes she was making to bring to Haley's tomorrow. Joe Foster was making out cards with money for the kids at the kitchen table. The home telephone rang and it was from an unknown number. "Probably another scam artist or someone wanting to sell us something," Sharon said. Joe agreed with her, but decided to answer the call, anyway.

"Hello," he said with a gruff demeanor.

"Dad," he heard on the other line.

"Jack?" he said, but not sure. "Jack, is this you?"

"Dad, it's me, Jack. I'm in Brazil."

"Where in Brazil, son? We've been trying to find you. Tell me exactly."

"I'm at a small resort. Dad, I've lost everything. I have no money, passport, nothing. I told the manager my family would pay for me to stay the night here. I need a place to stay."

"Of course, yes, of course."

Sharon was crying. She touched Joe's arm. "Put him on speakerphone, Joe."

"Jack, your mother wants me to put the phone on speaker. If we were to be disconnected, how can I get a hold of you?"

"I'm not sure, other than to call the hotel here. I can let you speak with the manager for details."

"Yes, put him on."

Joe hand signaled for Sharon to be patient and wait.

"Hello, this is André Silva. I am the manager at Pousada Penhasco. Can you please verify this is your son, sir?"

"Yes, it sounds exactly like him. We thought he might be injured or dead."

The man chuckled, "I can assure you he is very much alive. Perhaps a little rough around the edges, but alive."

"I would like to book a room for him until we can get him safely home with accommodations for food, whatever he needs while staying there."

"I can take care of that, sir."

"Great, give me a second here and I'll give you a credit card to use for his charges."

Joe gave the manager his payment details and then asked, "Also, can I get the exact name of the place and your phone number there?"

Yes, let me give you all the details. Joe copied them down. "Wonderful, that's good to know. Can I speak with my son once more?"

"Yes, of course."

Joe could hear Jack thanking the manager in the background.

"Dad, I'm so glad you answered the phone. I feel such relief that I got in touch with you."

"Are you okay? Are you injured?"

"I had some injuries and was helped by some local folk who nursed me back to my current condition. The worst thing I'm battling is a limp in my left leg and things seem foggy. I can't remember everything, Dad."

"Your brother, Jason, is in Brazil now looking for you with others. I am going to call his cell phone and let him know where you can be found."

"Jason is here?" Jack sounded surprised.

"Yes, he flew down to try and find you. Jack. You would not believe what we have all been going through. I'm putting you on speaker phone now with your mom."

Joe hit the button and said, "Are you there?"

"Yes, I'm here. Can you hear me?"

Tears rolled down Sharon's cheeks. "I hear you loud and clear, Jack. Oh my goodness, I wish I could hug you."

"I wish you could too, Mom. I don't know how I'm going to get back."

"Don't you worry, honey. We will get you back home to us and Haley."

"Haley -- who is Haley?"

Joe and Sharon looked at each other. "Your wife, honey. Haley is your wife."

"This is what I mean. My memory is shaky. I have a wife?"

"Don't worry about it right now. Let's just get you back in one piece for now."

"Dad, they're ready to take me to my room here at the hotel."

"Son, I wish we did not have to hang up. Do you know what your room number is?"

He could hear Jack asking the number of the room in the background.

"Dad, my room is going to be 1224".

"1224, okay. Hey, that's today's date. Jack, today is Christmas Eve." They waited for a response but there was none.

"You do remember Christmas, right?"

"Yes, of course. I just can't believe it's Christmas."

"You've been gone awhile. We will all have to catch up on what's been going on."

"Yes, we will. I have to go now. I love you both, and I'll wait for Jason to arrive."

"Alright son, damn I'm glad you made it and that you called."

"Me too! I love you both, Bye."

Joe and Sharon collapsed into each other's arms, both filled with tears of joy.

"God came through, Joe. Our son is alive."

"I have to call Jason right now," Joe said, suddenly remembering that he needed to send a text for possible privacy reasons.

"I'm not waiting to make sure he's receiving text messages. I've got to try and call him now. I'll use my cell phone. Hell, I'll step outside in the backyard just in case."

Joe Foster found his cell phone in the living room and stepped out the patio door to the backyard. He walked toward the back of the property along the fence line and pushed Jason's contact number.

"C'mon and answer Jay. I need you to pick up."

Finally, he heard "Hello."

"Jason, I'm so glad you answered. I need to let you know something. I've heard from your brother. He's alive and I have a phone number and address of the hotel he's been put up in."

"Dad, this is fantastic! Where do I find him?"

I'm standing out in the backyard just to be safe from eavesdropping. I will text you the location. I need you there."

"Of course, send me the details and I'm on it, Dad."

"Jason, he says he has a limp. Some natives helped nurse him back to health, but it sounded like he still has some issues, including his memory. He didn't know who Haley was when your mother mentioned her."

"Oh, wow … okay. Dad, he's alive and evidently walking around. Let me get off here and you send me that info. Who else can know this information?"

"We've got to keep it in our close circle. Do you mind if I tell Sarah and the rest of the family tomorrow at Haley's for Christmas?"

"It will be hard for me not to share this with Sarah, but yes, I'll keep quiet about it until tomorrow."

"Merry Christmas, son. I love you and so appreciate your efforts. Thank God you are in Brazil and can help your brother."

"Merry Christmas, Dad. I wouldn't have it any other way. I know Jack would do the same for me."

"Be safe and communicate often, so I don't worry."

"Will do, Dad, Bye."

Chapter 61 ~ Christmas

Wednesday, December 25, 2019

Days earlier, Sonya volunteered to put white lights along the walkway to the front door and around the entrance. Haley retrieved the poinsettia wreath she had hung the year before to adorn the front door. They had spent Christmas Eve wrapping the last of the gifts and preparing food for the next day.

The dining room table had been extended, and Haley had thought to go ahead and set the place settings. She placed a gold artificial tree in the middle for the centerpiece with tiny figurines from the manger scene around it.

"Didn't you tell me we had seven adults for Christmas?" Sonya inquired of her.

"Yes, that's right," Haley said.

"Okay, there are nine place settings at the table."

"Oh! I forgot to tell you. I put place settings for Jason and Jack. It's a gesture I thought would help. I wish both of them could be here. It is incredibly generous for Jason to miss spending the holidays with Sarah and his children to look for Jack."

"That's really nice, Haley."

"It's hard for me to celebrate Christmas without Jack, Sonya, even if he is somewhere unknown to us right now. Somehow, with the place reserved for him at the table, it makes me feel better."

A small children's table had been set up close to the dining room for Allison and Eli, with a gingerbread motif. Sonya also made a gingerbread house for them, which she would give them after they ate their food. Currently, it was hidden, because she knew how kids could be.

They freshened up and waited for everyone to arrive, while celebrating with Uncle Mike and Aunt Molly.

Christmas dinner was served very close to the time scheduled. Sharon, Sarah and Molly brought dishes to contribute. Joe and Sharon both seemed very jovial. In fact, Joe had whispered to Haley that he had a Santa surprise.

Sonya and Haley had decided not to serve wine or alcohol at the holiday celebration, but Haley had offered a prayer at the beginning of their meal when they sat down.

Eli and Allison ate like they were starving and Sarah was delighted they did so. Sonya presented the children with the gingerbread house and their eyes became large and they both giggled incessantly.

"Can we actually eat it?" Allison asked.

"Sure you can. You ate your food, didn't you?" Sonya said smiling.

Dessert consisted of pecan pie and a cream-filled chocolate cake with ice cream. Everyone made room for the delicious end to the meal.

As coffee was served to some, Papa Foster asked that everyone gather around the table for a Santa surprise he and Sharon wanted to share with everyone. As they approached, Haley was standing and he asked her to please sit down.

"Haley, Sarah and family, last night, Sharon and I were in the kitchen when the home telephone rang. It was a strange number on the caller ID, so we almost didn't answer. I'm sure glad we did. Jack is alive and he was calling home for help from Brazil." Audible gasps were heard throughout the home.

"Alive? Is he okay?" Haley asked, beginning to cry.

"Yes, I think so. He does have some injuries, but I'm not sure to what extent yet. But he's walking, talking, and sounding like our Jack," he said, proudly.

"Did Jason find him?" Sarah asked.

"No, but Jason is with him now and we have scheduled for a video call at 6:00 pm our time, so you can see for yourself. They will be calling your phone, Sarah."

"Now, for the bad news. He appears to have some amnesia. He says his memory is foggy and he did not know he was married or who Haley was," Joe Foster said, hoping not to upset Haley.

Instantly, Haley said, "I don't care about that! He's alive. This is a miracle! Hopefully, he will remember me at some point."

Sharon interjected, "I think he will, Haley. I don't see how he could forget you for long."

Everyone in the house buzzed with electric excitement, speaking to one another about how prayers had been answered and their wishes delivered.

Haley bent over the table and sobbed almost uncontrollably. "This is the best Christmas present in the world," she said tearfully.

Little Allison approached her empathetically and touched her arm. "Don't cry, Aunt Haley. Be happy, Uncle Jack has been found, and I bet my daddy's going to bring him home. Merry Christmas, everyone!"

"Merry Christmas!" they all reverberated in return.

THE END

Thank you for reading *A Dose of Murder*, Book 1 of The Big Pharma Series. The author loves to hear your thoughts and accolades. Please leave a written review when you have a moment.

In Book 2, *A Dose of Discovery*, you will learn of the extraordinary way Jack survived the horrific plane crash and uncover numerous secrets --- many leading back to Big Pharma.

If you have not done so already, download the free prequel novella to this series at www.lotusjames.com

Nestled throughout the world are corporate and government entities with the power to control the populace through the delivery of their products. In this series, the Foster family and their investigative contacts strive to:

- Solve murder mysteries
- Avoid surveillance
- Thwart personal threats
- Experience love
- Reveal greed
- Expose to the world

The diabolical plans of Big Pharma